YESTERDAY'S
MAGIC

YESTERDAY'S MAGIC

PAMELA F. SERVICE

Random House 🏠 New York

Text copyright © 2008 by Pamela F. Service
Jacket illustration copyright © 2008 by James Bernardin

Visit us on the Web! www.randomhouse.com/kids

Educators and librarians, for a variety of teaching tools, visit us at
www.randomhouse.com/teachers

Library of Congress Cataloging-in-Publication Data
Service, Pamela F.
Yesterday's magic / Pamela F. Service. — 1st ed.
p. cm.
Summary: In the twenty-sixth century, Heather is kidnapped by Morgan LeFay,
sending Merlin, Wally, Troll, and a dragon on a collision course with the reawakened
mythical beings of several cultures, while Arthur and his bride, Margaret,
continue their efforts to unite Britain.
ISBN 978-0-375-85577-1 (trade) — ISBN 978-0-375-95577-8 (lib. bdg.) —
ISBN 978-0-375-85578-8 (pbk.)
1. Merlin (Legendary character)—Juvenile fiction. 2. Arthur, King—Juvenile fiction.
3. Morgan le Fay (Legendary character)—Juvenile fiction. [1. Merlin (Legendary
character)—Fiction. 2. Arthur, King—Fiction. 3. Morgan le Fay (Legendary
character)—Fiction. 4. Wizards—Fiction. 5. Magic—Fiction. 6. Dragons—Fiction.
7. Animals, Mythical—Fiction.] I. Title.
PZ7.S4885Yes 2008   [Fic]—dc22   2007029873

For the "Writers by the Sea" —
Barb, Mary, Natasha, and Ellen

BRITAIN
TWENTY-SIXTH CENTURY

Five hundred years have passed since the Devastation—the nuclear war and social collapse that destroyed much of Earth's life and civilization. The nuclear winter that followed brought on a new ice age—expanding ice sheets, causing extinctions, and lowering sea levels. And another change has come as well. With the decline of technology, the forces of magic are returning to the world.

Most pre-Devastation nations have been obliterated. Humanity survives only in isolated pockets. In Britain, what remains of humanity is either terribly mutated or gathered in primitive warring kingdoms. Three misfit students at one of the few remaining schools become friends—Heather McKenna, Wellington Jones, and a boy known as Earl Bedwas. Mysteriously endangered, they discover Earl's true identity as the fabled wizard Merlin, magically rejuvenated and freed from centuries of enchantment. Pursued by the ancient sorceress Morgan Le Fay, they flee the school and seek an entrance to the Otherworld of Avalon. There they find and return King Arthur to a world much in need of the vision, unity, and hope that he once brought it.

Restored to youth, Arthur becomes king of the small territory of Keswick. Fighting battles and forming alliances with other rulers, including Margaret, the fiery Queen of Scots, Arthur and his followers gradually work toward reuniting Britain. Heather, Welly, and Merlin join in this— but also have their own conflicts with Morgan, culminating in a terrifying voyage back to London just before its nuclear destruction. Returning to their own time, they provide crucial help in a climactic battle between the army of Arthur and Margaret and the mutant and Otherworld forces led by Morgan.

The future for Britain now seems hopeful. But the world is larger than Britain. It holds more evil, more challenge, and more upwelling magic than these young warriors have yet imagined.

1

VOICES

Jaguars! the voice in Heather's head cried. *I actually saw one yesterday! It was much scarier, much sleeker, than the carved ones on the old temples. Have you ever seen a real jaguar?*

"No, I haven't," Heather said aloud.

Merlin turned from the ancient apparatus he was fiddling with. "You haven't what?"

Heather shook her head and felt the intruding voice slip away. "Nothing. I guess I was thinking out loud."

Standing up and brushing off his wool trousers, Merlin walked toward her. "You looked like you were a million miles away."

She nodded, pushing down the urge to tell him all about the voices, crazy as that would sound. "Yes, sort of."

Gently he kissed her on the cheek. "As long as you never go that far away without me."

She smiled teasingly up at him. "As if I'd ever want to." She knew she'd talk to him about the voices soon, but she hadn't thought it all through yet. For once, she didn't want to just saddle him with more problems. She wanted to offer some answers as well.

Changing the subject, she said, "So, have you figured out how that thing worked yet?"

Laughing, Merlin returned to the rusted metal device. "When this was a city park, I think people just turned this knob and clean drinking water shot out."

He gave the knob a sharp wrench. The pipe shrieked with the wail of a dying banshee. Then, with a single spurt of rusty water, it shuddered into silence. "Well, it was worth a try," Merlin sighed, letting go of the handle. "Imagine what this world would have been like before the Devastation—water pumped into every home and even to public drinking fountains in their parks. Civilization did do some great things before it blew itself apart."

Heather unhooked the leather water bottle from her belt and handed it to him. He took a swig, dribbling water down his chin through the sparse dark strands of a beginning beard.

"Think your beard will grow faster if you water it?" Heather laughed.

The boy shook his head. "It's like each whisker is thinking carefully about whether it really wants to do the beard thing. This reluctant beard drove me crazy the first time I was a teenager, and now it's doing it again."

Retrieving the bottle, Heather took a sip of her own as they continued walking. Now that York was filling up with guests for the royal wedding, they both liked to escape the crowded old city whenever they could. From behind the usual high pall of dust stirred by ancient bombs, the June sun shed a faint warmth. Snow lingered in shadowed spots, and a few soft twitterings floated in the air.

"Things are improving," Merlin said. "At least more

birds are coming back into the world, though they seem about as reluctant as my beard. I wonder if—"

A child's scream rose from behind a tumbled, vine-entangled wall. "Eek, a horrible mutie dog! Yuck, dog spit! Get him off me!"

"Rus," Heather and Merlin said together. Quickly they both clambered over the wall. On the other side were two girls. The younger was pinned down by a shaggy black and white dog, its two tails wagging, its two heads nodding as both tongues licked the girl's face. The other girl was timidly trying to tug the dog off.

"Rus," Heather commanded, "leave her alone! Maybe she doesn't want to be friends."

With a double whine, the dog jumped away and bounded over to Heather, thumping its paws on her shoulders, its two tongues licking her face.

"Down, Rus," Heather gasped. Then she spoke to the two girls, who were staring at them with wide eyes. "See, he really is friendly. Too friendly sometimes. You must smell like a person who loves animals."

"She does," the older girl said, helping the other up and dusting her off. "That's why we're out here where we shouldn't be, looking for Shadow. She's a feral cat Mia made a pet of, but now she's run off."

"I'm afraid fell dogs or muties might have eaten her," Mia said, looking at Rus warily.

Heather shook her head. "Is Shadow a fat gray cat with black swirly stripes?"

Mia's face lit up. "You've seen her?"

"Sort of," Heather said vaguely. "I think she's nearby. Let's look."

Merlin watched as Heather began walking west, over

the hillside, her thin blond braids swinging back and forth. The two younger girls followed like baby chicks. Holding Rus firmly by one of his two collars, Merlin followed as well.

After a few minutes, Heather suddenly stood still and closed her eyes. Then, opening them, she veered right and knelt beside a ridge of tumbled bricks. Hesitantly she peered over the top.

"Shadow's down there," she said, sitting back up, "in a little nest she's made for herself. If you look—very quietly—you'll see what she's been busy with the last few days."

Little Mia quickly knelt and peered over. "Kittens. Shadow has kittens!" Sitting up, she looked at her sister. "Nedra, let's take them all home."

Heather shook her head. "They're still too young to move. Let Shadow decide when it's time."

Nedra frowned. "But suppose she decides to go back to the wild. Shadow was a feral kitten herself once."

Heather nodded. "I'll talk to her about it. Tell her you two need her and her family." Lying full length on the ground, Heather inched her head over the bricks. She stayed that way for long silent minutes. Then she stood up, brushing dirt from her wool trousers and tunic.

"There. She says she still likes you, and she'll bring her kittens home when they're old enough."

"You talk to cats!" Mia breathed excitedly.

Merlin spoke up from his seat on a nearby pile of bricks. "Heather is very good with animals. Trust her."

"Heather?" Nedra questioned. Suddenly she smiled broadly. "Oh, I know! You're the sorceress King Arthur brought with him when he came to York." Then she clapped a hand to her face and looked at the boy. "And you must be her boyfriend, Arthur's old wizard, Merlin."

Mia giggled, jumping to her feet. "Papa says you can't really be that old Merlin 'cause you're so young, but Mama says he's daft, because everybody knows you magicked yourself young before you brought King Arthur back from the Fairy place. Nedra can work magic too! Not fancy stuff like that, though."

Merlin tilted his head. "You work magic, Nedra?"

"A little," Nedra said, a blush spreading over her dark skin. "Sometimes I can make hurt or sick things better."

"She fixed one of our lambs," Mia piped up, "just by talking to it and rubbing its broken leg, and she made Mama's fever go away just by singing."

Nedra blushed more deeply, then looked at Merlin. "Papa says we shouldn't talk about these things because it makes most people . . . nervous. But now Mama says that since our duke has sworn allegiance to King Arthur and Arthur has his own magicians, maybe it's okay."

Merlin smiled wryly. "Yes, just the idea of magic still makes some people nervous. But don't feel bad about having some power, Nedra. Now that magic is returning to the world, a lot of people do. You just have to learn how to use it."

Nedra nodded. "I know. It's scary sometimes. I wish I had someone to teach me." She looked hopefully at Merlin and Heather. "You wouldn't be looking for students, would you?"

Merlin shook his head. "We won't be staying here long enough. Once the royal wedding and festivities are over, Arthur and Margaret will be heading off again. There are still a few dukedoms to try making alliances with."

"But we have thought about setting up schools once things settle down," Heather added when she saw Nedra's smile fade. "Arthur has been talking with Earl about training people who show magical talents." She stopped, seeing Nedra's confusion. "I mean *Merlin*. I first knew him as *Earl* and still call him that."

As if to confirm this, a voice called from atop the ancient wall that surrounded the oldest, and the only still-inhabited, part of the city of York, "Earl, Heather! We just heard that King Douglas of Norfolk will be arriving soon. I'm going to watch from above the main gate."

"Right, Welly!" Merlin called back. "We'll join you."

"Welly?" Mia cried. "Is that the young warrior who fought all those battles with you? We heard a harper yesterday sing a song all about how brave he is."

Heather laughed. "When we were just schoolkids together, Welly never would have thought he'd be a hero in royal ballads. Now you girls better hurry home before your parents worry about you being outside the wall."

When the two girls scampered off, Heather, Merlin, and Rus headed back through the rubble of long-abandoned houses to where ancient and recently strengthened walls encircled the city of York. Merlin began talking about his doubts over King Douglas's loyalty to Arthur as High King, but Heather was hardly listening.

Hearing Nedra's worries about her budding magical powers reminded Heather of how miserable she'd been, only a year earlier, when she began discovering her own powers. Instead of talking to Earl about it right away, she'd been afraid of becoming an outcast from nonmagical people and had kept quiet—and scared. She shouldn't make that mistake again. This thing with the voices troubled her—even frightened her. What had just happened with that cat had somehow brought all her thoughts about it together.

"Earl," she interrupted, "I have a question, but don't laugh if it sounds silly. Seeing that cat made me think of it. Are there any jaguars in Britain?"

"Jaguars? You mean big spotty wildcats? I remember reading about them in the Llandoylan School library. But I don't think they're British. Somewhere from the pre-Devastation Americas, I think, the middle or the south. Why? You haven't seen jaguars, have you?"

"No, just heard about them. Are there any people still living in the Americas?"

Merlin frowned. "We don't know. The schoolmasters said there haven't been any communications across the Atlantic since the Devastation. But I don't think all the nations there had atomic weapons, particularly not in the south, so some people may have survived, the way they did here. In the north, of course, there would have been the advancing glaciers as well."

"But down where jaguars lived, there wouldn't have been as many targets for bombs, right? Or any glaciers?"

"Right. But, Heather, what is all this about?"

Twisting a braid nervously, she clambered over a pile of rubble. "I suppose I really should have told you about this earlier, but I didn't think it had anything to do with magic. Maybe it doesn't, and anyway, for a while I figured I was outgrowing it, but now it's getting worse. Well, not *worse,* really, because it's not *bad.* But stronger."

"*What's* getting stronger?" His voice rose in exasperation.

"The voices."

"Voices? Like visions with sound?"

"No, voices. Several of them. I've heard them on and off since I was little. I used to think of them as special imaginary friends—like most kids have. And since I didn't have many real friends, I liked having them pop into my mind. For the last few years, they've been kind of quiet, but now I'm hearing them more."

"What do they say?"

"Nothing grand, just like someone was chatting with you. What they're having for dinner, bits about family. Sometimes they do talk about spirits or supernatural creatures, like from Faerie or someplace like that. I was coming to think that maybe I was on a special 'wave link,' like the science master at school used to talk about, not with mechanical stuff but with other people. I figured I might actually run into some of these people now that we're traveling around the country. But I'm not sure now."

Merlin was watching her with his head tilted in concentration. "Why?"

"Because they don't always talk about stuff I think we have in Britain."

"Like jaguars."

She nodded. "And I'm not always sure they talk in English. I understand them in my mind. But the language some of them use seems off somehow."

Gently Merlin took her by the shoulders and sat her on a large concrete slab. "How many voices do you hear? And do you reply to them?" he asked, sitting beside her.

"A dozen, maybe, that I recognize regularly and sometimes bits from several others. And yes, when I feel them in my mind, I talk back to them."

"And you think maybe they are from different parts of the world, places where other people have survived the Devastation?"

"I'm kind of getting that idea."

A broad smile broke out on Merlin's thin face. He grabbed her hands and squeezed them. "Heather, this is so exciting! You may actually be communicating with parts of the human race we've totally lost touch with! I don't really understand it, though. It's not quite like any magic I'm familiar with."

After a moment's thought, he sighed. "But there are so many new aspects of this magic that's surfacing today! I have almost as much to learn as Nedra back there." He laughed ruefully. "Maybe we *all* need that magic schooling we've been talking about."

Just then the sound of a trumpet floated from over the city walls. Merlin shook his head and stood up. "Norfolk's party must be approaching. I'd rather work on this thing with your voices, but it looks like it'll have to wait a bit."

Heather called to Rus where he was snuffling under some stones, and the three of them made their way to a stairway in one of the wall towers. The guard saluted them, but Heather thought she noticed him quietly making a sign against evil as they passed. That didn't bother her as much as it used to. Magic still did frighten some people, but they also needed to get accustomed to it. In little ways, it was showing up more in people's lives each day.

They reached the top of the wall. Some distance along it, two figures gestured impatiently from the arch over one of the city's gates.

Plump, bespectacled Welly stayed standing and waving, but his companion loped toward them. On his short bowed legs, Troll finally scuttled up to Merlin. "Great Wizard better come. King acts worried about new guests. Sent Troll to find you." He proudly puffed out his skinny chest as Merlin began hurrying back along the wall.

"Not surprising Arthur should worry about Norfolk," Merlin said as they all rushed after him, "after they allied themselves with Morgan last year."

Half running to keep up with Merlin's long stride, Heather said, "But after Morgan's defeat at the Battle of London last year, most of her allies deserted her, right? I mean, not many even fled to the Continent with her."

Merlin nodded. "But I know Arthur has doubts about Norfolk's long-term loyalty. Anyone who can change sides as quickly as their King Douglas did bears close watching."

Soon they'd reached the point where the wall met the heavily fortified gateway over the main road. Guards with bows and spears were ranged in every embrasure, but clearly they had been ordered to simply watch and let the approaching party pass. Merlin, Heather, and Welly looked through one of the openings, and Troll scrabbled like a spider to the top of the parapet and peered over. The front of the party was just approaching the gate—ten mounted men, a dozen foot soldiers, and several wagons dragged by shaggy oxen.

"Judging by the crown on that helmet," Merlin commented, "it seems we have King Douglas himself here. Interesting."

Troll's gaze was fixed more on the back of the train. "And two big wagons. Lots more prezzies. Maybe Troll should get married so people bring him lots of prezzies too."

Heather laughed. "Maybe Troll should find a lovely lady troll first and think about the presents later."

The creature snorted. "Not really want wife. But prezzies good."

Ignoring their banter, Merlin remarked, "I don't quite like the feeling of this bunch. Maybe it's just that they were associated too long with Morgan and her Otherworld and mutie friends. But they have an unsettling aura about them." Frowning, he said, "I'm going to the Manor so I can be with Arthur when he greets them." Hurriedly he descended a narrow flight of stone steps.

Troll followed, but Heather stayed a moment, studying the newcomers for herself. From above, she couldn't see or sense anything clearly threatening, but there were definitely various degrees of mutations in the party. That wasn't saying much, she knew. All modern horses, due to radiation exposure, had mutated back to an earlier, three-toed form. Even the warhorses Arthur had been breeding for size retained the three toes. And after the destruction of Earth's protective ozone, the humans most likely to survive all had darker skin. The palest people she'd ever met were Merlin and Arthur—and Morgan—all of whom had originally lived long before the Devastation.

Still, although she didn't have Merlin's sensitivities, there was something about the party now passing through the gate beneath her that left Heather uneasy. There was some sort of mental stench about them, like when cooks use spices but fail to cover up the taste of rotting meat. Perhaps the fact that King Douglas had once been an ally of Morgan's was enough to explain it. Everything Morgan brushed against had a smudge of evil about it. With a shiver, Heather turned and hurried after the others. Behind her, Rus jumped up and stuck both heads out through an embrasure. He growled as the last of the Norfolk party passed underneath. Then with a whine he turned and trotted after his mistress.

2

PREPARATIONS

York's narrow cobbled streets twisted between buildings showing many centuries of architecture. Usually
Rus would range widely, darting up alleys and smelling
every cornerstone. But now he trotted close to Heather as
she quickly threaded her way to the Manor. The sprawling
building had known many uses in its days. It now served as
the residence of Basil, Duke of York, and the temporary
guest residence for King Arthur of Cumbria and Margaret,
Queen of Scots.

Admitted automatically by the guards, Heather hurried
through the now-bustling courtyard. She patted Rus's
heads and gestured for him to go to the kennels. Instead of
going, he whined and pressed against her legs.

Sorry, Rus, she thought at him, *but you really freak out
those girls I'm rooming with. We can stick together once we're
away from York. Arthur's party is a lot more used to you, after all.*
He kept whining, but she pushed him firmly in the direction of the Duke's kennels, then hurried up the back stairs
toward the rooms she shared with three ladies of Duke
Basil's court.

The three were all now in the common room primping

to look their best for the new arrivals. Heather figured she'd better at least change into a dress. She went into her own small room and pawed through a couple of crumpled linen dresses in her trunk before settling on a plain gray wool. She'd given up thinking that clothes could do much for her appearance. No matter what she wore, her body was still skinny, her face long, and her muddy blond hair thin and wispy.

She returned to the common room and studied herself in the room's one cracked mirror. Her frown slid away. She didn't care about all that so much now. She had once, but not anymore. She felt the new happiness bubble through her. She wasn't just the homely misfit lucky to have a couple of friends. Somebody *loved* her. Somebody she loved so very much.

She smiled at the other girls, who were giggling among themselves. They were several years younger than she and were all looking for husbands or already engaged. Heather knew that the dangers of her world and the difficult childbirths brought by lingering radiation meant that girls needed to marry far earlier than in pre-Devastation times. But plain and impoverished as she had been, she'd never held out much hope for being anything but an old maid at age fifteen, and well beyond. Now everything had changed.

When she'd first started rooming next to these girls several weeks ago, they'd acted both slightly afraid and wildly curious about her. They couldn't help asking what it was like to be not only magical but the girlfriend of the wizard Merlin. Not that they would have given him a second glance had he been just plain Earl Bedwas, as Heather had first known him. He was too gangly and skinny with far too hawklike a face to meet their definition of *attractive*. But power had its own attraction, Heather was learning, and these girls seemed to view her now with a mix of awe, pity, and envy.

"Come on," Heather said, undoing her braids and running a brush through her limp hair. "Down to the audience chambers. It looked like there were a few kind of cute guys in this last batch who might interest you. I saw them coming in." The fact that the party had also felt distinctly creepy she kept to herself.

Downstairs, the audience chamber was crowded with members of Duke Basil's court as well as with various guests. In addition to Arthur and Margaret's party, there were other dukes and kings and their followers who had come to York to acknowledge Arthur as High King, or at least to attend his wedding to Scotland's queen.

Heather slipped onto a small balcony just as Duke Basil walked onto the raised dais at the end of the room. Immediately he was joined by Arthur, Margaret, and other nobility in attendance. She saw Earl standing in the back to one side, a seeming teenager looking oddly out of place among bearded battle-scarred men.

As the host, potbellied little Duke Basil took center stage. However, clearly most eyes were fixed on the two beside him, the pair around whom old and new legends already whirled. Arthur, blond, bearded, and youthful, would catch attention anywhere even had the comparative paleness of his skin not made him stand out. But equally striking was the tall woman beside him. Margaret, Queen of Scots, had a head of flaming red hair and, as Heather and others knew, a temper to match. Though with her brilliant smile and flashing green eyes, she could be equally good-humored, and Heather was glad to call her a friend.

A trumpet sounded, and the crowd in the main part of the hall turned their attention from the dais to the doorway, where a dozen men marched in. Heather recognized some of those she'd seen earlier, including the crowned man who must be King Douglas. She tried, briefly, to be unbiased, but the man definitely made her uneasy. Most of her own magic had to do with animals, and she fought down a smile when she realized what animal Douglas made her think of. Weasel. Pointy whiskery face, close-set beady eyes. Even his walk had a sneaky, slinky quality to it.

"Duke Basil," the newcomer said in a high sharp voice, "thank you for welcoming My Majesty of Norfolk and my esteemed party to your noble city of York. Greetings too to the other worthies present here and most particularly to King Arthur and Queen Margaret. I know, Your Majesties, that we have not always agreed on the best future course for Britain, but events have unfolded as they have and must be accepted. I come to wish you happiness in your upcoming union and to bring you gifts and friendship from Norfolk."

Arthur stepped forward. "Thank you, Douglas. It is our hope that all enmities of the past can be forgotten and that all of Britain can once more be united in peace and friendship. Your presence here is surely a fine token of that future."

The speeches went on as every duke, king, and general present seemed to feel a need to proclaim something, but Heather soon lost interest. She saw Welly in the crowd below her busily scanning the assembly, taking his soldier duties seriously. When she glanced at Merlin, he looked severe, but that was his usual expression in a crowd, as if trying to seem wizardly even though he looked like a gangly teenager.

Finally the crowd adjourned for a meal and more speeches, but Heather skipped the beginning so she could check on Troll. She'd seen him slip into the room where Norfolk's wedding presents had just been unloaded onto tables with the rest.

"Now, Troll, just looking—no touching," she reminded him from the doorway.

He sighed. "Always just look. But sure Great King and Queen not need all this treasure. Maybe loyal retainers get share too. A little share?"

"Maybe. But none of it will be worth much if you drool all over it. The guards will keep it safe, so come on and let's get something to eat."

That idea seemed to please him almost as much as the gifts. He scuttled off to the dining hall with Heather following.

When she slipped into a seat beside Merlin at one of the long tables, she whispered, "I didn't realize trolls were so greedy about treasure. In the old stories, I thought that was just dragons."

He laughed. "True, nothing can beat a dragon for treasure lust, but they go for fine things like gold and jewels. Trolls just like stuff, the more glittery, the better. They never build up very big hoards because they're always stealing from each other. I'm sure that after the wedding, Arthur and Margaret will give away most of that haul. Troll will get his share."

After the meal, Heather was tired and would gladly have gone up to bed, but Merlin asked her to come with him. Arthur had called a few of his closest advisors to his upstairs room to discuss Norfolk and other matters. Heather didn't know what she could contribute but was happy just to be with Merlin. She settled into a chair by the fireplace. Despite the June thaw, a small fire fought off the biting evening cold.

"Notice how Douglas didn't actually say that he was offering you allegiance as High King," commented Otto, Arthur's burly general from Keswick.

Clarence, Duke of Carlisle, added, "How did he put it? 'Events must be accepted.' And he offered you gifts and friendship. Period. No allegiance."

Arthur nodded. "That's a start. At least he's here and not off across the channel with Morgan."

"Do you really think she is trying to regroup her forces there?" Margaret asked. "We did beat her rather decisively."

"Merlin?" Arthur said. "You're the expert here. What do you think our dear old friend is up to now?"

Frowning, Merlin touched his chin, then gave up, finding there was still no beard worth tugging at. "It's hard to read. She's expending a lot of energy cloaking her activities—that I can sense. But I don't feel there is any new army amassing. She still hates everything you stand for, Arthur—peace, unity, hope for a better future. But I expect she'll try some new tactic. It may not be for some time."

"And is her old ally Douglas any part of it?"

"He still has Morgan's stench about him. His very presence here troubles me. But I don't think he's directly involved in a plot. Still, it would be wise to detail men to shadow everyone in his party."

Otto laughed. "Do you take me for an amateur, boy?

I've already done that—even without a shred of magic. Now, let's talk about your plans for Nottingham, Arthur, since it's the next stop on your tour."

Heather was no longer listening. Otto and Merlin's bantering about the relative merits of "magic versus might" was an old joke. The fire dancing and crackling before her seemed far more compelling. And so did the voice. It blew into her mind like a crisp dry wind.

The temple building is almost complete, it whispered excitedly. *Tomorrow is the ceremony, and I'm supposed to carry the offering of milk to the statue, to the great bird who carries our prayers to the gods. What if I trip? What if the chosen cow refuses to give milk? The priestess says I'm a favorite of the spirits, but I'm not sure. Are you a spirit?*

"No," Heather said aloud. "I'm just a girl. But where are you?"

The voice in her head laughed. *Here; I'm here.*

At the same time, another voice answered. "Here. Heather, I'm right here. Where are *you*?"

Heather shook herself and looked up at Merlin. The rest of the room was silent. "Oh." Heather blushed, looking at the staring faces. "Here, I guess. But there was someone else here too."

Several of the others looked around nervously. But Merlin shook his head. "Don't worry. Whatever magic Heather is tapping into, it's nothing to do with Morgan. It's something . . . bigger, I think."

"Bigger magic than yours and Morgan's?" Otto exclaimed with mock dismay. "Gods preserve us. The world was a lot simpler when people could just fight each other straight-out."

Merlin smiled grimly. "And look where that got the

world." He gestured out the window as though at the blasted world beyond. "There's new magic about, and Heather's onto some of it. We just have to sort it out."

He smiled down at her, and Heather sleepily smiled back. She hoped they would sort it out—and soon. Having imaginary friends visit when you're a lonely kid was one thing. But having mysterious voices make her look like a lunatic during meetings of state was quite another. At the very least, she realized, she had to learn not to respond to the mental voices out loud.

Standing up, she excused herself to go to bed. Still, she thought as she left the room, thinking about jaguars or the girl with milk for the sacred bird was far better than dwelling on the weaselly, evil-shadowed King of Norfolk or the horrid, mind-warping sorceress Morgan Le Fay.

In the most recent of her fifteen years, Heather had seen more evil than she'd once imagined the world could contain. Sent to a boarding school when her mother remarried, all the adventure and all the evil she'd known as a lonely studious child had been in books. But events had thrown her life in first with schoolmate Welly's and then with Merlin's and Arthur's and with the forces that swirled around them. She liked to think now that she'd seen a lifetime's worth of evil, but a nagging ache in her bones told her that evil would always be entwined with her life. Still, unrealistic or not, she just hoped to keep it at bay awhile longer.

The entire town awakened extra early the next morning, the day before the Royal Wedding. Excitement vibrated in the air. Heather tried to ignore it, but tendrils burrowed under her blankets until she too had to get up and throw herself into preparations.

She knew Margaret and Arthur were embarrassed about making such a big deal of this, but the wedding was as much a political act as the union of two former enemies who had, despite everything, fallen in love. As Merlin had pointed out when the royal pair balked at all the ceremony, it conferred pomp and glamour on the concept of uniting. And that was what Arthur and Margaret needed to do first and foremost—unite Britain.

At first Heather helped in the kitchens. But she'd never had a smidgen of talent for cooking, so she figured it was better for all concerned if she did something harmless, like cleaning. Probably deciding she was more trustworthy than some, the head housekeeper assigned her to sweeping and dusting the room where the royal wedding gifts were displayed. She wasn't surprised to find Troll there too, crouched froglike on a window ledge gazing longingly at the ladened tables.

"Me not touch," he hastily assured her. "Just look." But Heather could almost feel him caressing everything with his eyes. She'd nearly finished her sweeping when Queen Margaret entered the room with Merlin and Welly staggering behind, arms laden with a new batch of gifts from a number of York's merchants.

The Queen looked at the full tables and shook her head. "I haven't a clue what we're going to do with all this stuff. How many goblets and knickknacks do two people need?"

"Give stuff out to loyal retainers," Troll piped up, his broad mouth stretched into a smile he clearly hoped looked very loyal.

"Obviously the answer," Margaret laughed. "And perhaps some *very* loyal retainers should have a gift now to keep them from bursting. Anything here, Troll, you'd like to wear at the wedding to show everyone what a valued courtier you are?"

Instantly Troll leaped down from the window and onto one of the tables where Merlin and Welly were trying to make room for the latest batch. With surprising delicacy, he picked his way through the piles until suddenly exclaiming and diving for something glittery. In moments, he'd adorned himself with a chain of rare ancient plastic beads, glinting in many colors.

"Perfect, Troll," Merlin said. "You look like a walking rainbow."

"No," Margaret said firmly, "it's a chain of office. The Order of Royal Bridge Protectors. Go on now and impress the masses."

Troll happily galloped off as the Queen said to the others, "I think we won't distribute the rest of this until most of the guests are gone, so we don't offend anybody. Oh, but wait, there was something that came in yesterday that's just perfect for you, Heather. It's around here somewhere. Ah, there it is."

From the clutter on another table, she pulled a pink plastic box with a white handle. On the side of the box was a faded picture of a white unicorn with a flowing rainbow tail. Carefully she handed it to Heather.

"It's beautiful," the girl whispered, "but I can't take it. That much ancient plastic is worth a fortune."

Margaret smiled. "But it's obviously meant for you. Look at the name stuck on the top."

Heather studied the gold decals. Some of the letters were partly missing, but there were enough left to clearly spell HEATHER.

Welly moved closer. "I know what it is. I saw one in an old book. It's a box that schoolchildren used to carry their lunch in."

"And before the Devastation," Merlin added, "it must have belonged to a girl named Heather. Obviously it *is* meant for you."

Margaret nodded. "Enjoy it. But now I'd better get back. And, Merlin, as one of those who thought that a big splashy wedding was a good idea, *you* clearly deserve no gifts for the rest of your life. I'd rather be in a five-day battle than put up with this. But I'm sure it will seem better once I can look back on it—far back." Sweeping her cape around her in mock anger, she strode from the room.

Welly chuckled, then looked at Merlin and Heather. "I hope you two are taking notes, and when you finally get around to the marriage thing, you do something a lot simpler."

"Count on it," Heather and Merlin said together. All three laughed as Welly left the room. Hand in hand, the other two were about to follow when Heather suddenly stopped and looked at one of the gift tables. "What's that? It looks like . . . Earl, is that a world globe, like they had in the Llandoylan library?"

With the precious lunch box tucked under her arm, she reached out to touch the battered ball. Examining the globe with her, Merlin shook his head. "It's staggering to see that this world is so large and we know such a tiny part of it. When I lived back in the fifth century, all we knew of the world was Britain and the other places that had once been part of the Roman Empire. But there's so much that not even the Romans knew. All the Americas, for instance. And now so much of it is beyond knowing again."

He sighed, then looked at Heather. She was staring at the globe in an unfocused way, one hand moving over its surface.

"Heather?" he said. When she didn't answer, he asked, "Is it voices?"

She shook her head but kept her eyes on the globe. "I think I'm getting some sort of feeling of where they are, the people with the voices. The jaguar boy—he's somewhere here." Her finger traced the narrow strip of land linking North and South America.

Then her hand slid around the globe and stopped at the green bulge of Africa. She squinted closer at the worn name printed there. "Zim . . . Zimba . . . no, Zimbabwe. The girl with the milk for the statue of the bird god. She's there. Earl, this is so exciting! Suddenly I can feel where they all are—here and here and somewhere along here." Her hands danced over the globe touching bits of Europe, Asia, and the Americas.

Impulsively she hugged Merlin and he hugged her back, tears glinting in his eyes. "This is so amazing—and comforting," he said. "To know that we in Britain are not alone. And maybe they know that *they* are not alone either. Heather, as soon as this wedding folderol is over, let's work on it. Let's see if more-regular communication is possible. That would be the best gift imaginable."

Heather nodded, then pulled away. "But speaking of gifts . . ."

"Would you like this globe? I'm sure Margaret and Arthur would—"

"No," she interrupted. "No, but I have a gift for you. I've been saving it till Midsummer. Well, actually, I've only just finished it, but Midsummer is a fine day for gift-giving. Since that's tomorrow, why don't you meet me just after midnight? I'll give it to you then, before we all get tied up with the wedding."

"Good. I'll meet you in the old abbey ruins. That's about as private as it gets around here. And, Heather," he said, kissing her lightly on the forehead, "I have a gift for you as well. What do you say we take Welly up on his suggestion and make these betrothal gifts?"

The next kiss lasted until a guard walked into the room with another load of wedding gifts. Hastily the two parted and went about their wedding-preparation duties.

In mid-afternoon, Heather took a break from helping plan the banquet seating chart and went up to her room. Kneeling down, she looked under her bed. She'd shoved the pink lunch box in there this morning, but she didn't touch that now. Somehow, lovely as it was, the thing made her feel a little uneasy. Maybe that was because it was a present that hadn't really been intended for her, maybe it was because it had probably come from darkened Norfolk, or maybe it was just because the original Heather who had owned it had died hundreds of years ago. Shoving disturbing thoughts aside, she pushed past the box and pulled out a long wrapped parcel.

The light slanting through her room's long narrow window was pale and gray, but when it struck the carved staff she was unwrapping, the wood glowed like polished gold. She ran her fingers over the carvings and smiled. It was as long as she was tall and had taken her months to carve. She'd never thought of herself as much of an artist, but she'd felt inspired when carving this. If magic had somehow been involved, it must have been the magic of wanting to make something beautiful for someone she loved.

Tracing one of the carvings with her finger, she thought about how much her life had changed since the day three years ago when she and Welly had played that adventure game beyond the school walls, had run into Earl and had begun an incredible real adventure. She smiled too remembering how she'd never given a thought to marriage being in her future. Many girls her age were already marrying, but she'd known she was too plain and penniless to interest any of the aristocratic boys at the school. And who would want to be tied to any of them anyway?

And now here she was, happily admiring an intended betrothal gift. But that was just one more unexpected turning in an amazing few years—enduring a quest for a supposedly mythical king, surviving bloody battles and magic attacks, discovering her own powers, traveling to the land of Faerie and briefly into a doomed past. She shook her head, recalling the simple plans she'd once made for her future. One thing she had learned since—life could be far too surprising to follow even the simplest of plans. But she hoped that, lurking darkness aside, she could at least hold on to her immediate plans for happiness.

With a last caress of the golden wood, she wrapped the staff in its tattered blanket and slid it back under the bed. It clunked against the lunch box, and she felt an odd jolt of power tingle up her arm. She frowned. Could the staff be invested with power already? It certainly couldn't be the lunch box. Could it? No. That was just a pretty gewgaw to carry someone's sandwiches.

Heather stood up and brushed the dust from her trousers, trying not to feel uneasy. She always felt uneasy around magic she didn't understand. Then she laughed at herself. Since she didn't understand *most* magic, she'd just better get used to it. And there wasn't a lot of magic Earl *didn't* understand. That thought banished her momentary unease, and smiling again, she hurried downstairs.

3

WEDDING

In a garden of the Manor, an old twisted oak spread branches over a stone bench. It was one of Duke Basil's favorite spots. Now he sat there with Arthur. Hand resting on his potbelly, the Duke shook his white-fringed head.

"Like I've said before, Arthur, I was skeptical at first of your claim to be *the* King Arthur, but your actions since then have assured me that, authentic or not, you are the man to unite Britain and end the fighting between all our petty little kingdoms and dukedoms."

Arthur laughed. "I appreciate your confidence, Basil, even if not your belief."

"Oh, I believe as much as I need, but I do somewhat draw the line at your teenage wizard. If you needed someone to play that part, couldn't you have chosen someone more . . . wizardly-looking? Older at least?"

When Arthur started to respond, Basil waved him off. "I know, I know. You're claiming he really is this old guy who took care of you when you were a child thousands of years ago. Whatever story you want to put out is fine with me. But the boy has practically accused King Douglas of still having dealings with the enemy. That suggestion based on this kid's vague suspicions and the order that all the Norfolk party be followed have not gone over well. A couple of Douglas's men caught some of my guards going through their personal things. I had to intervene and apologize or Douglas and his people might have walked out."

"Thank you for your diplomacy, Basil. That was well done. Did the guards find anything incriminating, by the way?"

"Nothing, though what that boy wizard wanted them to look for is beyond me. Ah, and speaking of the devil, I hope not literally, here comes the young man now."

Merlin was just entering the garden holding several rolls of parchment, orders for Arthur to sign. Arthur waved him over to the bench. "Merlin, Basil and I were just discussing your concern about Douglas and the Norfolk contingent. Is there something specific that's bothering you about them?"

Merlin frowned. "No. There is something amiss with them, but I can't pin down what. It could be just an echo of their earlier alliance, or it could be something more immediate but very well shielded. There are so many people in the city now and so many low-level, maybe even unaware, magic workers that it's difficult to sort out influences."

Basil gave a derisive grunt, and Arthur said hastily, "I'm afraid the Duke here is slightly skeptical of your wizardly powers. He was, after all, not with us at London or at the battle along the Wall or at other opportunities to see them demonstrated."

Merlin sighed at the not-unfamiliar situation. He nodded at Basil. "I am sorry, Your Grace, if my current appearance does not live up to my reputation. If it will set your mind at ease, I will be happy to perform some sort of demonstration."

Basil blushed and said, "No, no, that won't be necessary. Arthur's belief is enough for me. I wouldn't demean it by asking you for parlor tricks or whatever."

Merlin smiled thinly. "Thank you, Your Grace. It's embarrassing how many times I've had to transform something or somebody to make a point. But Arthur has asked me to do a little something at the wedding tomorrow—for public consumption primarily, but it should help."

After several more minutes, Duke Basil excused himself. When Arthur and Merlin were alone, the King looked at his friend. "I'm glad you restrained yourself there. I've heard about your giving King Nigel of Glamorganshire donkey ears. You know, that will *not* help my negotiations with that gentleman when the time comes."

Merlin hung his head. "I know—I couldn't help myself. Nigel is such a pompous ass." Then he looked up and grinned. "But don't blame me, Sire. I'm just an impulsive kid, after all."

"Don't give me that, old man," Arthur said, standing up. "The only thing young about you is the love light in your eyes when you look at Heather. You are planning to marry her soon, I trust."

"We are discussing it."

"Good. As sappy as it sounds, I'm so happily in love myself, I just want to see it spread around. Now let's get back to the others. And yes, I'll have my people continue watching the Norfolk contingent. They're still bothering you, I take it?"

"Yes. Like someone rubbing fur the wrong way. A feeling like there's something dark grating under the foundations—despite all the happiness on top. I don't feel this darkness moving, though, or getting any stronger. But it's there, like it's asleep . . . or waiting."

"Well, your concerns are good enough for me. We'll keep an eye on the Norfolk party. And we'll see how whatever you have planned for tomorrow convinces the Duke—and others—about your abilities."

As they walked out of the garden, Merlin said, "You've got to admit, Arthur, that if someone had spun a yarn like ours to you when you were first king, you might have doubted as well. You know, hanging out in Avalon or in a mountain for a couple of millennia, then coming back young again—that's fairy-tale stuff."

"Oh, I might have believed it, after all the training I had as a boy from that cranky old codger, that wizard what's his name. Merlin, was it?"

Laughing, the two returned to the bustle of royal wedding preparations.

That night, with the manor finally quieted down, Merlin and Heather met as planned in the ruins of the abbey, ruins that had been ancient long before the Devastation. Empty arches and broken walls traced dark shapes against the sky. A few of the brightest stars showed hazily through the high atmospheric dust. The night wind carried a chill hint of Scottish glaciers, but the two didn't notice.

Heather couldn't embrace or kiss him very easily since she was clutching a long loosely wrapped bundle behind her back, so she brought it out. "I made this for you."

Taking the bundle in both hands, Merlin peeled away the blanket. The hazy moonlight caught and silvered the long wooden staff, seeming to make the carvings move along its length.

Before he could say anything, Heather explained, "I know that after the Battle of London, you said you needed to try working with the new magic and stop using *things* like a staff to focus your power." She smiled. "But I've seen how twitchy that makes you. You always seem to be reaching for something that isn't there. So I thought if I made you a staff, working into it carvings of living things . . . and my own feelings, then maybe it would combine both the old and new magics for you."

Merlin traced his fingers over the carvings from the hawk head at the top blending through deer, squirrels, snakes, and horses. Below those came faces he quickly recognized—Heather's, Welly's, Troll's, Margaret's, and Arthur's. Twining vines wove between them all.

He struggled to break his speechlessness. "How . . . how . . . Heather, this is beautiful. I never knew. . . . There is so much life and power in this. *Thank you* doesn't begin to say it."

"I wasn't sure about the wood," she said, blushing happily. "But the time we all camped in that little oak grove near Oxford, I found this sapling that a storm had uprooted. It seemed right."

"Yes, oak has deep roots of power—as, it seems, do you." Gently he kissed her, then pulled back. "And if I accept this gift, are we officially engaged?"

She smiled teasingly. "Only halfway."

He laughed and pulled out a small cloth-wrapped package. "Then please do me the honor of completing the process and accepting this gift."

Even in the faint cold moonlight, the bracelet she

unwrapped glowed warmly. The red-gold band showed a delicate procession of running deer—antlers, backs, and legs blending and interweaving with each other in an intricate endless knot.

"This was my mother's," he said quietly. "Remember how at Glastonbury we found that hoard of treasure that the monks had hidden long ago after the fall of Arthur? All I saw at first was my Bowl of Seeing, but after our skirmish with Morgan, I dug up some of the rest to return to Arthur, and this was there. It must have been with my things when . . . when I left Camelot."

"It had been your mother's?"

He nodded. "She gave it to me when I went off as a young man to join King Uther. She told me my father had given it to her."

"Your father. You've never mentioned him."

"I never knew him. But he was Eldritch—as is the bracelet."

Reverently Heather slipped the bracelet onto her wrist.

Merlin smiled. "It fits as if it were meant for you. And perhaps it was. The Eldritch see very far indeed."

They spent a while longer warmly entwined in each other's arms. When reluctantly they parted, it was with mutual vows that their own wedding would be a great deal simpler than what they were expecting tomorrow.

The pink of dawn gave way to a rare blue sky, taken as a good omen by people who usually saw blue skies only in ancient paintings. There were many people up to see that dawn. Word had been spreading for weeks about the Royal Wedding. Crowds from within the city and from the countryside gathered early along the royal procession route between the Manor and York's ancient cathedral. Vendors hawked roasted potatoes and small souvenir stone carvings of Arthur's Dragon emblem and Margaret's Scottish Lion. Street musicians played fiddles, pipes, and drums while jugglers and puppeteers entertained the growing crowd.

At the Manor, all seemed loosely controlled chaos. Everyone was scurrying to put on their best, most impressive attire, groom their horses, and make a thousand final touches to decorations. Heather chose to wear a simple blue wool dress that one of Margaret's ladies had made for her. The only jewelry she wore was her purple glass ring and the entwining deer bracelet. Gretha, one of the York girls she was rooming with, offered eagerly to do her hair. Heather wasn't sure whether the end result, a swirled mound with one long lock cascading down her back, made her look elegant or ridiculous. But she admitted it made her look older.

The procession finally got under way around noon. Drums, trumpets, and bagpipes were followed by banner carriers. Then came troops of soldiers, including Welly, each proudly wearing Arthur's Dragon surcoat. When Arthur and Margaret appeared on their white and red warhorses, the crowd cheered wildly. Margaret, with her flaming red hair, golden crown, and green tartan gown, seemed like a figure from ancient stories. Beside her, a figure truly from those stories, rode King Arthur Pendragon, his golden beard and hair only slightly less bright than his crown, and his burnished armor and sword splendid in the pale sunlight.

Behind the couple rode Duke Basil of York and various dignitaries from around Britain plus members of their courts. Merlin could have ridden closer to Arthur, but he directed his black mare to walk beside Heather's gray. Heather thought he looked splendid in his simple purple robe, but she also thought he looked very nervous.

When the level of cheering waned slightly, she leaned over and whispered, "What's the trouble? This isn't *your* wedding."

"Thank the gods," he muttered back. "But Arthur's asked me to do something at the ceremony, something that involves singing. At least my voice has finally broken, but singing in front of hundreds of people is not my favorite thing."

"You'll do fine," she practically had to yell back as the procession entered the plaza in front of the cathedral and the cheering swelled.

When the wedding party finally dismounted and entered the cathedral, the crowd quieted. Those processing inside were awed into silence. Heather had visited ancient monuments before in her travels with Merlin and Arthur, but the vastness of this space with its great arches, pillars, and vaulted ceiling defied words.

When she squeezed Merlin's hand as he left her to go forward, it was clammy with nervousness. She smiled encouragement. Then she stood with the rest of the dignitaries and tried to shut out their whisperings and jostlings and just concentrate on the beauty and enormousness of the space. With pleasure she watched sunlight slant through the high windows and pool on the floor around her. Some of the ancient colored glass remained, tingeing the light with reds and blues.

Despite the number of people, the air smelled faintly sweet, and she was impressed by the lavish arrangement of flowers on the altar. She imagined that prior to the Devastation, an event such as this might have been laden with flowers, but their rarity now made this one display a real gift, a gift from the people of York. Looking beyond the altar, she caught sight of Merlin standing among the clergy of various religions who had been called to participate. She tried to look encouraging again but knew she was too far away.

Enthralled with the setting, Heather didn't pay close attention when the clergy began chanting, speaking, or singing. She focused forward again when Arthur and Margaret exchanged vows and then was suddenly riveted when she heard Merlin's clear deep voice rise up. He was singing in an ancient tongue that probably only he and Arthur had ever heard before. Yet the haunting melody itself contained more longing, love, and hope than any words could have held. As the song rose up, so did the visions it magically conjured.

Trees, lush and stately, such as seen only in ancient paintings, seemed to rise on either side of the altar. Their branches fluttered, releasing two winged creatures—a red dragon and a golden lion. Growing in size, they circled high into the cathedral vault, their sweet wild voices carrying Merlin's song. Then they glided through the great windows and rose above the building for the awed crowd to see. Singing and soaring higher and higher, they beat their wings, and a rainbow cascade of flowers showered down on the crowd.

The cheers that greeted this display were loud and delighted. Moments later, the cathedral doors opened and the High King and Queen appeared. The cheering shook the city's ancient stones. When Heather finally found

Merlin in the crowd exiting the cathedral, he looked tired but relieved—and happy.

"I can't believe you doubted yourself, Earl," she whispered. "That was incredible."

"I always doubt myself. I can't help it. But at least this demonstration may allay the doubts of a few others." Just then he met the gaze of Duke Basil, who had remounted his horse. The Duke nodded in an almost-awestruck way. Smiling graciously, Merlin nodded back.

The rest of the day and evening passed in a happy blur for Heather. There was the banquet, with rare delicious foods and many speeches—far too long but good-natured. Jugglers, acrobats, and musicians entertained. Then came the dancing.

Heather had never liked formal dances, whether at school or at the various courts they'd visited with Arthur. She felt she was as graceful as a lame horse—and about as attractive as one too. No one ever asked her to dance. Tonight, she realized as she was leaning against a wall pretending to enjoy watching the dancers, would be no exception.

As dancers swirled by, she saw Welly among them and gave him what she hoped was a cheery-looking smile. Earl, she noticed, was watching the musicians as always. No hope there. She refilled her glass of punch at the refreshment table.

When Welly finished his dance with one of Duke Basil's serving girls, he slipped over to the musicians and firmly grabbed Earl's arm. "Why don't you ask Heather to dance?"

The wizard turned paler than usual. "I . . . I don't dance."

"It's not difficult—you just move yourself around to the music."

"I'd make a fool of myself. People . . . Heather would laugh."

Welly snorted. "No, she wouldn't. And don't give me the line that dancing is beneath a court wizard's dignity. You're not a dignified-looking graybeard right now—you're a teenager. Heather looks like she really wants to dance."

Merlin glanced her way. "She looks lovely tonight. Lots of people, lots of better dancers, are sure to dance with her."

"No, they won't! Don't you get it? Lovely or not, no one will dance with her because they all know she's the Wizard's girlfriend and they're afraid you'll turn them into toads."

"Oh. I hadn't thought of that."

"Don't think at all. Just go dance." Firmly Welly pushed him toward the pillar where Heather was standing studying her punch cup.

When he approached and stammered out a suggestion that they dance, Heather looked up with surprised delight. "I didn't think you danced."

"I don't, as you will soon discover. But this time around, I'd like to try—as long as you promise not to laugh, or scream too loudly when I tromp on your feet."

"Agreed—as long as you promise the same."

Soon they were dancing with the rest, ignoring minor missteps and totally oblivious to what anyone else thought. From his vantage point, sweeping by with various partners, Welly watched contentedly as Heather's elaborate hairdo collapsed into a free cascade around her shoulders and both his friends' faces flushed with happiness.

The dancing went on late into the night, but finally even the youngest revelers tired. Margaret and Arthur had retired to their marriage bed. Very tired but fuzzy with happiness, Heather kissed Merlin good night and made her way to her little bed in the nook upstairs.

As her eyes slid closed, she suddenly jerked awake with thoughts of her bracelet. Should she sleep with it on? Suppose it slipped off in the night and got lost in the sheets and laundered? A silly fear, really, but maybe she needed a jewelry box for it. She'd never had enough jewelry before to need such a thing. Then she remembered the pink unicorn box under her bed. That might be just right.

Reluctantly leaving the warmth of her blankets, she crawled out of bed and fumbled underneath it until she felt the smooth plastic box and pulled it out. Sleepily shrugging away her earlier uneasiness, she opened it for the first time. A squat matching bottle was inside. It must have been for that long-ago Heather to carry her drink to school in. The pink top looked like it also served as a cup. Suddenly she felt she needed to see how it opened. Reaching for it quickly, she pulled at the top. Nothing. She twisted it one way, then the other. It unscrewed in her hands.

Blackness roiled from within. Oily blinding blackness filled her lungs and ears and eyes, drowning and smothering her, pulling her into itself.

4

PURSUIT

Dawn found York unusually quiet. Eating, drinking, and dancing had carried on throughout the town until long past midnight. But in one room of the Duke's manor, quiet hung in an unnatural, smothering cloud. Beneath it, Merlin lay in nightmare-racked sleep. More than exhaustion from the day before held him down. For hours, he'd struggled fitfully but helplessly to wake up. Finally, as the first finger of faint sunlight touched his window, he thrust himself awake. Sitting up, he gasped, blinking in confusion.

Being exhausted he could understand. There'd been the wedding, the draining illusion, and then the food, drink, and all that dancing with Heather. Heather! He knew at once the cause of his nightmares.

Bolting out of bed, he grabbed his fleece-lined jacket, then froze, staring at the wall. Outlined against the rough stone were the powdery remains of what looked like a squashed moth. He groaned. An oblivion spell sent to fly through his window. How had he allowed that to trap him? He'd been tired and distracted, but . . . Heather! She was endangered!

Running from his room, he charged upstairs, down a

hall, and burst into the girls' suite. He stepped quickly to Heather's tiny room but stopped at the doorway. The stench of evil almost choked him. Thrusting open the door, he stared. A sheen of oily blackness seemed to cover the walls, windowsill, and empty bed. Discarded on the floor lay the ancient thermos bottle and lunch box, their pink plastic surfaces now corroded and pitted. The reek of evil in the room was horribly familiar.

"Morgan!" he yelled. But he knew the sorceress and her victim were already far away. Somehow she had cast another spell, a shielded abduction spell, and encased it in that innocent-seeming gift, knowing that it would surely be passed on to someone named Heather. His Heather. And the King of Norfolk, her old ally, had brought it into the Manor!

Murderous rage seared through him. He'd incinerate the man! He charged only a few steps before stumbling to a halt in the girls' common room. No, he had to control himself, had to think. Douglas might have been an innocent carrier; he might not have known. And Arthur wouldn't appreciate his wizard killing a potential ally and asking questions later.

Arthur. Yes, he should tell Arthur. But no, that wouldn't help yet. He had to think, to calm himself; he had to concentrate on sensing where Heather was now, where Morgan had taken her.

Hearing giggles, he looked up. Two of the other girls were standing at the doors of their rooms. They were eyeing his nightshirt and bare feet. "Spent the night with your girlfriend, did you?" one asked teasingly. "That's nice."

"No!" he snapped. "If only I had. When did you last see Heather?"

"When she was dancing with you," the other answered, taken aback by his sharp tone. "Why? Is something wrong?"

Without answering, Merlin stormed from the room and headed back for his own.

Once there, he sat on the bed and closed his eyes. With a moan, he stood, grabbed the staff Heather had made for him, and sat back down. Running a trembling hand over the carvings, he told himself to calm down, to focus. He needed to forge a link with Heather; he needed to sense where she was.

A warm tingling spread into his fingers. Closing his eyes, he let the power and the love carved into the staff seep into his skin. Breath and pulse slowly calming, he focused his thoughts. Again he saw Heather's small room. He felt the oily stench of evil and saw how it clotted around the windowsill, then sprayed into the air.

Even there, it was traceable, like following the reek of a burning brand. It led him skimming over the moorland, swooping and gliding like a dread bird of prey. Visions came of an approaching coast, a rocky beach. Then a tumult of images, a black stifling cocoon, an impossibly hideous beast, and a face of timeless beauty and hate.

Snatches of sound came as well—a rhythmic crashing, a screeching cry, a light-chilling laugh. Suddenly a jolt launched his mind through churning spray, over jagged rocks and wrinkled gray sea. But even there, between sea and sky, the trail could be followed. Like the slime left by a huge hideous snail, it led east over the ocean, glinting with evil.

Slowly Merlin roused himself. He knew what he was dealing with now and where he must go. Looking around his room, he was suddenly aware that the morning had advanced. Quickly dressing, he grabbed his staff and hurried downstairs, heading directly to Arthur's room.

The guard at the door raised a surprised eyebrow when Merlin demanded entry, but nodded and knocked timidly on the door. Impatiently Merlin brushed him aside and barged through the doorway.

In one movement, Arthur roused from sleep, rolled over, and grabbed the sword propped against the wall. Beside him, Queen Margaret, red hair splayed over the pillow, mumbled in her sleep and pulled the blankets more closely around her.

For a fuddled moment, Arthur looked at Merlin. Then he sighed and leaned his sword back against the wall. "Merlin, if you didn't look so ghastly, I'd suggest strongly that you come back later. What's the matter?"

"Morgan or a minion has been here. She's abducted Heather."

"Heather? How . . . ? No, you only need tell it once. Call the Duke and anyone else you think advisable into the Council Room. We'll be there right away."

Merlin left the King to waken his wife of several hours while he himself rushed out and gave the guards the names of several people to fetch. Then he hurried to the rooms assigned to the King's guard. A few of the soldiers were already stirring, but on his narrow bunk, Welly was a large, solidly asleep lump.

"Welly, get up!" Merlin said, shaking him roughly by the shoulders. "Heather . . . Heather's been abducted. Morgan's involved."

"What!" Welly blurted. Abruptly he sat up, squinting at his friend. Fumbling for his glasses on the side table, he jammed them onto his face. "What . . . ? How . . . ?"

"Arthur's calling an emergency council. I'll tell you on the way."

After dragging on trousers, Welly practically had to run to keep up with Merlin. The wizard's explanations were angry and disjointed. Welly was glad when they finally reached the Council Room. A half dozen advisors were there already, looking sleepy and worried. Several more joined them shortly.

Arthur and Margaret, having hastily dressed and now seated in a pair of oak chairs, greeted the arrivals. "Apologies for calling you at this hour after so late a night," the King said, "but Merlin here brings alarming news. Morgan Le Fay is not conceding Britain to us after all, though that was always too much to hope for. She or an agent was here, within these walls, last night, and abducted Heather McKenna." As the exclamations died down, he continued. "I'll let Merlin explain."

Looking bleak, Merlin stood. "The abduction spell was cleverly wrought and concealed in one of the wedding gifts that Douglas of Norfolk brought in two days ago. It was selected as something that almost certainly would be passed on to Heather."

"Oh, no!" the Queen gasped. "I didn't . . . I wouldn't . . ."

"No, Your Majesty," Merlin assured, "there was no way you could have known. It was diabolically well shielded. If anyone should have known, it was *me*. And I didn't." He choked back a sob. "I didn't!"

Otto, standing nearby, slapped him heavily on the back. "Cheer up, boy. It's not your fault. That Morgan woman's the very devil. The first thing we have to do is arrest that traitor Douglas and wring the truth out of him."

There were several shouts of agreement, but Arthur

raised a hand. "The first thing we need to do is let Merlin continue."

Merlin nodded. "Thank you. But it *is* my fault. Had I not let myself become so diverted, I might have sensed something more than a vague threat. And it is possible that Douglas did not know what he was carrying. Morgan once had an ally's access to Norfolk and could easily have planted the box there without King Douglas's knowledge. Yes, certainly detain and question him—diplomatically— but what I must do is set out after Heather. Morgan is flying with her to the Continent, and the trail grows fainter with every passing moment."

Arthur stood. "Basil, King Douglas is a guest in your house. I'll leave his treatment to you, remembering, of course, that we need to secure Norfolk's friendship at some point. And, Merlin, I know you want to go after Heather, but have you given thought to Morgan's motives in this?"

After a moment's silence, Merlin nodded. "Heather has a budding talent for magic that Morgan may wish to use. Some of that talent is developing in surprising ways that I doubt even Morgan is aware of. But I admit, the most likely reason that Heather was abducted is to get at me and, by luring me away, to weaken you."

Duke Basil spoke up. "And knowing that, boy, you are still planning to go traipsing off?"

Merlin's face rippled with pain. He looked at Arthur. "If it had been Margaret abducted, wouldn't *you* go?"

The King nodded after a moment. "I would. And I wouldn't just send questing knights after her either. But, Merlin, you are needed here too. This enterprise we've engaged in—you are part of it. You always have been. When I was forced to go on without you before, some two thousand years ago, the whole thing collapsed."

"It's different now. We've built stronger this time. But I will return. I *must*. Just as I must find Heather."

"See that you do," Arthur said gruffly. Then he gave a grim smile. "And I think Morgan will find herself more than evenly matched in you, awkward teenager or not."

"So how do you propose to go chasing after the witch?" Duke Clarence of Carlisle asked after a long silence. "You said she was *flying* to the Continent?"

Merlin nodded. "She's probably using the mount we saw her on before, a sort of mutant flying griffin. I'll have to follow by boat and then overland. It will be infuriatingly slow, but though I can transform myself into a hawk, I can't maintain that form for long."

"Well, then, you'll just have to use our dragon," Duke Basil said, and several of his followers laughed.

"Dragon?" Merlin and Arthur asked together.

"Just an old legend," the Duke said, "a joke, really. There's a hill on the moors nearby that's supposed to be a sleeping dragon."

"Tell us about it," Merlin urged.

"It's just a story they tell around here. I believed it as a kid, like I believed in fairy tales or . . ."

"Or in tales of King Arthur," Merlin continued impatiently. "Go on."

The Duke blushed so that even his bald head turned brick red. "Right. Anyway, long ago, there was supposed to be this big white dragon that was harassing York. But that angered the giant boar that has always been York's guardian spirit, and there was a big magical battle. The outcome was that the dragon was cursed to lie asleep on

the moors until . . . I don't remember; something like . . .
until its mother came back."

"Not mother," another voice spoke up. "Midwife. The
one who birthed the dragon." A small dark man smiled
apologetically. "As York's chief Druidical priest, I have read
all the old texts, and the word used most frequently is *midwife* or *birther.*"

Intently Merlin asked the priest, "And when was this
supposed to have happened?"

"Judging by the verb forms used in the earliest version,
I would say sometime after the Romans departed but before the Vikings arrived."

"Ah," Merlin said, and the corners of his mouth
twitched in a grim smile. "It's a long shot, but worth a try."
He looked at Duke Basil. "Your Grace, if you can lead us to
that hill, I will test if there is any truth to the old story. If
there isn't, I've no choice but to ride to the coast and see if
I can find a boat to take me to the Continent. Can you take
me there right away?"

"Hold on, Merlin," Arthur said. "You can't go dashing
off on your own. If this is a trap, as seems fairly certain,
you'd better have a party of warriors with you."

"I travel faster alone."

"Well, a single warrior, then, to guard your back."

"That will be me," Welly said suddenly, trying to stand
tall and warrior-like. "I've done the back-guarding thing
before."

A figure that had slipped into the room without anyone noticing crawled from under a table and stood beside
Welly. "Troll go too. Me very tricksy. Good in fight with
nasty folk."

Merlin looked both touched and exasperated. "Friends,

I can't take you into this. I have no idea what lies ahead—except a great deal of danger."

"All the more reason why I don't want you to go alone," the King interjected. "Take Welly and Troll at least, Merlin." Then he turned to the Duke. "Basil, could you have some traveling provisions assembled and lead a small party to this storied hill? We'll probably find nothing in it, though, but rock and dirt. People are forever making up tales like that to explain odd natural features or to scare their kids into going to bed."

Within an hour, a small party of horsemen clattered down the streets of York and out the north gate. Those citizens already up and about after a day of celebrating watched with interest, particularly since the newly married king and queen were in the party along with their duke and the young royal wizard. The sight of what was apparently a troll riding behind a plump young warrior caused special comment, as did the fierce-looking two-headed dog loping alongside.

Riding north and west, they soon passed through the abandoned ruins of the once-large city. Before them stretched the Yorkshire Moors, the bleak treeless hills furred with gray-green grass. Little moved besides themselves and the occasional rare bird soaring in the tarnished sky. Hooves clopped over the hard earth, and the breath of horses and riders showed in puffs on the cold air.

Riding up between Merlin and the King, Duke Basil pointed to the west. "See that ridge there, like a raised scar on the horizon? That's Dragon Hill. My friends and I used to come here as kids and dare each other to kick it or stick a sword into the 'dragon's' side."

"Did you?" Arthur asked.

The Duke laughed. "I still believed just a little too much to risk that. But tell me, Arthur, in your . . . eh, earlier time, did you ever actually see a dragon?"

"I heard that there were still some about, and I saw evidence of them—villages destroyed and so forth. But no, I never saw one myself. What about you, Merlin? There was some story about you as a boy, the first time, having confronted several dragons."

Eyeing the hill as they rode nearer, Merlin nodded impatiently. "By then, most dragons had left this world and returned to Faerie. But not all. At that time, King Vortigern had killed the previous king with the help of Saxons he'd invited into the country, but the Saxons had turned against him and chased him into Wales. He tried to build a fortress on a mountaintop, but the walls kept falling down, and his court wizards—real charlatans they were—told him to sacrifice a boy with no father. That was supposed to be me, but any wizard worth the name would have known that the reason the walls kept falling down was that they were building over a cave containing dragon eggs.

"I told them that. They dug down, revealed a clutch of large eggs, and accidentally cracked two. The result was a couple of young dragons, one red and one white, swooping out, fighting and terrifying everyone."

Queen Margaret, who'd been riding nearby and listening, said, "A red dragon and a white one? And the one in Basil's story is white. Are the times about right?"

Merlin smiled at her. "You're following my thinking. York's Druid said it was after the Romans left, before the Vikings. That's about when Arthur and I were first around. If the local story is true, it's possible this is one of the dragons I met."

"And gave birth to," Margaret added.

"Well, *aided* in the birth, you might say."

By this time, they were quite near the little hill. "If you look at it right," Welly observed, "it does kind of look like a sleeping dragon, head stretched out one way, tail the other."

Troll, who was peering from behind him, said, "Trolls not like dragons. Dragons big and cranky and eat small folk."

"Small folk like trolls?" Welly asked.

"Trolls, people, cattle. Everything smaller than dragons."

Merlin had already dismounted. Waving back the others, he strode to one end of the hill. Rus stalked beside him until Merlin called to Welly to grab the dog and keep him away.

Unsheathing his Eldritch sword, the wizard held it high and jabbed it into the ground. Then, raising his staff, he began chanting in a language none of them knew. The horses fidgeted nervously, Rus howled from both throats, and the watchers moved back a greater distance to calm their mounts.

From there, it was harder to see what was happening by the little hill. The mists that often cloaked the Yorkshire Moors had risen suddenly and were clouding their vision. But mist could not disguise the vibrations they felt under their feet or the faint rumbling reaching their ears. The horses' nervousness was turning to panic, and everyone dismounted and held their bridles, trying to murmur soothing words. The rumbling only grew louder and drowned them out.

The vibrations in the ground grew to violent shaking. As everyone strained to see through the mist, it suddenly swirled away. The hill shook as if in the throes of a massive earthquake. The rumbling ended in a thunderous crack, the hill shuddered, and its turf covering broke open and flew apart. Flaming pieces of grass and soil showered down on the watchers, sending the horses into screaming terror.

"If only Heather were here," Welly cried as he clung to his rearing horse's bridle. "She can always calm animals."

Beside him, the Queen, struggling with her own stallion, called, "What about your troll friend? I've seen him talk with animals."

Looking around, they saw Troll cowering flat on the ground, hands splayed over both large ears.

Handing her reins to Welly, Margaret walked to the quaking figure and crouched beside him. "Troll," she said firmly, resting a hand on his shoulder, "you have an important Royal Duty here. You must talk to the horses so they don't bolt and leave the King and the rest of us stranded."

Troll looked up with fear-widened eyes. Then, fingering the plastic beads around his neck, he squeaked, "Right. Troll brave, do duty. Horses big hairy cowards." Scuttling to the first horse, he scrambled up its neck and began talking in its ear. He repeated this until all the horses had been reduced to quiet shivering.

The people in the King's party now weren't paying as much attention to the horses as to what was happening on the moor in front of them. The exploding dirt and grass had settled to the ground. The air smelled of hot dirt and singed grass. A cloud of dust still hung over the hill. Slowly it began to drift away, exposing raw white earth. No, the watchers realized. That was not earth. It was moving.

The white shape, nearly thirty feet long, twitched, then rippled with motion, as if muscles were flexing along its whole length. A long snaky neck rose up, a triangular horned head at its end. The mouth opened and out poured a bone-sawing screech and a sulfurous stench. The creature's sides shivered and, and in a renewed cloud of dust, great wings unfurled.

Standing below the rearing head, Merlin raised his staff and shouted, "Hold, Worm! Twice now I have freed you. This time, I claim my lawful debt of service."

The dragon curled its neck down, bringing its head so close to Merlin that the watchers gasped for fear of seeing their young wizard disappear in one chomp. Blazing red eyes looked at him, and the mouth opened, showing knife-sharp teeth.

"So," a rasping voice hissed, "it *is* you. The same meddlesome boy wizard. A little older, it seems, though that is a pathetic excuse for a beard."

"We are both a couple of millennia older, Worm. The world has changed a great deal since you were last awake."

The creature raised its head and through flaring red nostrils sniffed the air. "Yes, I can tell, and not changed for the better. Not many dragons about, that's certain." Again it stretched its huge white batlike wings. "So I'll just have to set off and look for an entrance to Faerie. Not much point in hanging around this wasteland. Nice seeing you again, boy."

"You too, Worm, but we'll be seeing a lot of each other until you have paid your debt."

"All right, you sniveling little lawyer. So I owe you. So I'll pay it. What have I got to do? Eat that little cluster of people and horses over there? Done." Stiffly the creature got to its feet.

"No! Leave them alone—they're friends. What I

require is your transportation services. I need to go search for another friend who's been abducted."

The dragon snorted puffs of sulfurous smoke. "You expect me to carry all those people? Forget it. I'm still a youngster, you know."

Merlin shook his head. "No, only two others are going. Besides, you shouldn't complain. You are indeed just a young dragon and haven't had much of a chance to see the world. Travel will give you that."

The dragon spat, a hot sizzling blob that splatted on the ground and steamed like molten lava. "And some fine world you humans have made of it. All right, you've trapped me. How long am I to languish in your service?"

"Until you have, at my request, returned me and my party to Britain."

Again the dragon snorted, producing twin plumes of smoke. "Agreed, you puny extortioner. So, let's get going. I'm intensely sick of this piece of moorland."

When the dragon, with Merlin at its head, began lumbering their way, Arthur ordered one of his men to lead the quaking horses a safe distance off. Then they all watched uneasily as the creature approached.

"As you can see, My Lord Duke," Merlin said as they neared, "childhood stories should never be discounted. Welly and Troll, if you still wish to travel with me, come over and meet our transportation."

Speechless, Welly and Troll stepped slowly forward. The dragon eyed them as steaming strings of saliva dripped from its mouth. "Tasty."

"Worm," Merlin admonished, "these are my companions and are to be protected, not harmed. But, Welly and Troll, you are both free to change your minds."

"No," Welly squeaked after a moment. "You and Heather might need me. I'm coming."

Before Troll could answer, the dragon hissed. "Don't count on that little scuttling one. Trolls are feckless cowardly sneaks, not good for much—except eating. They *are* nice and crunchy."

Troll whimpered, but Merlin spoke to him. "Don't worry, Troll, the dragon's pledged to transport and protect me and mine. Dragons do honor bargains—though, as you said, they are cranky."

The dragon was no longer paying attention to Welly and Troll. Lowering its head toward the others, it fastened its red gaze on Arthur. It sighed in a cloud of steam. "The Pendragon. I am honored. Even in the egg, I heard you were coming. Greetings."

"Greetings to you, mighty dragon," Arthur said, struggling to keep his voice steady. "It is my wish that you follow my wizard's instructions. The girl they seek is a member of my court and my friend."

The dragon raised its head. "As you wish, Pendragon. Your wizard is an uppity youngster, but I am bound to him—for the time being."

With much grumbling, the dragon squatted down and allowed bags of provisions that were brought from the horses to be loaded onto its back. Merlin secured them with magical bands, then he, Welly, and a reluctant Troll climbed onto the humped back and settled into saddle-like depressions among the broad white scales. Merlin extended the magic security bands to the riders as well.

Again the dragon unfurled its wings, this time to their full impressive width. As the others hastily stepped back,

Arthur called up, "Take care of yourself, Merlin. We need you. Bring yourself and the others back."

"I'll try, Arthur. Morgan cannot be allowed to win. *We* know that. We need to let her know that too."

Rus had been turned over to one of the soldiers, but now the dog broke away and, running forward, began barking frantically. The dragon lowered its head and squinted at the creature. "Right, I hear you, dog," the dragon hissed, "but no way am I going to carry the likes of you—squirming, flea-ridden, remarkably ugly thing that you are. Though if you *really* want to help your mistress, you could become a little snack to give me energy."

"None of that!" Merlin snapped. "Someone hold Rus. We'll bring Heather back, Rus, I swear it."

Gripping his staff firmly, he rested it along the dragon's back. Behind him, Welly was torn between clutching the scales and clutching his glasses. Then he remembered his glasses had been enchanted to stay on his face, so he used both hands to grip the scales as tightly as he could. Behind him, Troll closed his eyes and slid his long flat fingers into every crack among the scales that he could find.

On both sides, the huge wings gave a few gentle flaps, then with one powerful thrust jerked them into the air. Welly groaned and Troll squealed, but nothing could be heard above the thrumming of dragon wings.

Below, the group gasped in awe at the sight, then watched silently as the dragon rose into the sullen gray sky. Smaller and smaller the figure became, until it might have been confused with an oddly shaped bird. Finally it disappeared in the murky distance.

"Well, Pendragon," Duke Basil said apologetically, "I've

more than learned my lesson. I'll never doubt the old tales again."

Arthur shook his head. Grabbing Margaret's hand, he headed toward the horses. "Old stories are fine. But the problem with stories when you are living through them is that you don't know how they will end."

5

CAPTIVE

Darkness. Seemingly endless darkness into which only vague disturbing noises and a sickening sense of motion penetrated. Thoughts and feelings were smothered in the darkness—all except fear. Then even that faded into nothingness.

It was a faint rustling that pulled her up from the dark. Heather lay still, eyes closed, mind slowly wakening. There was the rustling again. Slowly she realized it came from under her. She twitched a leg, and the rustling returned. Gingerly she felt about with her hand. She was lying on what felt like a thin mattress, a mattress stuffed with rustling straw.

Her eyes seemed almost glued shut, but she struggled to open them. Above was a ceiling of gray stone. A small black blot on the ceiling broke loose and dropped toward her. Instinctively she raised an arm to fend it away, but the shape stopped just beyond her reach. Heather blinked and tried to focus. Then she screamed. The scream came out only as a rusty croak.

The thing hovering above her was—a bat? She'd seen bats in books but thought they were all extinct. She wished this one was. Its black leathery wings fluttered up and down, keeping it in place above her. Between the wings was a hairy body and a horrid face—a grotesque almost-human face, huge tufted ears, squinty eyes, turned-up snout, and a wide mirthless grin filled with needle-like teeth.

To make it worse, the mouth opened wide and it spoke. "Awake. Good. Report."

With that, the creature flew out of her sight. Woozily Heather sat up. She was in a room, a small round room, its walls and floor the same cold gray stone as the ceiling. The bat thing was nowhere to be seen. It must have flown out of the room's single window. She couldn't see anything through the window's glassless arch but pale gray sky. It was daytime. How many days?

Startled, she looked down at herself. She was wearing the same blue dress she had worn at the wedding. The dancing. The pink box under her bed. Heather groaned as it all came back in a jumbled rush. What had happened? Where was she?

She tried to stand but dizzily dropped back onto the crackling mattress. Very slowly she tried again and wobbled to her feet. Six cautious steps brought her to the wall. Gratefully she leaned against its cold stone. Then she looked out the window.

The light was low. Not knowing what direction she was looking, it could be either morning or afternoon. A tiredness in the hazy light suggested afternoon. If so, the position of the sun smudge told her she was looking west. But west from where?

There were mountains, tall, craggy, almost-bare mountains. Here and there dark mangy spots might be trees. Heather thought back to her geography classes in school. These mountains looked taller than anything she thought they had in Britain. Even the Scottish Highlands in the pictures hadn't looked like this, and anyway, those were under glaciers now.

She shivered. Not in Britain, then. What was there beyond Britain? Not much, she thought, not anymore. But yet, there had been those voices scattered around the globe. And now there was this place.

Leaning across the thick chest-high windowsill, she tried to see more of this place. Below stretched a bare rocky mountainside. Standing on tiptoes, she wriggled farther out. A rugged stone wall, unbroken by other windows, dropped many stories to the ground. Above, it rose a short distance to end in crenellations against the gray sky. She could see nothing but sky to her left, but to her right, the stone wall curved away, then abutted another stone wall, straight and featureless.

Turning back to the room, she studied it, but there was little to see. The mattress was the only furniture. In the far wall was a metal-studded wooden door. Without much hope, she staggered across the room. The door was locked. She tried the little opening magic that she knew. But it dribbled off like a feeble spray of water.

Trembling, she walked back and sank down on the mattress. Only then did she let the building despair overwhelm her. She'd been abducted to someplace unimaginably foreign. She was a prisoner in some ancient stone building. And she didn't know why or where or what might happen next.

Sobbing, Heather dropped her face into her hands. Something hard pressed against her cheek. Earl's bracelet!

She still had that. Clutching the metal circlet, she felt its warmth, almost like she was holding Earl's hand in hers. Somehow he'd help.

The pale daylight was fading from the window when the door suddenly clanked open. Startled out of a hopeless stupor, Heather turned to see a plate of food slide across the floor as the door slammed shut again. She stared at the plate a moment before getting up and walking cautiously toward it. Bread and some pale green mashed stuff. Her stomach grumbled at the sight. How long had it been since she'd eaten anything? Days, surely. But did she dare eat this?

Shaking her head, she kicked the plate. It skidded across the floor, clacking against a wall. Not until she knew what was going on. The food could be poisoned, drugged, or magicked. She had to know who had brought her here and why.

Another hour passed. A sullen sunset was replaced by a hazy splotch of moonlight behind high clouds. She heard another rustling. It wasn't coming from her mattress but from the base of the wall where she'd kicked that plate. She stared through the gloom and made out two shapes. Moving shapes. Rats, she realized—investigating the rejected food.

Be careful of that food, she thought at them. *It might be bad.*

She felt their startled thoughts. *Smells good. Hungry.*

It could be poisoned or have bad magic.

She felt mental giggles. *Live here. Get to know poison and bad magic. This clean.*

Well, then, it's yours. But be careful.

Heather looked at her guests more closely. One was

smaller and gray-white. A female, she felt. The male was a darker gray. They shared the food without fighting, stopping occasionally to clean whiskers and muzzles with the back of a paw.

When they'd eaten every crumb, they both nodded toward her, then scrambled off to what must be their hole in the wall, a small chink of greater darkness.

Wait. I'm trapped here. Where is this?

The rats stopped. *Big stone fortress,* the female answered.

Stone fortress in mountains, the male added. *Bad place, but food's here. Have to be careful or bad things make food of you.*

Heather sighed. A stone fortress in the mountains didn't tell her much. But she could hardly expect rats to know geography. *What sort of bad things?*

Again, giggles. *Every sort. Flying bad things, crawling bad things. Human bad things baddest of all. But you're a human, right?*

I try to be.

Thought so. If flying bad things come through window, don't let them bite. With that, both rats vanished into their hole.

Uneasily Heather looked out her window and gasped. The hazy moonlight showed a cloud of small black shapes fluttering just beyond the arched opening. Sharp hungry squeakings scratched at her mind. But they didn't fly in, almost as if an invisible screen kept them out.

For ages, it seemed, she watched the threatening cloud, but nothing changed. Finally, exhausted, frightened, and very cold, she lay down and struggled to fold one end of the thin mattress over herself. But she still couldn't sleep. She tried to think back over the things she'd read at Llandoylan School, searching for any clue about her whereabouts. The school had collected surviving books from all over, and she'd been perhaps the school's biggest bookworm, reading almost everything that didn't fall apart in her hands. Of course, fiction had been her favorite, but sometimes it was hard to tell what the pre-Devastation people thought was true and what they made up, because their real world was so different from hers. But still . . .

Suddenly a memory jolted into her mind, and she fervently wished it hadn't. She'd read a book once, set in some place on the Continent. Eastern Europe, maybe. At the beginning, there'd been a stone castle in the mountains. This really scary guy, a count or something, was keeping another guy prisoner there. And there'd been bats. Awful bloodsucking bats. Vampire bats.

Shivering from cold and fear, Heather got only fitful sleep that night.

The fluttering shapes beyond the window disappeared with the pale orange of dawn. Shortly after, the door rattled open a crack and another plate of food slid in before the door slammed closed again. Heather unrolled herself from the prickly mattress and stared at the plate. She was hungry enough now to risk eating just about anything. At the whisper of tiny footsteps, she turned. The rats were peeking out of their hole.

I must eat something, she thought at them. *But I'll share. Half for you, half for me.*

They crept fully out and waited patiently while Heather brought the plate back to her mattress. Breaking the bread in two, she used part to scoop up half of the green glop. It tasted like boiled leaves, but her stomach welcomed it, then growled in complaint when she put the remainder of the food down for the pair of rats. But she had said she'd share.

Finally, meal finished, the rats were gone and Heather was alone. She clutched her bracelet, trying to draw comfort from its presence. Then, lying back, she attempted to clear her mind. If only she could hear some of those voices now, that would be some company. But she'd never actually *tried* to hear them, just waited until they intruded on her. She wished she and Earl had been able to experiment. He'd been so excited by the idea that she could contact people living elsewhere. Well, now she had nothing else to do. She could try.

She closed her eyes and tried to think cool, calm nothing. Reaching out to animal minds came naturally to her, but this was different. She imagined her thoughts stretching out like weeds or tentacles waving around in the water, searching, reaching, trying to catch something. She thought she caught a hint of the voice that talked about jaguars, ancient temples, and annoying sisters. But those thoughts were busy elsewhere, not wanting to talk.

For a moment, there was another voice she hadn't heard often. It seemed scared and alone too. *Aunt Gutra told me to stay quiet in here. There's danger outside. But it's dark. Are you someplace happy today?*

No, Heather answered back. *I'm not. I've been taken somewhere far from home. I don't know why.*

Silence followed. Then, *I'm sorry. At least I'm home. And the danger always passes in a little while. Be brave. That's what Aunt Gutra always says: Be brave.*

She lost contact, and Heather found herself drenched in sweat. This was a lot harder now that she was trying to reach the voices than when they just came on their own.

From what she remembered feeling when she'd looked at the globe, that particular scared voice was way off in South Asia someplace. It still felt distant, though perhaps not as far away as before, but that gave her no clue where *she* might be. For a choking moment, Heather was overwhelmed with longing to have Earl with her. He could help her with this; he would know what to do, what was happening. And he could get her out of here, surely. She didn't even know what to try. Clutching her bracelet, she repeated what the voice had said: *Be brave.*

Tired from trying to reach out with her mind, she just lay back, closed her eyes, and drifted into a half doze. That's when a new voice cut into her with painful intensity. *Close. You're close. Why?*

Excited, yet cringing against the mental pain, Heather thought back, *I'm a prisoner in a stone castle or something. I was kidnapped. I've talked to you before, haven't I?*

A couple of times, I think. You sound much nearer now, though. Are you hurt?

No. Not yet. But I don't know why I'm here.

The voice stayed silent a long while, and when it came back, it was much weaker. *Sorry, I'm not good at this. Can't keep it up. You take care.* Nothing more came, and when she tried probing with her thoughts, she found blankness. But at least she'd had some contact. And if this person really was near, maybe he could help, though she didn't see how. Besides, his idea of close might just mean that he was closer than the guy near the jaguars. Well, anyway, Heather thought, at least she wasn't the only one who wasn't very skilled at working this thought-message thing.

The day dragged on. Nothing more touched her mind except fear and boredom. For long spells, Heather stared

out the window at the bleak rugged landscape. She supposed these mountains had been forested before the
Devastation. Then they wouldn't have looked so repellent.
She wondered if anything lived near here. Were there
bands of muties like in the wildest areas of Britain? If a lot
of bombs had been dropped in Europe and if this *was*
Europe, wouldn't the mutations be even worse? And were
there any clutches of normal people left? She tried not to
think about what was living with her in this castle, if that's
what it was. The stench of magic was obvious, and it
wasn't the good kind.

An occasional bird, or something with wings, traced its
way across the steely sky. Earl had always said that with
her magic affinity for animals, transforming herself into
one should come easily to her. But that was another one of
those things they hadn't had time to work on, what with
all the traveling with Arthur, trying to unify Britain. Earl
himself could become a hawk, but he said it was never easy
for him. Trying to turn herself into a bird now, when she
hadn't a clue how to do it, would probably be disastrous.
The rocks far below looked awfully hard and sharp.

It was mid-afternoon when the door lock clattered
once more. Heather had been lying on the mattress again,
trying to sleep now that it was less cold. Abruptly she sat
up and stared at the door. Out of the corner of her eye, she
noticed the rats also peering out hopefully. Then the door
opened fully, and she saw the face she most feared and half
expected.

"Morgan," she whispered.

"Yes, my dear. Heather McKenna, it's so pleasant to
meet not on a battlefield or in some silly battle of wills. I'm
delighted to have you as my guest."

"Guest, right," Heather muttered. She'd dealt with Morgan before and knew she had to guard herself against that lulling persuasive voice.

The woman stepped into the room. Again Heather was struck by her perfect beauty. Slender girlish figure, moon-white skin, lustrous black hair. There'd been a time when Heather had pined for a fraction of such beauty, and she'd come close to betraying everything to get it. But that, she knew firmly, was over.

"So sorry about the transportation," Morgan said soothingly. "It must have been a little stifling. But I hardly thought you'd accept a polite invitation."

"You got that right."

"Come, come. We need to put old enmities aside. The world has changed, you know. In fact, that's what I wanted to talk with you about."

Heather just stared at the woman, not answering.

"When I last talked with our mutual—acquaintance, Merlin, he told me that you had a newer type of magic, one that was different than what we from the old times wield. I certainly can feel that you have power, and that intrigues me. Power is something to be valued, and with the world changing as it is, it is so important to wield it well. Don't you agree?"

Heather kept stonily silent.

"You aren't making this any easier, you know. I am making you a very attractive offer. Magic is the future of the world now. I am suggesting that you join me. With your new powers and my ancient ones, there is so much we could do for this poor battered world."

Heather was surprised she had the courage to laugh, but she did laugh. Derisively.

"Oh, I know we've had our issues," Morgan continued, unruffled. "But don't dismiss my offer out of hand. This world is so badly shattered, it needs power—intelligently used—to unite it. That could happen if you joined me."

Heather stood up and glared angrily at her captor. "Issues? You said we've had issues? Trying to kill me and my friends, invading Britain with your loathsome armies, trying to undercut all the good that Arthur is doing— I consider that more than *issues*. I consider that pure evil, and I want nothing to do with it!"

Now anger edged Morgan's voice. "You may be power- ful, but you're a fool too. Letting Arthur and Merlin cor- rupt your mind like this. They have their own agendas, their own visions of the world. But theirs are weak visions, distorted by their outdated ideas. They can't begin to grasp the enormity of this world and the challenge of reviving and uniting it. Come with me, and I will show you the great potential of what we can do. *We,* you and I. Old and new powers united, strengthening each other. Not the frayed plans of a couple of has-beens mired in their own dimming dreams."

Heather felt the warm weight of the bracelet on her wrist and tried to draw strength from it. "Morgan, I would rather work for the dimmest of their dreams than further one of your nightmares. Go look for some other partner, one of your own vile kind, like that werewolf you used to hang out with. I'm not joining."

"Clueless young fool!" Morgan's anger manifested in a whirlwind of dust through the room. "I could *make* you work for me. A willing partner is more useful, but zombie slaves have their value too. You may have power, but you've scarcely a clue how to use it. Your supposed friend

Merlin was clearly too jealous of you to train a potential rival. I could teach you skills you cannot imagine, give you strength and power and beauty. Or I could crush you like useless vermin!"

With that, she thrust a hand toward the base of the far wall, and with a frightened squeak, a rat was yanked into the air. It was the darker, male rat, and he hung suspended in the air in front of Morgan, his legs and tail flailing.

Help! he called into Heather's mind, but when she jumped toward him, Morgan flicked a blast of power at her that sent her sprawling against the stone wall. Dazed, trying to shake her eyesight back into focus, Heather watched as, with a cruel smile, Morgan made a small clawed gesture toward the rat. Abruptly his writhing stopped. Instead the body crumpled in on itself. Blood, mushed flesh, and bits of fur dripped onto the floor. Finally the empty rat skin was released from the air and dropped onto the steaming puddle.

"Don't mistake me, Heather dear. Join me and we can work wonders. Cross me and your end will be far less merciful."

Sweeping from the room, Morgan slammed the door with the finality of the tomb.

6

EASTWARD

It took a while for Welly to force his eyes open and even try admiring the view. In the distance beyond the rolling moors was the dark sweep of ocean. This did not increase his comfort. He couldn't swim, and water in any quantity made him nervous. Though, he realized, if he fell from this height, drowning wouldn't be the major problem.

Talking might fix his attention elsewhere, but the wind of their passage made that difficult, and anyway, he was keeping his mouth clamped closed. The dragon's swooping gait churned his stomach, and he didn't think it looked good for a warrior of King Arthur's to get airsick.

Then all his attention was fixed on staying aboard. The dragon suddenly pulled in its wings and dropped like a stone for long moments, ignoring its passengers' cries. Abruptly the wings snapped out again, swooping them into a smooth glide that skimmed along a few feet above the moor. A cluster of dark shapes dotting the grass suddenly scattered, bleating in panic. Without missing a beat, the dragon's head snaked down and with perfect aim scooped up a fleeing sheep. Its bleating was silenced as fangs clamped together. Rising higher, the dragon continued its course to the coast.

"Hey, those are some poor farmer's sheep," Welly called to Merlin. "We shouldn't let the dragon do that."

Merlin glanced back at him. "One doesn't 'let' dragons do things. They're controlled by their instincts and their code of honor. Period."

"But you're a wizard."

"Which is why I know not to meddle with dragons more than I have to. We're just along for the ride, and lucky to be doing that."

Riding behind Welly, Troll only groaned and held on tighter. He was very aware that trolls and sheep were about the same size.

The surf-fringed coast was close enough now to throw the sound of crashing waves into the air. Skimming toward the last cliff edge, the dragon suddenly folded its wings and glided to a smooth landing. Dropping the sheep carcass on the grass, it turned a bloody head toward them.

"Breakfast time."

"It's afternoon," Welly objected feebly.

"Hey, fat boy, I haven't eaten in two thousand years. And my appetite's a lot bigger than one sheep's worth—so watch it."

"Let's stretch our legs," Merlin suggested pointedly. "The North Sea has shrunk a lot since the Devastation, but it's still a demanding crossing."

"Yeah," Welly muttered. "And let's get away from the breakfast table."

Staggering stiffly onto the ground again, Welly stayed well back from the cliff's edge. Staring across the gray water, he could just make out a dark line along the horizon. "Is that Europe?"

Merlin nodded. "What's left of it. Well, the bare bones of the land should be the same, but the nations that people created there are probably long gone. I only left Britain once before. A trip to what later became France. It was beautiful then. I wish I could keep remembering it that way. But we can't. Heather's somewhere in Europe now."

"Can you still see the trail or whatever?"

"I can sense it, but we must hurry. After 'breakfast' is over, of course. We're lucky this is a baby dragon. Otherwise it might have stopped to eat the whole herd."

For a moment, Welly thought about their mount, feeling very glad he hadn't met a grown-up dragon. "But I don't feel right just calling it 'dragon.' Doesn't it have a name?"

Troll hissed and Merlin put a hand on Welly's shoulder.

"Never ask about dragons' names," he whispered. "Creatures from the Otherworlds keep their true names secret."

"Oh, so our pudgy little warrior is impolite as well as ignorant," the dragon said, coming silently up behind them. It paused to wipe its bloody muzzle over a tuft of grass. "But yes, I would prefer you use some name—and certainly something other than 'Worm.' How about 'Blanche'? It suits, I think. Yes, you may call me Blanche."

"You're a girl?" Welly said, astonished.

"Doesn't this kid know anything? It takes boy things and girl things to make baby things. Right? I was kind of hoping that 'Red' and I could pair up when we got older. But now he's probably off in Faerie with bevies of eligible young dragons, and I have to go off on this ridiculous world cruise."

"I thought Merlin said you and the red dragon were fighting."

"So? That's how dragons show interest in one another, numb brain. Better get on now, all of you, before I forget this code-of-honor thing and skip out for Faerie right now!"

Quickly the three scrambled onto Blanche's back and were soon winging over the gray wrinkled expanse of ocean. Troll had his eyes shut the entire way; Welly kept his open but focused on the opposite shore. Merlin forced himself to look around but unhappily recalled the days when unfiltered sunlight sparkled on the water and when colorful boats and white seabirds skimmed over the waves.

He knew the world was slowly recovering. Gradually the atmospheric dust was thinning, giving them more glimpses of blue sky and producing some earlier thaws. Some plants and animals thought extinct had even been seen. But he knew things could never be quite the same. He sighed. Perhaps it was a good thing that there were so few alive who could remember the world as it once was— and truly mourn the loss. There was just himself and Arthur—and Morgan. He wondered, though, if she didn't really prefer this twisted world as it was now. It certainly gave more scope for her brand of magic.

The European shore was bleaker than the one they'd left. Dry grass covered the ground only in spotty patches. Seaside villages showed up as crumbling ruins, and larger cities were rusted skeletal remains.

But the ruins weren't totally deserted. A few shapes scuttled into shadows as they passed above. Muties, Welly realized with a shiver. Muties or, worse—creatures from the darker Otherworlds. He'd met some of both with the armies Morgan had recruited to attack Britain.

As the sun was lowering toward the horizon behind them, Blanche banked into a loop and circled down to where a couple of rocky cliffs enclosed a now-dry river valley. Her riders climbed off, already shivering in the coming night.

Welly buttoned his fleece jacket and commented to Merlin, "I'm surprised it wasn't colder riding up there."

"Dragon fire. It's always smoldering inside. Keeps dragons and their passengers, it seems, nice and warm. I guess we have to camp here for the night. Much as I want to, we can't ask Blanche to fly nonstop."

"You've got that right, magic boy," Blanche said from behind them. Welly whipped around, astonished that something as big as a dragon could move so silently. She snorted a laugh at his surprised look. Smoke puffed from her nostrils. "And I'm not going anywhere until I get a proper meal. Thought I noticed a herd of something lurking over there. See you."

With a few beats of her wings, she was up and gliding over the eastern cliff, her white shape astonishingly bright in the dusk.

"Firelit white isn't exactly made for stealth," Merlin observed. "But she's what we've got, and anyway, if I can sense Morgan, she can probably sense me. Stealth may not matter."

Soon he, Welly, and Troll were huddled around a small magically started fire eating rations brought from York. That outpost of civilization seemed awfully far away to all of them now. Emptiness and silence pressed close around them—as did the cold and dark.

Twice Merlin started to say something, then lapsed into awkward silence. Finally he got up, paced around the fire, and abruptly sat down again. "Welly, I'm awfully glad you insisted on coming with me. . . ."

"And Troll too," their associate added.

Merlin nodded impatiently. "Yes, I'm glad you came too, Troll. But this is something different."

"Oh, me get it. Private human-to-human talk. Troll go to sleep." Wrapping himself in the blanket he'd draped over his shoulders, Troll rolled up like a bug on the far side of the fire and immediately began snoring.

Weakly Merlin smiled, then he looked again at Welly. "Like I said, I'm glad you came, but I feel guilty too. Not just for putting you in danger, and gods know there's certainly enough of that. But because . . . well, because of Heather. Me and Heather, I mean . . . Because we're . . ."

"Hold it, Earl. Are you thinking that I'm jealous of you two? Of your being a couple?"

"Well, you and Heather were close friends at Llandoylan long before you got tied up with me. You've been through a lot together, have risked a lot for each other."

"And for you, Earl. Hey, Heather and I are *friends*. But she's more like my sister. I saw that you two were made for each other long before either of you dummies realized that." Welly stopped and nervously began plucking at a few brittle strands of grass. "It feels sort of weird talking about this kind of stuff, but I'd do anything for Heather, and I want to see her happy. You make her happy." Welly blushed and flicked a few pebbles into the fire, watching the sparks fly. Then, taking off his glasses, he began polishing them on a sleeve.

"Besides, now that I'm one of King Arthur's famous warriors, girls come flocking." He laughed awkwardly. "Well, sort of."

"True, I have seen you with some very fetching ones."

Welly's firelit face turned even more ruddy. "Yeah, well, they've been okay, but not really what I'm looking for, I guess. The right one's out there somewhere, probably. I'm young yet, I suppose."

Merlin nodded. "You are. But I'm not, not really. One long lifetime and a bit of another, and Heather is the first person I've felt this way about. There was Nimue, of course, but that was different—enchantment was involved." He paused and his voice dropped. "What I feel for Heather amazes me every day. And if I can't save her from that foul creature Morgan, I don't feel this life's worth living anymore."

He stared silently at the fire for a moment, then continued. "I know what Arthur said about this abduction being a trap. But I can't help it—I've got to try and save Heather. And I'm grateful that you're here to help . . . and that you understand."

"Of course I understand," Welly said.

"And Troll understand too," came a squeaky voice from across the fire. "But enough mushy boy talk. Sleep time—before fat white worm come back and burp yucky dinner at us."

The two boys had no sooner rolled up in their own blankets than the dragon glided back into their camp. Red smeared her white neck and chest, and her noxious burps produced clouds of smoke.

"Wild mutant cattle are not bad, really," she announced, delicately picking her teeth with a claw. "Those

extra heads and legs make them extra crunchy. I suppose
you want to be off at dawn, wizard boy?"

"Or earlier," Merlin replied, trying not to breathe the
putrid dragon breath.

"Right, then. I won't need to stop for breakfast—
I brought back a couple of extras. But don't even think
about sharing them. They're *mine*."

"Absolutely," Merlin assured her. "All yours."

They were in the air again by dawn. To Merlin, the trail
they were following still glinted slimily through the sky.
Below it, spreading light from the east showed a bleak
landscape. Crumbled villages and abandoned towns gave
way to glassy plains where cities had disappeared under
balls of nuclear fire. Their southeasterly route took them
over some of these and skirted others. That evening, they
flew longer than planned so they could camp in a relatively
less-desolate spot.

Blanche went out foraging again, and the others ate an
almost-silent meal around their small fire. Over a dark
ridge, the night sky still glowed faintly from radiation, like
the ghost of city lights that had once twinkled there.

When the depressing silence grew too heavy, Welly
asked Merlin, "Is the rest of the world all like this?"

Merlin sighed. "I can't believe it could be. Supposedly
the nuclear nations destroyed each other's cities, and social
collapse devastated much of the rest. But some countries
never had nuclear arms or, like Britain, had abandoned
them by the time the war broke out. We know that muties
roam the Continent. But tucked away in places, there must
be surviving pockets of less-mutated humanity as well.
When Morgan brought her armies from here, they in-

cluded not only muties but also darker creatures from the Otherworlds. So all of those gates between the worlds are not sealed, and that in itself means there must be enough life in *this* world to attract creatures from the Other."

Merlin took a bite of the dried mutton that made up their dinner and thought about what to say next. "Besides, Heather seems to have moments of mental communication with magic workers elsewhere. There appear to be survivors scattered over the world."

"What? She never told me about that."

"No, she really just figured it out in the last few days. If only we'd had time to work with it before . . . I can only hope that Morgan doesn't learn about that, or whatever she has in mind for Heather could be even worse." Angrily he slammed a fist down on the gravelly ground. "That's why I begrudge even these short rest breaks. But dragons are tricky to work with. You don't dare push them too far."

"Dragons!" Troll snorted while huddling closer to the fire. "Don't know which worse. Riding overgrown worm or sleeping here. This place full of ghosts."

Welly nodded and shivered, but Merlin looked sharply into the surrounding darkness. Clutching the hilt of his sword, he whispered, "And perhaps something more solid than ghosts as well."

In the smoky black night, patches of deeper darkness flowed silently toward them. Here and there, the low firelight glinted on what might be an eye or a fang. Quietly Merlin gestured at their campfire. It blazed into a column of violet light. Squeals and growls broke the silence as the light showed a closing circle of creatures. Most seemed more animal than human. Skin flapped from the bodies or glistened with sores. Eyes and limbs were missing or oddly multiplied. Some shrank back from the light or scurried away, but some crouched, ready to spring.

Jumping to his feet, Merlin swept his staff toward the nearest group. Purple fire shot from its tip, charring a few creatures before they left the ground. Welly pulled out his sword and sliced into a translucent many-armed creature loping toward them.

Troll hurled rocks at the enemy, then fumbled in his bedroll for his small dagger. Suddenly he squeaked and grabbed at Merlin's coat. "More, lots more coming!"

Merlin swung around to see a pack of hairy creatures charging from behind a pile of boulders. Before he could even raise his staff, the pack was engulfed in a spray of flame. The remaining creatures looked fearfully into the sky and scattered.

"I can't leave you helpless incompetents alone for a minute, can I?" Blanche said as she settled to the ground and folded her wings. "The muties around here aren't nearly as tasty and have really bad attitudes. Let's sleep a bit and move on as soon as we can."

"I heartily agree," Merlin said. "And thank you."

She snorted a gout of flame. "If I let the one I'm bound to get himself killed, my debt will never be properly canceled. One of those honor things. Now sleep."

"Should we set watch?" Welly asked as they rolled out their blankets.

Flopping on the ground, Blanche encircled the three with her neck, body, and tail. "I don't think they'll be bothering you any more tonight. Not with *me* around. So stop jabbering and sleep."

Merlin didn't find that easy, tired though he was. But

he also didn't find the stench of dragon breath nearly as disturbing as the distant glow of the dead city. Rolling over, he turned his back on that and eventually drifted into troubled dreams.

For several days, they followed the course Merlin sensed trailing into the southeast. Gradually they saw less outright destruction, though the land below looked bleak and largely lifeless. Some scraggly trees appeared, and occasional figures moved in the landscape. These scuttled for cover as the shadow of the dragon passed over. In other circumstances, Merlin knew, he ought to find out what sort of creatures these were—muties, Otherworld denizens, or perhaps somewhat-human survivors. But no time could be spared for that now.

Finally one late afternoon found them threading their way into mountains. Merlin wished he had paid more attention to European geography, but as their course was now more east than south, he guessed these were the Carpathians. Here some more trees survived, and they glimpsed planted fields where a few huddled settlements cowered under cliffs or were tucked into narrow valleys. Merlin didn't sense any other than normal magic about them.

As they climbed higher among the mountains, Merlin became alert. The trail he had been following for days had, at times, nearly broken, but now it was thickening into more of a rope than a thread. Heather and the magic that had abducted her both felt near at hand. Their exact goal became clear as they glided through a mountain pass and saw an only partly ruined stone castle on the mountainside ahead.

Merlin leaned forward and called to the dragon, "That's it—where we're headed."

"That's obvious enough, wizard boy. The place reeks of magic. So what is your great rescue plan?"

Merlin hated to admit that he didn't have much of a plan, not until he knew the situation here. "We could start out by simply swooping down where Heather is and seeing if we can grab her. What do you think, Welly?"

"A frontal attack? Might work. Obviously approaching on a bright white dragon ruins our chances at stealth."

"Well, *sorry,*" Blanche huffed. "Next time you can walk."

Ignoring her, Merlin clutched his staff and closed his eyes a moment. Then, opening them, he focused on a tower on the building's far right. "See that tower, the tallest one with the conical top? That's where Heather is. We might as well make straight for there, to test their defenses if nothing else."

They felt Blanche's growl rumbling through her whole body. "I didn't sign up to be caught in the middle of a magic workers' battle."

"You didn't sign up at all," Merlin reminded her. "You were drafted. And those are the orders—unless you can think of something better."

"Besides turning and flying back home? All right, in we go."

Their steady pace suddenly changed as the wings beat blurringly fast and the dragon shot forward like a spear. The wind of speed blew any shrieks away as they quickly closed in on the tower. Merlin, clutching a dragon scale with one hand and his staff with the other, thought he caught sight of two figures at its arched window.

Suddenly they jerked forward as the dragon furiously backstroked with her wings. Veering abruptly sideways, she circled around and hovered some three hundred feet from the tower. "Magic barrier," she gasped. "Nearly splattered myself like a moth against it."

"I'll try to crack it," Merlin yelled, pointing his staff. A thin beam of purple light shot forward, then shattered into harmless sparks. Concentrating, he increased the power. Purple tendrils spread over the invisible wall, but no cracks appeared.

"Uh-oh. Trouble!" squeaked Troll from the back. "Bats!"

Merlin kept focused on the barrier, but Welly looked up, drawing his sword. "Bats? That's not exactly a big threat."

"No! Troll knows. These bad bats. Vampire bats!"

Frantically Welly began swinging his sword as the cloud of darting black shapes closed in. Most stayed out of reach, though with sickening splats, he hit a few. Twisting her neck, the dragon sprayed the air with flame—incinerating bats but nearly choking her riders.

Suddenly the barrier dissolved of its own accord. A bolt of green power shot from the tower window. The dragon veered sideways, and Merlin, hanging nearly upside down, shot out a purple bolt that knocked aside the green.

A hail of green fireballs followed as the dragon dodged. Merlin frantically deflected them. Suddenly Blanche shrieked, tearing the sky with pain. "My wing! Going down!"

She flipped over and in a ragged spiral dropped downward. Dizzily her riders glimpsed a knifelike ridge of rock and the boulder-strewn ground beyond. Barely able to hold on, Merlin couldn't focus on any target. He felt hope-lessly vulnerable. As his sight swirled past, he glimpsed the tower room glowing green. A massive bolt of power shot toward them. Miraculously, it suddenly seemed to jerk aside, missing them by a few feet and slicing off the top of a rock pinnacle. Then their fall took them over the ridge, out of sight of the castle.

With a shudder, Blanche opened her half-folded wings, and their plummeting slowed. They came to a rough land-ing on a rock ledge at the base of a cliff. After realizing they had indeed landed, not crashed, the three passengers crawled off and sat dizzily on the ground.

Troll was the first to recover. "Dragon tricksy. Big faker!" he cried.

"I am not!" Blanche insisted. "I've got a huge hole in my left wing, and it really hurts! But I *did* have to get us out of there. We were, as the saying goes, like sitting ducks."

"Good strategy," Welly grumbled, "if it hadn't nearly dumped us all on the rocks."

"Well, it didn't, did it!" she snapped. "You lot may not be good for much, but at least you ought to be able to hold on."

Shaking away the last of his dizziness, Merlin stood up. "Let me look at your wing. I'm not much at healing magic, but maybe I can—"

"Don't you touch it, meddlesome boy! I'll deal with it myself."

Sitting on her haunches, Blanche folded her left wing forward, holding it up to her snout. A ragged hole was scorched through the leathery membrane. Black drops of blood welled from the edges and dropped, hissing, onto the stony ground. The dragon grunted. Little gouts of flame burst from her lips and caressed the wound. The bleeding stopped and, to the amazement of the watchers, the gaping wound slowly shrank. Finally the white surface of the wing, though rough in that spot, was again unbroken.

"There," Blanche said smugly. "I'll fly again, though no thanks to you and your insane aerial battles. If you ask me—"

With a sharp crack, the ground suddenly fell away from under them.

7

VIEW FROM THE TOWER

Days had passed since Morgan stormed out of the tower prison. Desperately Heather wanted out of this place, and she was furious with herself for not being able to get out on her own. But she wasn't sure if she wanted to be rescued—not by Earl.

Morgan hadn't believably explained why she'd been brought here. Surely, Heather realized, her own magic wasn't strong enough to be of much use to as powerful a sorceress as Morgan. There must be some other reason, and Heather was very much afraid that she knew what it was. She hadn't been stolen just as a magic worker—but partly as bait.

If all this was also a trap to lure Earl here, then she was putting him in tremendous danger. The solution was becoming inescapable. It might be better if she just gave up and agreed to join with Morgan—while trying not to really help her very much. Then Earl could live the life he was meant to—helping Arthur build a united peaceful Britain.

The idea brought tears stinging to her eyes. How could she face the rest of her life without Earl? Well, at least,

Heather realized grimly, if Morgan was involved, it was likely to be a short life.

After Morgan had left, Heather helped the female rat move the remains of her mate back into the wall. Heather knew that most people didn't think animals felt things as deeply as humans did. But she was certain they did. Those two rats had been mates for life. And now the little female felt terribly hollow and alone—that feeling filled Heather's mind whenever she picked up her thoughts. Heather continued to share her meager meals but placed the food right by the rat hole to reduce the risk if Morgan should sweep in again.

As she had for days, Heather moved to the window and looked again at the stone walls, wondering if she dared climb down. The pale afternoon light showed only shallow dark cracks between the stones. There seemed no way she could do it unless she could turn herself into a lizard. Her mind had played around with that, picturing a lizard, picturing her own hands as tiny lizard feet. But she didn't dare. Earl had warned her about how dangerous animal transformation could be. Without practice, she could turn herself into a hybrid monster—or a quivering blob of dying flesh.

The door clattered open. Heather jumped but forced herself not to look around.

"No word of greeting, my dear?" Morgan said silkily. "No matter. I'm sure we'll work together well in time."

Heather felt the woman come stand beside her and smelled the faintly sweet perfume she wore—mustily sweet, like a whiff of dead things. Morgan put a cold hand on her shoulder, and Heather shivered.

"Yes, keep looking westward, dear. We should be

having a reunion soon. I believe your crazed elderly sweet-heart will be arriving any minute."

Brushing Morgan's hand aside, Heather spun around to face her. "So this is a trap, isn't it? You just snatched me to use as bait!"

Morgan's green eyes snapped with annoyance, then she laughed. "Disappointed? You really thought I would go to all this trouble to snatch a run-of-the-mill child witch to work as my special partner? You think far too highly of yourself, my dear."

Laughing again, Morgan paced around the small tower room, then she turned back to her prisoner. "Actually, I'm being somewhat unfair. So unlike me, I know. Merlin did seem to feel you have some special new breed of power. And, foolishly infatuated though he is, he remains rather sharp about such things. With the world changing, I can use all the extra help I can muster. And I am sure that once this unpleasant episode is over, you and I can work together—to our mutual benefit."

Heather glowered at the floor but said nothing. Morgan sighed and continued. "I admit to having a hard time in Britain lately with Arthur and Merlin back to their old ways. Getting Merlin away from there and disposing of him once and for all will make my life a great deal easier. And you, my dear, will help in that as well."

"Never!"

"Oh, how melodramatic you are! You don't have to do anything—just be here. The farther I can lure him from his home ground, the greater my chances against him will be. The old magic—Merlin's magic—works like that, giving you greatest strength on your home turf. But I've spent the last several centuries traveling the world, what's left of it, and I'm quite at home anywhere."

Heather wished she could wipe that smug smile off the woman's face but could think of nothing biting to say. "So where are we now? Where is this dreadful castle of yours?"

"It's not my castle, really. I just use it sometimes. A gate to one of my favorite Otherworlds is here. No doubt you've noticed my little flying friends? I'm keeping them out of your room—for now. You wouldn't be much use to any of us drained of blood."

Involuntarily Heather glanced over her shoulder. Morgan moved beside her to look out the window. "Yes. Keep an eye on that low gap between the mountains. I sense he'll be here quite soon. He's moving a little faster than expected, but I suppose we'll see why soon enough."

Heather stared at the saddle between two jagged mountains. She was torn between longing for Earl to come for her and wanting to warn him, to urge him to turn back. If only she could communicate with *him* instead of the scattered voices that randomly dropped into her mind.

Clasping her hands, hoping Morgan wouldn't notice, she clutched Earl's bracelet and tried to conjure up his face—pale and thin, heavy dark eyebrows, perpetually mussed black hair, hawklike nose, and lustrous dark eyes.

Don't come here, she thought. *It's a trap. Turn back, turn back. I love you.*

She concentrated hard but felt nothing. She scowled. What good was having power if she didn't know how to use it? But getting Morgan as a tutor was not the answer.

The mountains had become a dark silhouette against a dusky sky when Heather's straining eyes picked out something moving over the pass. A white speck in the air slowly coming closer. She felt Morgan tensing beside her and knew the sorceress saw it too.

"How extraordinary," Morgan exclaimed. "He's using a dragon. They're so hard to find these days, to say nothing of getting one to cooperate. Your boyfriend never ceases to amaze me. That's what makes our little feuds over the years so interesting. But all good things must come to an end."

She turned and looked at Heather. "I'm happy to have you observing, my dear. Very educational. But I really can't have you interfering." Rapidly she wove her hands through the air, and suddenly Heather felt herself enmeshed in prickly bands of force. She struggled to tear them away but could scarcely twitch a muscle.

Helplessly Heather watched as Morgan, chanting to herself, began drawing a green glow out of the air. The glow solidified into a pulsing emerald globe. Casually letting this hang in the air beside her, Morgan leaned out the window.

"Good backup, but first let's bring out my special defense forces." She opened her mouth with a long piercing cry, followed by a string of chirps and yips.

Her head frozen in one position, Heather at first saw no change. Her sight was fixed on the mountain gap and the approaching speck of white. But it was more than a speck now. Great batlike wings were visible along with a snaky head and tail. It *was* a dragon! Despite herself, Heather was awed. A real dragon. How had Earl managed that? *Please, oh please, turn back!* Again she felt her thoughts stay trapped in her mind.

Now a subtle difference came over the air as if clear water poured down a glass pane. The dragon had picked up speed and was shooting toward them. Suddenly, with frantic backpedaling, it swerved aside, and Heather could see that it indeed carried a rider. No, several riders.

"Too bad, that speeding worm saw the barrier," Morgan commented. "It would have been quite entertaining to see it collide. Well, prolongs the fun."

A bolt of purple energy launched from the dragon's back and shattered against the nearly invisible barrier. Several more came. Tendrils of purple spread over the surface, but nothing cracked. Then the flying figure was engulfed by a black cloud, a cloud that swelled and shrank and fluttered at its edges. Bats, Heather realized. Thousands of bats!

The dragon swooped and dove, then suddenly loosed a stream of fire, tearing ragged holes in the cloud. Wind blew them the reek of burning bats. Morgan raised a hand and the barrier melted away.

"Enough of this," she cried, shooting a blast of green power directly at the dragon and riders. It was met by a beam of purple. Volley after green volley was deflected until the twisting, dodging dragon suddenly shrieked, flipped over, and began spirally down.

"Now we have them!" Morgan cried, reaching for the green ball that pulsed with power in the air beside her. "Just waiting for the right moment."

Heather couldn't even scream her fury. If only she could attack Morgan, destroy her aim! A small furious thought bit into her. *I can!*

Out of the corner of her eye, Heather saw a gray shape streaking their way. *Yes, rat, bite her!*

Morgan reached back, ready to hurl the ball.

Now!

Just as Morgan thrust the ball forward, the rat sank her teeth into the sorceress's ankle. Morgan jerked, propelling the ball slightly askew. Furiously Morgan looked around, but the rat had already dived for cover under Heather's skirt. Then the sorceress looked back at the sky. "Missed! But no matter. They're going down. Pity to lose a dragon like that, but the riders are done for. At last."

The silence that settled over the mountains seemed louder than all the explosions and screechings. Heather's eyes stung with the afterimages of light and with tears that couldn't fall.

Finally Morgan broke the silence. "Well, that's done. Almost a shame, really. Still, that old wizard's a devious one. I'll send out a crew to make sure he's finished. And fresh dragon meat—now there's a delicacy."

She headed for the door, then turned and looked at Heather, still standing frozen before the window. With a flutter of her hands, she dissolved the invisible bonds. "If you have melodramatic grieving to do, get it over with. I've business to attend to here. Then, when the timing's right, we'll be leaving. You should be pleased, you know. I was telling the truth—the first time. I do have a use for you other than as bait."

The door closed before Heather's body realized it could move. Then it slowly sank to the floor. Sympathetically a small rat crouched and watched as the girl violently rocked back and forth, choking on sobs and the tears now pouring from her eyes.

In time, Heather knew, she'd have room for guilt and for hate. Now all she felt was bottomless despair.

8

UNDERGROUND

Dust swirled around them in choking clouds. Clutching his staff, Merlin staggered to his feet, surprised that various parts of him weren't shattered. The dragon's sudden weight must have broken through the roof of some underground cave.

As the dust settled, Merlin saw reddish lights some distance to his left. They weren't bright but were enough to hint at the figures holding them. It was hard to tell, but they looked human—mostly.

He needed a great deal more light. At a word, his staff radiated an intense purple. It cast a violet glow on the white mound beside him. The dragon's head was raised as she stared at the distant row of lights. A rumbling vibrated through her, not a purr—a growl.

"Is everyone all right?" Welly's voice rose from the far side of the dragon.

"I'm fine," Merlin answered, keeping his eyes on the distant shadowy figures. "Troll?"

"Troll not hurt. Scared. This trip, Troll always scared. Not like lights." Skittishly he drew his knife.

Blanche rose to her feet still growling while Merlin

walked around her to join the others. He and Welly drew their swords as the figures holding the lights began slowly walking their way.

"Hold!" a voice called across the echoey cavern. "Intruders, declare yourselves."

The dragon's growling grew in volume, but Merlin put a hand on her flank. "Wait," he said quietly. "Whoever these people are, they don't feel dark—not as dark as the things we met outside. Maybe they know something that can help us get to Heather."

He raised his voice. "We are travelers from a distant country. Our enemies are outside, not here. If you wish us to leave, we will."

The speaker leading the others was much nearer now. He was thin, palely purple, and had long white hair. They were all armed with swords. "No leaving now. We must take you to Baba."

He made a quick gesture and two figures stepped to one side. They manipulated some mechanism in the semi-darkness, and suddenly a cranking and grating shook the cavern. Dust and pebbles rained down on them. Looking up, they saw a black panel sliding across the opening, cutting them off from the grayer night sky.

Blanche shifted uneasily, and Merlin cautioned her again. "Wait. Like you said, we were sitting ducks up there. It might be useful to learn where we are and who this Baba person is.

"Baba is your leader, then?" Merlin asked loudly.

"She is."

"She? Does she go by any other name? Morgan, perhaps?"

The advancing man spat on the ground. "The foreign witch? Do not insult us."

"Ah. Then we will do you no harm if you do none to us. We will meet with your leader."

"You are our prisoners, not our guests—until Baba says otherwise."

"Should we go with them?" Welly whispered to Merlin.

The wizard turned to their other companion. "What do you say, Troll? You're more familiar with the denizens of the current Otherworlds. What do you feel about these fellows?"

Troll wrung his long hands. "Some local muties, some from Otherworlds, some both. But not *bad* bad. Not like Morgan."

Merlin nodded. "That's what I feel too. Let's meet this Baba person."

Sheathing their swords, he and Welly stepped forward. Troll skulked along in their shadows, sticking his knife back into his sash. Blanche rose to follow.

"You three, yes," the white-haired man said. "But not that . . . animal."

"Watch it, grub," Blanche said, her words wreathed in smoke. "Treat me with respect, or I treat you like dinner."

"She's one of our party," Merlin told the startled-looking man. "Where we go, she goes—if she fits."

The man and the others backed away. "We'll see what Baba has to say. Come, then." He hurried ahead of them down a high wide hallway. The other light holders walked even faster.

Striding along with more confidence than he felt, Merlin studied the walls and ceiling. Smooth surfaces that must have been white once were now grimy and splotched with mold. Pre-Devastation architecture, he guessed. At regular intervals on the ceiling were contraptions that he supposed must once have been light fixtures. They were dark now. That made him want to look more closely at the lights their guides—or guards—were carrying.

He squinted ahead. The men, though armed, were clearly not anxious to be close to the intruders. The more Merlin focused on their red-tinged lights, the less he liked them. They looked a lot like glowing human skulls.

As they proceeded down the corridor, faces peered out of doors on either side. Some were pale, but not pre-Devastation pale. They were almost translucent, like creatures living under rocks. Merlin realized that the reason the white-haired man looked slightly purple was that his blood vessels were showing through his skin. Did these people live underground all the time? And what sort of place was this, anyway? Impatiently he filed these questions and tried to keep track of their route as they turned from one corridor into another and another. Their footsteps echoed dully through the dim maze.

Finally they rounded a corner and found the light holders clumped around a closed door. It was larger than the other doors they'd passed, and instead of a dirty white surface it was brightly painted. A vibrant red background was covered with multicolored flowers, animals, and birds.

The white-haired man knocked timidly. In a flurry, the painted figures on the door rearranged themselves. A crabby-looking chicken seemed to open its beak and squawk, "What?"

"O great Baba, the mighty and esteemed Yaga. As directed, the intruders on the hangar hatch have been apprehended. They claim to be from 'a distant country,' wherever that is. We bring them here for your questioning."

A painted duck pushed the chicken aside and glared into the hallway. Finally it quacked, "Ah, two humans and a troll. Interesting. Aha! And a dragon. *Very* interesting."

The chicken pecked at the duck, shouldering it aside, and squawked, "Right. Send the three smaller ones in. Madam Dragon, I fear you are too large for my office. I'll have someone bring you a bowl of munchies. Will fried bats do?"

Blanche grunted at the talking door. "In large quantities, yes."

"Done," the duck quacked. "Door, open! Kitchen staff, bring the bats!"

The door flung itself open, and the light carriers bowed the three travelers in. Merlin looked back at Blanche, who seemed content to sit down and await the promised goodies. Then he stepped through the door.

It was a large office, though not dragon-sized, and very cluttered. Shelves, chairs, and tables were piled with books, dolls, wood carvings, glasses, and teapots. In one corner stood a high wooden tub with a wooden pole sticking out of it. It looked to Merlin like an enormous mortar and pestle, though he couldn't imagine who could use such a huge thing for grinding. A number of chickens and ducks wandered through the room, and several cats draped themselves over pieces of furniture. In the center of the space crouched a huge wooden desk, equally cluttered, and behind it sat someone small.

Stepping forward, they saw it was a little old lady. Very little and very old. A bright flowered scarf tied around her head barely contained her riotous gray hair. Her face seemed entirely made up of wrinkles except where a long nose protruded from the middle and bent down, almost meeting the upturned chin. Two beady black eyes watched the three as they approached.

"Well, well," she cackled, "nice of you to drop in."

This was all getting too confusing for Welly, and being confused made him angry. "We didn't exactly drop in by accident, did we? We landed in some sort of trap."

The woman shrugged. "Not really. You and that great heavy dragon thumped down like invaders on our hangar door. Of course we caught you! And if our lookouts hadn't reported that you were fighting the castle folk, we probably would have considered you enemies and killed you on the spot."

"Or tried to," Welly said meaningfully, placing a hand on his sword hilt.

Baba chortled. "Oh, of course, that was before we knew we had such a formidable warrior in our midst. Give it a break, kid."

Then she turned her beady eyes on Merlin. "But *you* are a different matter. Foreign travelers, you say? Where from?"

"Britain," Merlin answered simply.

"Right. I've heard of some interesting goings-on there. Oh, wait. The meddling witch who moved into the castle is British too, isn't she? Friend of yours?"

Troll jumped up from where he'd been cowering behind Merlin. "No way! She nasty nasty witch! She stole Nice Lady, and we got to rescue her!"

"Hush," Welly whispered urgently. "How do we know whose side this old hag's on?"

Overhearing, Baba laughed. "Right, kid. Never trust nobody that nobody sent. So why should I trust *you*?"

Troll hopped up and down impatiently. "Because we

got to rescue Heather. Get her and Merlin back to Arthur before Morgan does more nasties. That why!"

"Well, at last someone's coming out with useful information," Baba cackled. "I've heard something about you lot—from my Otherworld connections. It's not everybody who'd mess with that Le Fay woman. Down here, we try lying low when she's in residence. I've worked too many centuries trying to keep this ragtag lot going to let that gadabout foreign witch with dreams of grandeur mess with us.

"But you, boy, I know you now." Jumping up, she skipped around the desk and pointed a knobby finger at Merlin. She wasn't much taller than Troll, but with her layers of fringed shawls and flowered skirts she was twice as wide. "The age thing fooled me at first—and that feeble little beard. We've heard about you and that Arthur fellow even in our Otherworld—and we're a pretty provincial lot."

Merlin tried to respond but couldn't break into her flow of chatter.

"Ah, now this girl you're after . . . I bet that's the same one little Ivan came running to me about. He's got this new talent coming. Mind speaker. Wave of the future, that is. He's not much good at it yet. No focus. But he said there's another of his kind nearby, held prisoner or something, and I bet it's your girl."

Merlin felt a thrill of hope and watched impatiently as the woman hopped about like an excited flea, the fringe on her shawls whipping around. She continued, "So now we better help you. Can't let Miss Rule the World get hold of that talent, can we? And as the saying goes, 'The enemy of my enemy is my friend.' Always worked for me."

Reaching down, she grabbed a chicken, whispered in

its ear, and flung it fluttering toward the door. Momentarily it vanished and a cackling chicken voice was heard outside ordering someone to go fetch Ivan and bring him to the dining hall.

"Come on," Baba said, bustling to the door before anyone else could get a word in. "Got to feed guests—and do some plotting and planning while we're at it." Merlin frowned but followed. He didn't want to take the time to play grateful guest, but obviously this person knew things that might help.

Outside in the hall, the painted chicken and duck were still squabbling on the door. Baba gave them a slap and gestured to Blanche, who was just licking the last bat out of a large tureen. "Come along too, deary. I'm sure that just whetted your appetite." With that, she bustled down the corridor, followed by the visitors and several guards clutching glowing skulls.

After a few paces, Baba fell back to walk beside Blanche. "A real British dragon—what an honor to meet you, ma'am. We have a preference for firebirds in my neck of the Otherworlds, but dragons always piqued my fancy. China had its share too, you know, but that place got hit even worse in the Devastation, and most of its Otherworld folk cleared right out."

As they hurried along, Welly slipped up to Merlin and whispered, "Is the old lady crazy or what?"

"Or what," Merlin answered. "I think she's a big-time supernatural sort. If only Heather were here. She read a lot more about other countries and their legends than I bothered with."

"I wish she were here too," Welly agreed. "But if she were, we wouldn't be. I mean . . ."

Before Welly could sort this out, Baba scuttled up to join them. "Quite a stroke of luck it was, finding this place after the Devastation. I nearly ran off myself, like most of our Otherworld types, when this world got so crazy. But there were survivors. We weren't as lucky as you British lot. Only one of your cities got hit, I'm told. But even here, not everybody died in the blasts or the chaos afterward. So I stayed behind with a little ragtag band of survivors, hoping to find a place where the radiation wouldn't kill or mutate them too bad. And we found this place."

"What is it?" Welly managed to slip in.

"A big underground bunker. A city almost. Apparently some government and military big shots built this hideout in the mountains in case war broke out. But I don't think most of them got to use it. They were killed right out, or maybe from the radiation or the plagues. But they'd stocked the place with food and books and bunches of gadgets, most of which don't work anymore. And I introduced some touches of my own."

"Like glowy skulls?" Troll offered.

"Always worked for me," she chuckled. "Used to set them on poles around my house. Discouraged unwanted visitors. But the magic here is not all mine. There're new magics popping up all the time helping us deal with stuff. Maybe someday soon we'll move back onto the surface. The folks living here now can handle a lot of radiation— even developed some useful mutations. But after generations underground, they're looking kind of sickly."

She broke off into cackling laughter. "Never thought I'd end up this maternal. Ha! There even used to be stories about me eating children. I never did—well, not much, anyway. But I kind of fell into this group-mother role, and you got to do what you got to do. Ah, here we are, in the dining hall. It's between mealtimes, so there's lots of room. I know you're in a hurry, but you got to eat and we got to talk." She motioned them to seats at long tables and bustled off to see about their food.

"*We* have got to talk?" Welly muttered as they sat on the long smooth bench. "Where does the *we* come in?"

Merlin nodded. "Talks a lot, but I guess she doesn't get outside visitors much."

Troll was sitting on top of the long table tapping its smooth whitish surface when Baba came back. With her were several translucent people carrying a big steaming bowl of something gray. Others timidly placed a large pot of something red in front of Blanche, who had tucked herself into a corner of the dining hall.

Baba handed out spoons and smaller eating bowls to her guests. "Eat up. Mushrooms. We grow lots of different types here. Even before the Devastation, it was a big local crop. They do well underground. Ah, here's little Ivan. Let's hear what he has to say."

Just let *him talk,* Welly thought as he spooned a quivering gray mushroom into his mouth. He bit down cautiously. It was slimy but tasted rich and nutty. He scooped more into his own bowl.

The young boy walking toward them was short with the same see-through skin as the others and with eyes almost as big as Troll's. He looked very nervous and shy.

"Come on, boy," Baba said. "Don't freak out. These are special guests. Tell them what you heard. You know—in your mind."

The boy sat at the table and without looking up said, "I'd heard that voice a few times before, sort of faint and far away. But a couple days ago it was real loud. It hurt my head."

He lapsed into silence until Merlin prompted, "And what did the voice say?"

"That she'd been kidnapped from someplace foreign and didn't know where she was. She wasn't hurt, but she was scared. That's all. I'm not very good at this."

"Yes, you are," Merlin said encouragingly. "You're miraculous. Can you reach her again?"

"I don't know."

"Try, boy," Baba urged. "It's important."

"Be like hero in old stories," Troll offered.

Ivan's smile spread until it was almost as wide as Troll's. "Like the stories Baba tells us?"

The old woman grinned, her eyes almost disappearing among the wrinkles of her face. "Like the Prince saving Vassalissa the Beautiful."

Nodding, Ivan crawled onto the table, curled up beside Troll, and closed his eyes. For a while, they watched the boy apparently sleeping. Then Baba motioned for them to eat their mushrooms and ignore him.

Troll was just serving himself a third helping when the boy abruptly sat up. Startled, Troll dropped the ladle, splattering the others with mushrooms. Ignoring this, they all concentrated on Ivan. Eyes wide, he huddled there trembling.

"Well?" Baba snapped impatiently. "Did you reach her?"

Troll wrapped an arm around the boy. The shivering subsided and Ivan nodded. "She's *very* happy you weren't killed. I described who was here and she is even happier. She's afraid she's being taken away someplace else soon.

She thinks the woman has some scary plans for her. She wants me to tell you that you should go back home and forget about her. She says that just knowing you're alive makes it easier for her to deal with whatever Morgan is planning."

Ivan closed his eyes a moment, then looked directly at Merlin. "But I don't think she means it. Not deep down."

Merlin stood up. "Whether she means it or not, we're going after her. Now!"

With a clawlike hand, Baba grabbed his sleeve and yanked him down. "No, you're not. Sleep first. It's still night out there, and that's when the truly nasty Otherworld types that hang out here are worst. I don't think even a famous foreign wizard like you could take them all on."

"But . . . ," Merlin began. Welly poked him and pointed toward Blanche. The dragon was fast asleep, her head in the empty bowl, each snore filling it with little puffs of smoke.

"All right," Merlin said reluctantly. "We could all use some rest. But only until dawn. We can't let Morgan spirit Heather away without a fight—or a clue where they're going."

"Judging by the performance tonight," Baba observed, "I'd say you need some sneakier tactics. But I haven't lived like a mole for centuries without developing a few pesky tricks. I think we can get you a lot closer to your friend than you managed on your own. Get some sleep. I'll work on it."

The travelers wanted to stay together, so accommodations were found for them all in an empty storeroom large enough to house even a dragon. Blanche grumbled fiercely when they awakened her to move, but she'd no sooner lain down again than she was asleep.

Merlin was certain he'd never manage to sleep. Lying down, he clutched the smooth carved staff, sensing it would somehow make him feel close to its maker. At least he could pass the time thinking of her. But soon he slipped into blackness and jumbled dreams.

Others needed him, cried for his help, but he could do nothing. Heather, wrapped in fear. Arthur, embattled by enemies, hopelessly outnumbered. They both called for him, but he was trapped in darkness. The darkness became a cave. Enchanted in the heart of a mountain, voices cried to him for centuries, but he could not answer. Voices died away as their speakers turned to dust, forgotten except by him. But one voice remained. One taunting laughing voice. Morgan Le Fay knew she was winning. Just as Merlin knew he must not let her win.

9

UPWARD

Roused a few hours later from his troubled sleep, Merlin felt only vaguely refreshed. Suddenly remembered purpose brought him to his feet. He joined ever-chattering Baba in rousing the others. Welly groaned, Troll whined, and Blanche snorted in a way that threatened to incinerate them all. But eventually they stumbled from the room, led by several guards with glowing skulls and the seemingly tireless Baba.

"No time like the lovely predawn to start adventures," she said cheerily. "I can't wait till I can take my own people up to see a real dawn again. Ah, well, I'm nothing if not patient. Now, where I'm taking you is not the scenic route. There were passages that the makers of this place started building, then abandoned. Maybe they ran out of money; maybe the wars caught up with them before they were finished. Early on, we walled them off—partly because they were clammy and yucky and partly because they are just too close to the old castle and all the evil that seeps from there. But because they *do* lead close to the castle, they're a good route for you now."

Merlin nodded. "If we can sneak into the place, I think

I can find where she's being held. The closer we get, the more I sense her nearness."

They turned several corners, and suddenly the wide corridor came to an end. In front of them was a wall of closely packed rubble, slabs of broken concrete mixed with soil, twisted metal furniture, and odd machinery. Wires coiled out of broken metal boxes like severed blood vessels.

"Just shift some of this garbage away," Baba said, "and you're into the unfinished parts." She looked at Merlin appraisingly. "Your magic or mine, boy? Or do we let the dragon do the heavy lifting?"

"I don't lift," Blanche snarled. "I smash. Stand aside, punies!"

The others scrambled away as the dragon smashed her massive tailquarters against the makeshift wall. It sagged, and a few chunks of concrete and rusted metal fell away. Another blow and the whole structure collapsed. The dust cleared to show a ragged hole large enough for even the dragon to pass through.

Baba stepped forward and peered into the darkness. "Haven't been in here for centuries. I doubt it's gotten a lick better since it was walled off. Oh, well, there's no adventure without a little danger."

She turned to the small group of her guards that had accompanied them. They clustered together looking less than eager for adventure. "Here, give our guests some lights. And you stay here and guard this opening till I come back. We don't want anything nasty slipping through."

As she climbed through the gap, glowing skull upraised, additional skulls were passed out to the others. Welly took his reluctantly, wishing he somehow didn't have to touch it. But even its grisly glowing face was better than the thick blackness beyond. Blanche took a skull in one clawed foot and examined it contemptuously. Then she clambered through the gap in the wall, tossed the skull onto the floor, and kicked it ahead of her down the passage like a football. Her glowing nostrils provided all the light she needed, but the game was entertaining.

Troll scampered on ahead, raising his skull here and there to examine the walls. They were straight and feature-less except for damp patches of moss and pale glowing fungi. Occasional wispy shadows flitted on ahead of their advancing lights, but the shadow-casters never showed themselves.

Baba and Merlin walked together while the witch eagerly imparted a torrent of magical advice. After a lecture on potions against radiation sickness and how to ward off vampire bats, she turned to the subject of Morgan.

"Of course, I don't know as much about her as I should. Whenever she shows up, we try not to draw her attention. Not that *I* wouldn't be a match for her, mind. . . . Well, maybe she's just a *teeny* bit above my league. But my folks here would be easy targets for her shenanigans and for her horrid Otherworld friends."

"Have you any advice for how to deal with her?" Merlin managed to squeeze in.

"Basically, my advice is *not* to deal with her. But that's not an option for you, is it? This castle of hers isn't really hers, of course, but she's been using it on and off for centuries, since well before the Devastation anyway. Its original owner was a great pal of hers. So creatures who like her style are all over the place. And of course, there are all sorts of mutants. Radiation was quite severe in this part of the world. Really amazing what it did to some things."

Their little party had been walking for some time down the dark passage, their footfalls echoing hollowly off the damp walls. With every step, the air seemed to get colder and heavier. And the smell of stale mildew increased. At last the passage ran into a rough wall of natural stone.

"End of the line," Baba said briskly, "unless you want to blast your way through miles of solid rock. I'm sure, of course, Madam Dragon, you could make quite a dent, but fortunately you don't have to. We're right under the old castle here, and the passage's ceiling is quite thin in this spot."

Merlin gazed up at the ceiling. "Yes, I can feel it is. Are you coming farther with us?"

Baba sighed. "No, dear boy, I fear I cannot. How I'd love to get a crack at some real adventure again. But my pathetic people here would be lost if I go off adventuring and get myself reduced to a quivering blob of magicked gunk. I confess, my magic's rather the provincial kind. Good for frightening babies and making houses walk on chicken legs, but I'm no match for Morgan and her ilk. I wish you the best, though. It's heartening to know there are others in the world I might actually *like*. Maybe we can keep in touch—even get together once this world straightens itself out a bit. Ta-ta!"

Briskly she shook everybody's hand or claw, and in a flurry of flowered shawls and skirts, Baba bustled down the hall. Merlin watched her light shrink to a gray dot and vanish. Then he sighed and turned his attention back to the corridor ceiling.

"Baba's right," he said, putting down his glowing skull and igniting a brighter purple light along his staff. "The rock is very thin here, and there's the base of some large structure just beyond it. All we have to do is break through."

"Right," Blanche said, drawing in a deep breath.

"No! No blowtorch here," Merlin cried. "We need a little more subtlety."

"Suit yourself, boy," she said, letting smoke dribble unused from her lips. "I'm just along for the mindless-brawn role, it seems."

When Troll tried to comfort her, she moodily sent him away coughing in a cloud of smoke.

Flipping his staff around, Merlin raised the pointed end to the ceiling. A narrow purple beam of light shot up and slowly etched a pencil-thin circle in the stone. The large circle completed itself, but nothing happened. Reversing his staff, Merlin impatiently battered the circular section with a broad purple beam. The rock shivered, cracked, and broke loose, smashing to the floor with a thunderous boom and an explosion of dust.

"Oh, master of subtlety you are," Blanche snorted.

Chagrined, Merlin waited until silence and dust settled again. Nothing seemed to move beyond the opening. He hoped they were far away from the parts of the castle where anything lived that could hear them.

Welly stared into the opened darkness ten feet over their heads. The feeble glow from their skulls didn't chip into it. "Now what?"

"You people would be hopeless without me," Blanche snapped. She grabbed Welly with a clawed foreleg and abruptly lifted him through the opening. Troll and Merlin followed; then, with a jump and a sculling of her wings, Blanche joined them, barely managing to squeeze herself through the hole.

"You might have made it a little bigger," she snarled at Merlin. "Just be glad you have a young lithe dragon like me to work with. Though, underfed as I've been since joining you, I'll be lucky to ever be a big strapping adult."

"Chronic complainers often don't survive to adulthood either," Merlin grumbled as he led the group away from where the floor was ominously creaking around the hole.

Merlin and Blanche had left their skulls below, but the light from the remaining two and from Merlin's staff showed they were in a large stone vaulted room, dark and damp and empty. A small window high in one wall let in a thin sliver of predawn light. At the far end of the space, a narrow flight of stairs was carved into the wall, disappearing through a narrow opening at the top.

"Looks like you'll have to stay down here, Blanche," Merlin said. "I'm sorry; I know you can be subtle, but you're a little large for sneaking around castle passageways."

"Fine," she grumbled. "I'll just catch up on my rudely interrupted sleep."

Welly frowned. "Don't sleep so hard you can't hear us if we need you."

"Ignorant human. Dragons sleep with one eye and both ears open—to guard their treasure. *Not* that I've been given any chance to gather treasure on this adventure."

Leaving her grumbling, Merlin, Welly, and Troll headed for the stairs. They were steep and had no railing. Merlin and Troll had no trouble, but Welly's fear rose with every step. He pressed himself so close to the wall he scraped off rock dust, but he still felt he was teetering on the edge.

At last the stairs opened into another, smaller room. The vaulted stone ceiling was lower, and the main furniture seemed to be curtains of cobwebs. Seeing no doors or further stairs, Merlin stood in silence a moment, trying to locate the direction where he felt Heather to be. Then he led them to the right. The hanging cobwebs were thick and sticky. The more they pushed through, the more the clinging whiteness seemed to wrap around them. Hearing a squeal behind him, Merlin spun around and saw Troll almost totally cocooned in white. Welly, struggling to free his sword, wasn't much better off.

Looking down, Merlin saw white tendrils spreading over his own body, wrapping themselves around his legs and chest. Clutching at his sword, he fought to pull it loose from the scabbard, then slashed at the smothering webs. The Eldritch blade sliced through them. Like smoke, the torn webs writhed and curled away. Freeing himself, Merlin staggered to Welly and sliced the webs from his friend's sword arm. Next he carefully cut loose the struggling troll. The webs didn't give up but kept flapping and slithering toward them.

"Better run!" Merlin called, and led the way, slashing whiteness as he went.

After steady hacking, they broke free. The vault ahead of them was clear of cobwebs. Troll had lost his skull in the struggle, but by Welly's light and the glow from Merlin's staff, they saw that the only objects in the space ahead of them were several large rectangular stone boxes. Most were set back in shadowy niches, but as they passed close to one, Welly studied it and shivered. Its stone lid was partly shoved away. Inside, he glimpsed a scatter of brittle white bones.

Behind him, Troll groaned. "No like this place. Want to be somewhere else."

Welly tried to sound brave and comforting, though his voice broke. "The floor's slanting up, so we're headed somewhere else." Then he hurried to be a little closer to Merlin. "But, Earl, those were really humongous spider-webs. And where there are spiderwebs . . ."

"There are usually spiders," Merlin finished for him. "And they're here too. I can sense them. But they don't like the light. Keep hold of that skull, and, Troll, keep up."

Instantly Troll was nearly plastered to the back of Welly's legs. "Small spiders nice and crunchy. Big ones creepy. These big?"

"Very," Merlin said, gesturing into the darkness on their right. Two red eyes stared at them, disturbingly far from the floor. Welly took a hesitant step forward, thrust-ing his glowing skull toward the eyes. Briefly he saw a cluster of long hairy legs, a swollen belly, and a glint of fangs before the dog-sized creature scuttled back into the shadows.

Merlin increased the level of purple light glowing from his staff. "We seem to be safe enough in the light, but let's get out of here."

Welly had just opened his mouth to agree when he caught sight of something hanging on the ceiling above where the spider had been. A shapeless, sickly yellow glob. Suddenly with a slurping sound it dropped from the ceil-ing. Fierce hissing erupted. Their light showed a tangled mass of hairy legs and yellowish blob rolling over and over. Rolling their way.

The three spun around and quickly headed in the di-rection they'd been going. The floor was more steeply

slanted now and slippery. Very slippery. Welly felt slick-
ness under his boots. He leaped ahead, trying to find surer
footing, but the floor was so slick he slid back. Flailing
his arms, he took another step and fell. Facedown on the
floor, he realized the stone was covered in slime. Rolling
over, he was suddenly looking into a large face. Two eyes
on stalks, a slit sharp-toothed mouth, and smooth, slimy
yellow skin. A giant slug!

"Gross!" he squealed, and tried to sit up. The mouth
split open and slime spewed out, thick yellowish putrid-
smelling stuff, like the creature was endlessly blowing its
nose at him. Welly gagged as the mucus covered his face.
He reached up, trying to peel it away. More slime engulfed
his hands, gluing them to his face. He flopped away like a
fish, tried to stand, and again slid to the floor. Slime flowed
over his legs, sticking them down.

Welly tried to scream, but it only came out as a muffled
gargle. Through the slime encasing his head, he heard
other screams and thumps. He hoped to hear the saving
sound of a sword cutting through this horrid slick cocoon.
Nothing.

The gluey coating was hardening now; he could barely
twitch a muscle. Then, through his blinded eyes, he
thought he saw the light level rise. The temperature certainly did. The hardened mucus all over his body started to
heat up. It bubbled like soup, then began to drip away.

Gasping, Welly staggered to his feet. Merlin, himself
half engulfed in slime, was shooting heat from the tip of
his staff. The large blob near his feet quivered and heaved.
Troll burst forth. "Yuck, yuck, yuck! Troll hate slugs! Not
even good eat. Yuck! Oh! Hot slug juice! Ouch, ouch!"

"Sorry," Merlin said as he boiled away the last of the

slime encasing his own legs. "There wasn't time for delicate temperature control."

Just then Welly felt a drop of slime fall on his head and slither down his cheek. He looked up. "There're more on the ceiling!"

Half a dozen glistening slugs, each a yard long, stared back at them with their wiggling eyestalks. "Run!" Merlin cried as he raised his staff and sprayed the ceiling with searing purple heat. Six shriveled yellow husks dropped to the floor. The light showed other glistening forms lurking in the shadows. Merlin turned and raced after the others.

Troll was now clinging to Welly like a backpack. They passed several hardened translucent lumps that looked like giant spiders were entombed inside. They also saw a scattering of empty yellow skins lying about like popped and wizened balloons.

"Looks like we stumbled into a major slug-versus-spider war," Merlin said as they continued up what had now become a steep ramp.

Welly shook his head. "I suppose we shouldn't pick sides, but if there's anything I hate worse than spiders, it's gross things like slugs. Especially giant mutant ones."

Still clinging to Welly's back, Troll shivered agreement. "Yuck!"

Finally the ramp reached another floor. A wider corridor continued to slant upward, but more gradually, following a slow spiral. Through the outside wall, occasional slits let in pale gray light. The other side of the corridor was made up of small cell-like rooms, empty except for chains, bones, and a few heaps of rotting foul-smelling stuff they didn't want to examine. They hurried forward.

"I don't understand," Merlin whispered. "We made

enough noise down there to wake the dead—literally. Where are the guards, the denizens of this castle?"

"It's daytime now," Welly suggested. "Like Baba said, maybe they don't get about in the day."

"Something does," Troll squeaked, peering over Welly's shoulder. His big ears twitched. "Something with claws running this way."

After a moment, the others heard it too—large clawed feet charging down the sloping corridor toward them. By now they had passed the last of the cells and were in a wide empty hallway. Weak dusky light through a narrow window showed something small streaking their way and something much larger following. The pursuer looked like a cross between a giant cat and a magnified lizard. And it looked hungry. The object of its hunger pelted toward them and, without stopping, leaped on Merlin and scrambled to his shoulder.

Thrown off balance, Merlin couldn't fend off the pursuer. Lunging forward, Welly jabbed at it with his sword, raking a thin red scratch across the creature's side. Hissing, the beast swerved aside and crouched, preparing to leap on Welly.

Steadier now, Merlin slashed forward with his staff. The creature's tail caught fire, and with a howl, it turned and raced back up the corridor.

Awkwardly Merlin turned his head and looked into the face of the animal on his shoulder. A pale gray rat. It squeaked and chittered at him, but Merlin shook his head. "I don't speak animal. Heather does, not me."

"Troll do too." With that, Troll climbed down from Welly's back and leaped onto Merlin's. He thrust his face toward the rat, which cringed back against Merlin's neck.

Then the little creature began squeaking and chittering again. A couple times Troll answered back. Finally Troll jumped down and squatted on the floor.

"Heather gone."

Merlin went cold. "Gone? How?"

"Rat friend of Heather. Hours ago, very bad woman, must be Morgan, take Heather away. They get on very very bad beast and fly off. Direction just south of where sun rise."

Merlin frowned with confusion. "But . . . but I feel Heather here. Above us, in this building."

Troll nodded. "That trick. Morgan snip bit of Heather's hair—put it in funny blue flame. Not burn, just floats in air."

"A decoy spell!" Merlin spat. "I should have known. It gave off enough of Heather's essence to make me feel she was here. If I'd only probed . . ."

"Never mind, Earl," Welly said. "Morgan deceives everyone. Did the rat say any more, Troll?"

"Say Heather not want us to follow. Too dangerous."

"As if *dangerous* weren't part of this whole picture," Welly muttered. "Anything else?"

Troll grinned. "Rat say *she* hope we do follow. Heather nice person."

"And so we will!" Merlin said. "Troll, thank the rat and ask her if there's anything we can do for her."

From where he sat, Troll chittered, and from Merlin's shoulder, the rat chittered back.

"Food nice," Troll translated.

Chuckling, Merlin gently lifted the rat from his shoulder, put her on the floor near a comfortable-looking hole, and fumbled in a sack tied to his belt. "Baba gave me these before we left. I hope rats like dried mushrooms."

He placed some by the rat's twitching nose. Instantly she gobbled them up. Merlin nodded and put down the whole bag. With a parting squeak, the rat dragged the bag into the hole and disappeared.

"Where to now?" Welly asked. "Back to the dragon?"

"Not much choice. Which means, of course, back through slime-spewing slugs and clinging spiderwebs."

"Or not!" Troll cried. He'd clambered up the wall and was looking out the little slit of a window. "Dragon out there!"

"What?" Merlin rushed to the window. The large white dragon, with shallow thrusts of her wings, was hovering just outside.

"Numb ears!" she shouted at them. "Troops of guards are after you. Their tromping woke me up. Dragon hearing's honed against treasure thieves."

"I don't . . . ," Welly started to say just as flapping footsteps were indeed heard. From the far end of the corridor, the singed cat-lizard led a troop of gangly hairless near-humans. Whether muties or Otherworlders, Welly couldn't tell, but their swords and axes made that unimportant. More and more kept coming.

"Stand back," Merlin ordered wearily, and raised his staff.

"No, *you* idiots stand back!" Blanche bellowed from outside. In moments, there was a shivering crash and the wall buckled. Another crash, and stones fell away, leaving a ragged gap in the wall. The advancing soldiers blinked against the dust and flood of gray light. Squinting through it himself, Merlin saw the white back of the dragon rising and falling just outside.

"So jump already!" Blanche yelled.

Gripping his staff, Merlin did. He landed with a thump and began sliding off before his desperate fingers grasped a scale and he hauled himself up. Trembling, Welly followed, Merlin's hand catching him before he slid far. Troll hesitated—until he heard the clicking tread of the cat-lizard. Then, squealing, he launched himself into space, landing squarely on top of Welly.

Before they'd scarcely settled, the dragon veered away from the castle wall. "How did you get out here?" Merlin called over the rushing wind.

"Left another hole in the wall below," she answered. "Well, that's what ruins are good for—ruining. Where to now?"

"Southeast. To a girl who doesn't want to be rescued and really hopes that she will be."

"She's not the only one who hopes that," Welly added.

"No, indeed," Merlin said, mentally adding a small gray rat to that list. "No, indeed."

10

TEMPLE

Heather was curled up in tear-stained sleep when Morgan swooped down on her in the middle of the night. "Mourning period's over. Time to go."

Heather glared up at her through red, darkly circled eyes. Hearing that boy's voice in her mind last night after watching the battle beyond the tower had lightened her heart—but not her hatred of Morgan. "Your scouts . . . ?"

"Found nothing. And I was *so* looking forward to dragon steaks. The wretched underground dwellers must have hauled off the bodies. But just in case . . ."

Swiftly Morgan brought up a knife and sliced off the tip of one of Heather's frazzled braids. Muttering, the sorceress wove her fingers around it until the strands were enmeshed in a globe of blue light. With a flick, she set it bobbing in the air.

"I doubt there's anyone to pursue us now, but precautions never hurt."

"I'm not bait anymore?"

"I've got other uses for you now, my dear, and frankly, more important business to attend to. Get moving. The timing is finally right."

She yanked Heather to her feet and dragged her toward the doorway.

"Wait!" Heather cried. Twisting out of her grasp, Heather dropped back to the mattress and fumbled for her boots. She shot a glance to the base of the wall and saw the rat's whiskered face peeking out.

Find Earl. Tell him. . . . Try to tell him. . . .

I know, came the silent reply. *Hear your thoughts. I tell him. Be safe.*

With her boots only half on, Heather was dragged to her feet and out the door. Once the sound of footsteps disappeared, the rat scurried from her hole and climbed a wall to sit on the broad windowsill, watching to see what direction her friend would be taken.

When they climbed out onto a flat-topped tower, Heather shrank back. Morgan's mount waited there. The reddish mane that surrounded its beaked face seemed tipped with flame. The creature shifted uneasily on slender legs, pawing the stones with clawed feet. Its split tail switched like an angry cat's, and the folded wings seemed to hunch impatiently along its sides.

"Choose," Morgan commanded. "Ride behind me or travel as you did here, in a black cocoon." She gestured to the right, and Heather saw several wizened figures holding a cloud of darkness. She recognized the stifling smell.

"I'll ride," Heather managed to say.

Moments later, they were soaring over the broken battlements of the half-ruined castle. No lights showed as its dark crouched shape dropped away into the night. Heather hated having to touch Morgan, let alone clutch her around the waist. But it was that or plummet into the mountainous darkness.

The wings beside them beat a steady rhythm, but cold and fear kept Heather fully awake. Finally she wrestled up enough courage to ask, "Where are we going?"

After a long silence, Morgan answered. "I have business with an old . . . acquaintance of mine. You see, while your precious Merlin was stagnating in that mountain, I was free. The old world offered a lot of scope for one with my interests. I traveled quite a bit, met a number of most interesting characters. When the Devastation came, that world changed, and I admit to not traveling as widely. After all, there's not nearly as much of the world worth visiting. But on the whole, most changes I've seen have been very much to my liking."

Morgan would *find a blasted world to her liking,* Heather thought angrily. But she decided this might be the time to ask a long-nagging question. "I know how Earl . . . Merlin kept alive in that mountain, cycles of reversed aging or something. But what about you? You're not immortal."

The laugh in front of her was high and cruel as a bird of prey's. "Not exactly. But close enough—now. There are types of magic that your prim and proper former lover wouldn't touch. But they are very powerful. The types of magic I might just share—if you join with me. Think of it, Heather. Think what you could do with many lifetimes."

Heather did think, and shivered. She'd rather have one lifetime with Earl than many with the likes of Morgan. Remembering now what Earl had once said about Morgan, she shivered even deeper. Morgan had prolonged her life by having dealings with death. Heather didn't know quite what that meant, but it sounded deeply wrong.

For days and nights, they flew on, stopping for brief periods to let the beast rest. Heather sometimes slept where she rode, feeling now some sort of magical strap holding her on. Mostly she looked down at the land passing below. Mountainous and snow-covered, some of it. A few huddled villages, a far greater number of ruined cities. Other stretches were just blasted glassy plains or cindery craters in the ground. Between these, though, she spied patches of green, even occasional scatterings of what looked like flowers. This part of the world seemed to be slowly recovering, just like Britain was. But in her present circumstances, even that didn't cheer her very much.

They rose higher now so as to clear rows of ice-encased mountains that glinted like giant crystals. From things Morgan had said and her own hazy memories of geography classes, Heather figured these must be the Himalayas. And beyond them, she thought, was India. All exotic-sounding places she'd hardly believed in, let alone thought to see. She certainly hadn't wanted to see them like this, as a captive heading to an unknown and probably horrid future.

Slowly they dropped lower again. The ground below was rocky and still mountainous. Scraggly vegetation spread over it, choking what now appeared to be a vast complex of ruined stone buildings. Gliding lower, they landed gently at the foot of a cliff pockmarked with caves.

The bands around her loosened, and stiffly Heather dismounted. The cloak of warmth they had ridden with dissolved as well, and she shivered in the cold. Looking around, she saw only ruins. But once, those buildings must have been gorgeous, she realized. Intricately carved stone was piled into towers and walls, pinnacles and buttresses. All were now strangled by thick gray vines, vines that sprouted only a few sickly green leaves.

She glanced back at the cliff and noticed that some of

the caves were half closed by recent-looking walls of rubble. From behind them, a few dark heads peered out.
Suddenly words tickled her mind.

You here? With an evil one?

Heather recognized the frightened distant voice she'd
heard in her mind nights ago! But now it didn't feel distant. *Not by choice,* she thought back. *Can you help me?*

Frightened. Silence. Silence broken by Morgan ordering
her to follow.

Heather did, stumbling into the gloom as ruins rose
around her. To keep both fear and hope at bay, she studied
the stone. Every inch was carved. Now worn by weather
and time, only a few shapes were recognizable. Animals,
birds, flowers, and some things that might have been
humans—except for the hideous heads or the unusual
number of arms. Surely these ruins were very old, older
than muties anyway. Had Morgan brought her to another
gate to Otherworlds? Or were these very ancient temples
to mythical gods? Or both?

Morgan's nails gripped her shoulder and shook
Heather back to attention. "We're here," she snapped. "Be
silent now. Do as I do."

Had she detected a note of fear in Morgan's voice?
Heather wondered. What were they facing that could
frighten Morgan Le Fay?

They passed between two carved doorposts into a large
dimly lit room. Sickly sweet smoke clouded the air.
Through it she saw flickering flames in hanging pierced
metal lamps. More intricate carvings covered these stone
walls, but Heather's attention was drawn to the living figures. On both sides, they clustered. Most were small, bent,
and dark. A few seemed human. Others were muties, but
some could never have mutated that way. Even muties

never sprouted horns, or saber-like fangs, or heads that clearly belonged on animals.

Heather shivered. Untrained or not, she had enough magic to sense the presence of Otherworlders, and of overwhelming power—power that seemed partly evil and partly something else, something deeper and older than evil.

"Morgan Le Fay and companion," Morgan announced imperiously. "Take us to suitable rooms. Your mistress is expecting us."

At this, a bent old man wearing a dark wraparound robe bowed and led them away. Heather followed Morgan closely, careful not to brush against anything. The ancient power around her felt thick and dark as soot. They climbed stone stairs that were worn in the center by generations of feet and padded along arched corridors. At every landing and corner, they passed guards whose swords looked only slightly more threatening than their grotesque horns and fangs. At last a wooden door was flung open and they entered a room that was more than "suitable." The word that came to Heather's mind was *sumptuous*.

Looking around, Morgan seemed to sigh with relief. "This will do," she said haughtily to the stooped, wrinkled attendant. Bowing, he backed out of the room and closed the door.

Laughing, Morgan threw herself down on a divan. "One can never be quite sure with our hostess, but indeed, we do seem to be welcome. Timing is everything with her. Phases of the moon and such determine which side of her personality rules."

Heather puzzled over that for a moment, then gave up and studied the room, trying not to like what she saw. That was difficult. A richly patterned rug carpeted the floor, and large soft-looking pillows were scattered about it. Brass filigree lamps hung from the ceiling, swaying in a breeze from an open grilled window and casting speckles of light around the colorful room. By a pair of divans, a low brass table held real glass bottles and goblets as well as several plates of tempting-smelling food. Tapestries hung on the walls except where arched openings suggested other rooms beyond.

Morgan leaned forward and examined the table. "Ah, honey cakes. There are few enough flowers and bees left to make honey. Kali does not stint herself—or her guests."

Heather sat carefully on the other divan, feeling dirty, out of place, and uneasy in this room. "So Kali is the name of a woman you came here to meet?"

Morgan munched a honey cake and delicately licked her fingers. "Yes, but 'woman' is hardly the term. Kali is a Power, one of the strongest denizens of any Otherworld to maintain residence in this world. She is very, very old."

"Older than you?"

Morgan laughed. "Oh, a great deal older, but we share some common interests."

That didn't sound hopeful to Heather. If this Kali person had much in common with Morgan, no help could be expected there.

Picking out a cluster of grapes, Morgan said, "Come, eat some of this food. I'm sure your pathetic 'feasts' with King Arthur had nothing to compare with these delicacies." When Heather still hesitated, she snapped, "Don't be such a suspicious fool. Why would I want to poison you now? We have plans."

Finally Heather gave up and nibbled at some of the cakes and fruit. She hated to be disloyal to Arthur and Britain, but the food was amazingly good.

After Morgan had eaten her fill and drunk several glasses of juice, she pointed to one of the adjacent rooms. "There's a bath in there. Go clean yourself and get rid of that disgusting wool rag you're wearing. I'm sure new clothes are ready for us. And wash your nasty stringy hair. Remember, to some, the person you're meeting tomorrow is a goddess."

That was disturbing. Heather was getting used to dealing with magical persons and had even met the exquisitely wonderful Lady of Avalon. But an out-and-out goddess might be a very different matter.

Much of Heather's uneasiness, though, slipped away when she went into the next room and lowered herself into the golden tub filled with warm scented water. When Heather finally pulled herself out, Morgan pointed to another room with thickly mattressed beds and flung her a soft white nightgown. Morgan went to take a bath of her own, but Heather fell asleep the moment her head touched the down-filled pillow.

The relaxing luxury of her night, however, was soon disturbed. Only darkness showed through the grilled window when itchiness in her mind prodded her awake. *I am sorry,* the voice said, the one she'd heard earlier. *I was frightened. We all are, always frightened. But you are special. I can hear you. I must not let you be hurt.*

Where are you?

Nearby, in the caves. We all must work for Kali. Sometimes it is frightful work. But we are born to it. You are not. You must leave here, leave the dread temple. Leave before it is too late for you.

I want to leave. But how?

Silence. *I do not know. Are any coming to help you?*

No, Heather struggled to admit. *There should not be. I told them to not try to rescue me. It's too dangerous for him . . . for them.*

Again silence stretched in her mind. *Then I will try to help. But there is little I can do. Danger is everywhere.*

This voice was gone. Heather tried to call it back, but the only noises in her head were her own thoughts. Not pleasant ones. She wished the voice had been more specific. What was the danger? Well, she could guess at it. Morgan clearly wanted her to join with her in some way, to teach her this new magic Heather supposedly had. Earl had told Heather that her magic was indeed a new type, dependent more on life—on the web that binds people together. And there was this strange mind-talking thing that was developing. She didn't think Morgan knew about that—which was probably good.

No longer sleepy, Heather sat up in bed, wrapped herself in her soft blanket, and thought. This danger the voice warned of—that might be it. Heather didn't feel that her own magic was very strong, but if it really was so different, then letting Morgan gain any of it would be dangerous— to the world. Earlier, Morgan had talked about using power to rebuild the world. But any future world Morgan could envision would not be one Heather wanted to share.

Still, Heather didn't see how her magic could easily add to Morgan's. After all, she hardly understood it herself. How could she teach it to Morgan—even if the sorceress tried to force her to?

When dawn was just paling the sky, Heather slipped again into sleep. She didn't wake until Morgan's sharp voice sliced through to her. "Up! Nearly time for our audience, lazy child! There's a suitable wardrobe in that closet. Choose quickly."

Sleepily Heather climbed out of bed and walked to the closet. On a long bar hung a dozen colorful dresses, each more wonderfully embroidered than the last. Her hand lingered on an emerald-green one, but Morgan pulled out another and thrust it at her.

"Here. Red is more appropriate for you today. Dress, and we'll do something with your ridiculous hair."

The dress was beautiful, brilliant red embroidered with squiggly patterns of black and gold. It almost hurt her eyes to look at them, but *wearing* the dress, she wouldn't have to. Heather slipped it on, enjoying the amazing light feel of the material. She noticed that Morgan too was wearing a new dress, black embroidered with red and set with hundreds of small mirrors. In it, the sorceress looked, as always, shapely and elegant. Heather sighed. Despite her own dress and the fancy hairdo Morgan suddenly conjured for her, Heather knew that beauty and elegance were not meant to be hers.

"Those gold sandals," Morgan said, pointing, "are much more suitable than your old scuffed boots. Put them on."

At that, Heather balked. "This place may be elegant, but it's cold. I'll keep the boots on, thanks."

The woman shrugged, fastening her own jeweled sandals. "It hardly matters now."

They were no sooner ready than the stooped old man from the night before was at the door. "Follow. The great Kali, the Duel Goddess, the Destroyer, the Great Mother, the Giver and Taker of Life, awaits."

The attendant scurried ahead, and Morgan confidently followed. Heather wondered if there was any way *not* to follow. She liked the sound of this Kali person less every minute. But Heather was sure that blindly dashing down some other corridor would only lead to one of those fanged guards forcing her back.

Heather soon lost track of their turnings and the stairs they climbed up or down. But the farther they went, the more she was aware of a sound, a throbbing drumbeat vibrating through her feet and into her ears like the heartbeat of a mountain.

At last they passed through an arch onto a balcony where a broad stairway led down to a huge high-vaulted room. The drumming came from there. Beyond shadowy pillars, Heather could just make out the drummers and twisting, gyrating dancers. That was the only movement in the vast space. Then abruptly the drumming stopped. The figures melted into the shadows, and Heather uneasily followed Morgan down the stairs. The old man did not come with them.

The room was very large and very empty-feeling. At first she thought the floor was covered in mist, but when she stepped into it, Heather realized it was ash, a sea of gray ash. At times it was nearly knee-deep. As they waded through, Heather noticed gray sticks and lumps sticking up through the ash. Bones! She tried not to touch any but winced whenever she felt something brittle crunch under her ash-enshrouded boots.

In the middle of the room, broad stairs rose out of the ash, and gratefully Heather climbed them. They led to a dais curtained off with billowy black drapes. Suddenly the drapes curled aside like writhing flames, and Heather saw Kali.

Sitting on a bone-encrusted throne was a gigantic woman, maybe twenty feet tall. She was black. Not human black, but the black of deepest midnight. And she was nearly naked. Shapely in a way that would have made flat-chested Heather envious had she not been so horrified by the rest of her.

Kali had four emaciated arms, adorned with bone-white bangles. Her long necklace seemed to be a string of human heads, their necks still bleeding over her bare black body. Around her waist, a coiling snake held up her short skirt, a skirt of severed human hands. Under a wild crown of disheveled black hair, Kali's face was beautiful and horrible. Her lips and flicking tongue were blood-red. She stared coolly at Morgan and Heather with all three of her eyes.

Stopping at a broad landing near the top of the dais, Morgan bowed. "Great Kali, Revered Goddess of Death, Great Mother, Destroyer and Giver of Life, I, Morgan Le Fay, greet you once more."

Kali continued to stare at them. Heather shivered under the glance of the third eye set in the middle of the woman's forehead. Then the goddess spoke in a voice like cascading ice, sharp and cold.

"Greetings, Morgan. You have done well since last we met. So much death and destruction passes in your wake. It pleases me. But who is this beside you?"

"A minor magic worker, but young and imbued with new power. I mean her to share in my life."

"Ah. Yes, it would be time. Your deeds continue to earn my aid." Abruptly she stood up, spewing new blood from the skirt of severed hands. She gestured to gargoyle-like figures crouched on either side of her throne, figures Heather had taken to be more carvings. "Bind her!"

Instantly the creatures sprang at Heather. Before she could flinch aside, her hands and feet were bound with stout black ropes. She screamed in protest, but Kali only laughed, a deep rocky laugh. She gestured again and two more grotesque figures stepped from behind the throne, each carrying a white bowl. One, filled with bubbling red liquid, was handed to the goddess. The other, an empty one, was placed on the flagstone in front of Heather. She stared down at it and realized it was a bowl made from the top of a human skull.

With one hand Kali made a complicated gesture, spreading and curling fingers. With another she reached beside her throne and grabbed a long curved sword, its blade already dripping blood. With her remaining two hands, she raised the bowl to her lips and drained it.

Crying wildly, the goddess flung the empty bowl into the surrounding sea of ash. Then she leaped over the heads of the watchers, spraying them with blood from her skirt and necklace. Landing on the ash-shrouded temple floor, she began to dance. Again drumbeats echoed in the hall. Great ashy clouds rose and swirled as the giant goddess danced wildly around the floor.

Terrified, Heather struggled with her bindings, but Morgan only smiled and shrugged. "Kali does enjoy herself. She's the goddess of death, and life as well. But the moon is dark now, and anyway, these days the death aspect is definitely her favorite. She's been getting so much more of that in the last few hundred years."

"And you work for her!" Heather yelled accusingly.

"Oh, no. I am very much my own person. But we share common interests, and perhaps together we and others similarly inclined can nudge the world into becoming even more to our liking. Kali has indeed given me a little friendly help now and then."

"I understand now. That's what Earl meant when he said you had extended your life by having dealings with death."

"Why, yes; how perceptive of him. But life and death are two parts of the same thing. One can't have—or extend—life without death. And that is where you come in, my dear."

"You didn't want to learn my magic at all."

"No, I want to *absorb* it. If I just feed off the death of some non-magical person, it doesn't do me nearly as much good. But if you are half of what Merlin claimed, you should give me quite an edge."

By now, Kali's gyrating dance was drawing her closer and closer. The drums shook the hall like an angry heart. In horror, Heather watched as the goddess and her bleeding sword approached the bottom step. Heather's eyes dropped to the empty skull bowl at her feet and then raised to Morgan's greedily smiling face.

Morgan, she thought with a blast of hate. The sorceress had deliberately deceived her, almost been nice to her. How had she fallen for it again? All that sisterly talk about new clothes, baths, and honey cakes. What a monster this woman was!

Heather closed her eyes and wished desperately for help. She knew there was none outside to call upon. She had only the magic within her, but that had proved of little use up to now.

Yet there would be no more *now* if she did not act.

11

SACRIFICE

As they soared southeast, Merlin could barely sense the dark trail that they had followed before. It was there, but only faintly, as if Morgan was either convinced he was dead or had other things in mind besides luring him. The thought made him both more hopeful and more worried. If she was concentrating on her plans for Heather and not him, the result might not be good.

What drew him on mostly now was Heather herself. He could sense her, feel the bracelet he'd given her still clutching her wrist. And the staff that she had given him seemed to yearn for the way they were heading.

And it wasn't just a sense of direction that led him on. Along this trail flowed a growing sense of urgency. Tired as he was, he didn't want them to stop and only did so when Blanche refused to go another flap farther without food and a nap. Then she'd swoop down on some scraggly unsuspecting herd, snatch a beast, and land to crunch it before curling up for a brief sleep.

Troll, after gobbling his rations, would immediately drop to sleep beside their magic-conjured fire. Merlin and Welly usually took longer to fall asleep—talking to ease their worry and impatience. During their first brief rest stop, Welly asked a question that had increasingly been bothering him.

"Earl, we're clearly in a very distant, very foreign country. But I *talked* to people back there, or heard them talking to each other, and I understood them. I thought people in all these foreign countries spoke different languages."

"They do, and the languages are probably even more different now that peoples are cut off. Your understanding them is no surprise—not to me, anyway, but I guess I never told you, what with all the business when we left Avalon."

"Never told me what?"

"Remember when I asked the Lady to give Arthur the gift of languages so he didn't have to struggle learning the way they speak in Britain now? That language had been changing for two thousand years, and he was always such a dunce at languages, I knew it would take him forever. Folk of Faerie, like Troll, naturally have the gift of languages, but we humans don't. The Lady agreed and suggested she give you, Heather, and me the gift as well. I said fine but that I doubted we would need it. She just looked at me and said that we never could be sure."

Merlin sighed and rolled over with his back to the fire. "The Eldritch have an uncanny way of sensing the future. I wish it was a trait that I'd inherited. Now sleep. As soon as the dragon's finished digesting, we're off again."

As their journey continued, Merlin's sense of urgency grew, and their rest breaks shortened. Blanche insisted on meals, but at his urging she would just swoop down, snatch some fleeing animal, and munch it in the air.

At times, the land was too barren to see anything for her to snack on. On several of the mountains they flew over, glaciers had advanced far down the slopes, driving away any people or animals who might have survived there. Over one bleak icy stretch, when Welly was wishing he had an even heavier jacket, he heard Merlin mutter, "Faster. We've got to go faster."

At that, Blanche snaked her head back to them. "Be my guest, hawk boy. Sprout wings and carry the others." She snorted smoke and set them all coughing. "Just give the word that my honor debt is paid, and you'll see me fly plenty fast—out of your lives."

"Sorry," Merlin managed to say between coughs.

"You should be. Where was the other place that batty Baba person said used to have dragons? I've half a mind to cut off there anyway and check it out. Maybe there are some good-looking male dragons still hanging around."

Welly squeaked in alarm, but Merlin held up a hand to quiet him and spoke to the dragon. "If you did that, you'd break the dragon code of honor, and no self-respecting male dragon would have you. Besides, you wouldn't want to miss the end of this adventure, would you? All the dragons in the old days had sagas or adventure tales revolving around them. When you get back to Faerie, you ought to have something to tell about your extra two thousand years in this world."

She snorted, drifting more smoke their way. "Don't try to outsmart me, boy. As it happens, curiosity is another dragon trait. And I really would like to know how this story comes out. But don't press me. I can always make up the ending if I have to."

After a time, they left snow and glaciers behind. The mountains ahead were lower. In patches, meager forests covered the bare rocky soil, and small villages showed some human or mutie life. Merlin felt they were close now, and he cautioned the dragon to fly lower.

Hours earlier, the sun had set behind them. The night sky was unusually clear. Tarnished starlight gave every-thing a ghostly cast. More mountains appeared ahead of them. When Blanche complained it was time to rest, Merlin urged her to go on just a little farther.

"See that mountain that stands by itself, the one with the flattish top?"

"Yep, and it's a lot of wingflaps away, in case you haven't noticed."

"I have, but you're a strong young dragon. I know you can do it. Heather, I sense, is somewhere just beyond that."

Grumbling steadily, Blanche continued winging toward the mountain. As dawn just grazed the east, they began their circling descent to its summit. They landed on a rough plateau surrounded by jagged pinnacles. Snow crouched in patches among the rocks, and the air, once they climbed stiffly from the dragon's back, was thin and bitterly cold.

"Doesn't look like there's a lot of breakfast just waiting around for me," Blanche growled. Impatiently Merlin an-swered, "Look around for rock rats or whatever, but don't stray far. I need to get an idea of where Heather is and then act quickly. I sense there isn't much time."

"Time for what?" Welly asked as he followed Merlin toward the far edge of the plateau.

"I don't know! But there is something truly evil brew-ing, and Heather's in the midst of it. We ought to be able to see down into the valley once we get to those boulders at the edge of the plateau."

As they neared the boulders, shadows detached themselves and stood before them. People, wearing robes, holding swords. Merlin and Welly drew their own swords, and Troll pulled out his long dagger.

"Who or what goes there?" a voice called from the edge of the boulders.

Merlin ignited his staff with light. "I ask you the same." Behind them, the three could feel Blanche taking a few protective steps forward.

Gasps and mutters were heard from the crowd in front of them. "Surely these are gods or spirits," one said. "This may be Vishnu coming to curtail Kali."

"Or Shiva," said another.

"Or Rama, the hero."

Another chimed in, "No, this must be Surya, god of the sun. See his light and the celestial bird he rides."

A woman stepped up. "Well, surely the one behind is Hanuman, the monkey god."

Troll jumped forward indignantly, waving his dagger. "Me not monkey! Me Troll, brave warrior!"

Behind him, Blanche spat a glob of flame that landed just in front of the foremost speaker. "And I am no bird!"

Merlin raised a hand as the group cowered back. Quietly he spoke to his companions. "Let's not start a fight here. I don't sense anything dark about these people— except fear."

Then he stepped forward and spoke to the dozen or so people who the spreading dawn now showed them. "We are not gods or spirits. We are foreign travelers seeking a companion of ours who has been stolen away and, we believe, taken here."

"I know who they are," said a small voice. A little girl in a ragged dress pushed her way through the crowd.

"Patma?" one man said. "Go back to bed."

A silver-haired woman grabbed the girl's hand. "No, listen to her. She Sees things sometimes—and Hears them. What do you know of them, Patma? Are they demon servants of Kali?"

The girl shook her head, swinging her dark braids back and forth. "No, Aunt Gutra, they have nothing to do with Kali. There is a girl who a witch-woman brought for Kali. These people here have come to rescue her. But they must hurry. It will happen soon."

"What will happen?" Welly blurted.

"The sacrifice," the girl answered as she rushed forward and grabbed Merlin's hand. The wizard suddenly looked even paler than before. "Come, I can take you near there."

One man stepped to bar their way. "These are strangers. Is it wise to show them our secret ways?"

The silver-haired woman slapped the man on the arm. "You old skeptic. Clearly these are beings of power. If Patma trusts them, they are to be trusted." Then she turned to Merlin. "Excuse us, but we live here in the shadow of Kali's temple and are ruled by fear. We serve her and her followers because we must, but we are not hers—not when she is in her dark moods. Since it is often our children whom she takes, how could we be? Follow Patma."

The little girl quickly led them to the boulders and through a low doorway concealed between two of them. Endless-seeming stairs led down, lit by narrow gashes in the rock wall. Here and there, passages branched off, but Patma ignored these. Then she darted into one that led straight for a while and then dropped again. Soon they were passing through a series of small caves with their openings overlooking the sprawling ruins below. The cave walls were adorned with carvings and colorful paintings, but the travelers saw these only as intricate blurs as they hurried by. Then came more down-spiraling stairs, more, larger caves. Finally they stopped at a door concealed behind a seated figure of a fat person with a long nose, tusks, and flapping ears.

"Ganesh," Patma said as she patted the statue's carved stone toe. "May he bring us luck."

Behind that door, the passage became low and narrow. There was no natural light, but as Merlin started to light up his staff, Patma whispered, "No light. We will be in the temple precincts soon. There are demon guards about."

After long minutes shuffling forward in the dark, the ceiling dropped lower. They were forced to crawl. Welly hated tight places, and only the thought of Heather in danger kept him from totally losing control. For Troll, dark underground places reminded him of home. Merlin's thoughts were focused on Heather. He could feel nothing but her fear.

At last the passage ended between the feet of another statue. Patma poked her head out first, then darted out, motioning the others to follow. As Welly did, he glanced up and saw that this statue had many arms, tusks, horns, and a fierce scowl. He was glad it was only a statue.

For some time, they had been feeling a pulsing in the stone floor, growing louder as they advanced. Now in the narrow hallway down which Patma led them, they could hear that it was drumming. It grew louder and more insistent with their every step. Abruptly the hallway ended in a balcony. With columns and carved stone balustrades, it overlooked a great open hall. Tiers upon tiers of balconies circled the hall, but all except theirs were empty.

Crouching behind the balustrade, they peered through the stone grillwork. Far below, the vast floor seemed covered in gray mist or powder. Rising out of it were stone stairs leading to a throne. It was empty now, but below it, Merlin saw Heather standing in a long red dress, her hands and feet bound. Beside her stood another familiar figure. He quivered with anger. Morgan Le Fay.

Both Heather and Morgan were standing still, watching another figure, a gigantic grotesque woman dancing wildly over the gray swirling floor. She was black as deepest night and all four of her thin arms waved madly, one brandishing a sword that steadily sprayed what looked like blood.

The drumbeats grew more frenzied. The dancer drew steadily closer to the dais—and to Heather. Sword now held upward, step by menacing step, the dancer advanced.

Heather closed her eyes, shutting out the advancing figure of Kali. She must do something *now.*

Animal magic, that was all she felt sure of, but there were no animals near to help her. Transformation. Earl had warned of its dangers, but nothing could be worse than the danger closing on her now. She felt the heavy comforting weight of Earl's bracelet on her wrist.

Furiously she concentrated, and the first animal that came to mind was the rat. Pale gray fur, long whiskered snout, bare whip of a tail, and tiny feet—pink, clawed, and made for scurrying. She knew that rat, every fiber of it. She would be that rat—she *was* that rat.

Shrinking and fading, convulsing inside. Bonds fell uselessly away from her small form. Scrambling over them, Heather the rat pelted down the stairs between

Kali's pounding legs. She dove into the sea of ash. Herself gray as ash, she scampered across the floor, leaving a long powdery plume in her wake.

She heard thumping footsteps as Kali chased after her. Gray camouflage was of little use if she couldn't see where she was going. Desperately she scrabbled above its choking pall. Crouching on an empty skull, she stared around. Everything looked so large and far away to her rat eyes. Where was a wall, where escape?

Heather squealed as claws bit into her shoulders and lifted her into the air.

12

ESCAPE

Heather writhed, trying to break loose from the talons' grip. Then, looking down to the ash-covered floor, she realized that a drop from this height would kill her rat self. Hanging still, with pain gripping her sides, she saw that she and her captor were rising, passing tiers of carved balconies. A hawk's fierce black eye stared down at her, its beak opening in a raucous cry. They continued to rise, not returning to the dais.

A green blast of energy careened their way, but the bird dodged and closed in on one balcony. The bolt shattered stone on the wall below as they swooped over the carved balustrade and shot like an arrow into a narrow dark passage. Heather could just make out shapes fleeing before them through the darkness. The flapping wings of the creature that held her barely missed the walls.

Suddenly they veered around a corner. Ahead, figures huddled at the base of a large grotesque statue. Before she could even focus on them, the thing that carried her swept low and let her loose. She rolled over until she bumped up against a stone wall. Blinking her rat eyes, she looked fearfully at the bird of prey, now crouching beside her. Its features blurred. She shook her head, but the image kept dissolving. It became a man. No, a boy, really. Earl! She tried to call his name but was still trapped in the rat's form.

Merlin pressed shaking hands around her furry body. "Easy, Heather. Transformation back is often harder than the first change. Close your eyes. Relax. Think about yourself, your human self. Remember what you were wearing, remember everything that's you. I'll help."

She tried to imagine the person she saw in the mirror. She'd never been too pleased with that image, but she longed for it now. She could feel the force of someone else longing for it as well. Dizziness overwhelmed her. Her body was tingling, twisting, expanding. Her suddenly larger lungs gasped for air. Then she was lying on her back, looking up at Merlin. Looking through clearly human eyes.

"Welcome back," he said with his familiar lopsided smile.

Swiftly she sat up, burying herself in his embrace.

"Sorry," said a young voice beside them. "But we must get out of here!"

With Earl's arm around her shoulders, Heather stood. She saw a small dark-haired girl with big worried eyes. Beyond them were two people she recognized. "Welly! Troll! You're here too!"

"Patma's right," Merlin said, helping her totter forward. "We've got—"

"Too late!" the little girl squeaked as four sword-wielding guards, hideous with horns, fangs, and scaly blue bodies, lumbered around a corner.

Quickly Merlin jumped in front, pushing the others

behind him. He held up his staff, but the approaching guards laughed. "Little boy fight demons with stick!" the largest grunted in a thick guttural voice. "More food for Kali!"

As the lead guard lunged, Merlin swung his staff. The blast of purple energy bowled the guards over, rolling them like balls down the corridor and around the corner. Merlin followed with several more blasts, setting a wall of fire burning across the hallway.

"Quick," he whispered, "into the passage." Already Patma was leading the others through the narrow opening under the statue. Merlin was the last to crawl through, but just before closing the entrance stone, he sent a sound spell down the main corridor in the direction away from the fire. When the demons broke through, he hoped they would follow the phantom sound of running footsteps away from the hidden route their prey had really taken.

After interminable crawling, the passage rose again and finally exited at the feet of the elephant-god statue. Again Patma rubbed the stone toe, and muttered a prayer of thanks. "Now quick, up to the mountaintop. They mustn't know we helped you." She dashed off again through the series of caves and up steep twisting stairways.

At the foot of one staircase, Heather nearly collapsed. "Sorry, sorry. I feel like a squeezed rag," she gasped.

"It's the transformation," Merlin assured her. "It's exhausting even if you have total control. Shall I carry you?"

Heather laughed weakly. "No, I've got claw marks in my sides from your carrying me earlier." Still, she gratefully accepted Merlin's supportive arm around her waist.

The caves and stairs passed in an endless blur until finally, panting for breath, they all emerged into the cold mountain air. Staggering from among the boulders, they stopped and stared. Ahead, on the flat mountaintop, sat Blanche the dragon, surrounded by a circle of softly chanting people. Around her white neck hung a garland of purple flowers, and in front of her was a large wooden bowl piled with now cleaned and cracked bones.

The dragon looked up and blew a lazy smoke ring their way. "Had success, I see. I too. These dear people are quite convinced I'm a god."

"And you haven't tried hard to dissuade them, I take it," Merlin said, striding forward.

"Why should I? Their goats and little cakes are delicious."

Hurrying over to her, Welly said, "Well, say goodbye to your flock, because there's a real goddess down there, to say nothing of Morgan, and I'm sure *they'd* love dragon steaks for dinner."

"Yes, hurry! Go, go, go!" Troll said, scurrying up onto Blanche's back.

The silver-haired woman stood and walked toward Merlin. "You have succeeded. We are glad. But you must indeed go now."

"What will happen to you if they learn you helped us?"

"They won't. We have our ways of concealment."

"You should have seen *his* ways, Aunt Gutra!" Patma said excitedly. "If anyone's a god here, he is. Changing shapes, big purple fire!"

"Nothing divine," Merlin laughed. "Just magic. But you have seen magic growing here too."

The old woman nodded. "And Patma here is among the best at it, if we can just teach her calmness."

The girl sniffed. Heather whispered to her, "Thank you

for being with me in my mind when I needed a friend, when I needed hope."

The little girl smiled. "You had lots of friends. See, they didn't leave you." She gave Heather a tight hug. "Let's talk when we can. I can teach you to have hope, and you can teach me to be brave."

"Deal," Heather said, hugging the girl back. "Though you're plenty brave already."

The old woman slipped off her own fur-lined jacket and draped it over Heather and her flimsy red dress. Thanking her, Heather let Merlin lead her to the dragon and help her onto its scaly back.

"Another weight to carry," Blanche grumbled once her passengers were on board. "I may up my rates."

"What, a great god like you?" Merlin said. "Surely you can handle anything."

"Humph!" Blanche got to her feet and spread her wings, sending the circle of her admirers scurrying back.

Merlin called down, "Thank you all, but quickly now, go back. I don't know your Kali. Perhaps, as a goddess, she is less petty. But Morgan Le Fay is big on vengeance."

The dragon lumbered into a trot over the rocky plateau. Then, with great thrusts of her wings, she soared into the air. The people below stared in awe for a moment, then hurried into the concealment of their rocks and caves.

"Keep low," Merlin cried over the wind of flight. "We don't want to be seen from the other side of this mountain."

"You dare order a god around?" Blanche said even as she dropped lower.

"Hey, dragon," Welly called. "They thought we were *all* gods or heroes or something."

"Right! Troll monkey god!" Troll frowned to himself. "What is monkey?"

Heather, who was now riding between Merlin and Welly, answered. "The books say they were very clever little creatures. Maybe there still are some around here, but I'd rather not stay to find out."

"Right," Welly echoed. "Can we go home now?"

"Yes," Merlin said. "Arthur is waiting. And Morgan's goal is still to destroy him."

"That's not her only goal," Heather said.

Merlin craned around to look at her. "What do you mean?"

"I'm not sure. Morgan was so full of lies. But she did keep talking about increasing her power and somehow . . . reshaping the world."

For long moments, Merlin remained silent. Then he growled, "Yes. I see it. Morgan and Arthur's conflict has always been about Britain. But Britain is not the whole surviving world—not the way we thought."

"So how does that change things, for us, I mean?" Welly asked.

"If there are indeed clusters of humans, muties, and Otherworlders scattered over the world, then it can perhaps be united. United either by Morgan's kind or by Arthur's."

Troll's eyes widened even more. "So back to Arthur! Tell him!"

Quietly Welly added, "Morgan will want to stop us from doing that, won't she?"

Merlin nodded. "She'll be after us with even more than vengeance in mind."

Blanche broke in. "Great. Here I am, happily flying along—but *where to*? Give me some directions, can't you?"

"The world is round," Merlin answered. "I've learned that much since I was living before. We could go either way. But taking a different route might make it harder for Morgan to follow. She's spent lots of time in Europe and probably has more allies there. So let's head the other way. East."

Abruptly the dragon veered right, leaving her passengers white-knuckled and gasping. "East it is," she called. "Though I sure hope you're right about this world-being-round thing. Sounds daft to me!"

13

STEPPE

Mountains frosted in snow, glaciers shouldering their way down desolate valleys, and then came deserts. At first the deserts looked dry and natural, like they had been bleached that way since the beginning of time. Then came deserts with twisted ruins poking through the sand— ruined places where people had once lived. Finally came bleakness beyond the concept of desert. Lifeless glassy plains, too blasted to hold even a hint of former cities.

Blanche's admirers had loaded bags of offerings on her back before their departure. Now the travelers had smoked meat, bread, and dried fruit to sustain them. In much of the land they passed over, not even the sharpest predator could find anything living below.

The more days that passed, the less certain they were of pursuit. But their brief rest stops on land were not cheerful ones. The dead surroundings were too oppressive. At one stop, a chill camp on a bare ridge of red rock, they discussed again their route home.

"I wish I had paid more attention to that globe," Merlin admitted.

"Troll liked globe. Almost took globe, not beads, as

prezzie from Queen. Still like beads best." He gleefully twirled his string of iridescent plastic beads.

The dragon snorted, melting the sand in front of her nose into shiny rivers of glass. "Your ridiculous beads wouldn't tempt even the poorest dragon. Not that I've seen even a glimmer of gold or jewels on this grand world tour. You all probably saw lots in that fancy temple, but did anyone bother to snatch up a few trinkets for your loyal dragon? Not on your life!"

"That's exactly it, you greedy dragon," Welly snapped. "We were mostly running for our lives."

Trying to soothe tempers, Heather turned the talk back. "Well, Troll, you spent time looking at that globe. What would you say about where we are now?"

Troll beamed at being asked such an important question. "China!"

"Or what's left of it," Blanche grumbled. "Not exactly the dragon paradise that crazy Baba woman prattled about."

"There certainly isn't much here," Merlin said. "What do you sense, Heather? Any voices?"

"Nothing here," Heather said with a shiver. "It feels totally dead. Maybe north of here . . . I don't know for sure. But it feels less bleak somehow. And I think that's where one of my voices is—the one who used to talk about horses. So some humans must still be there."

Then suddenly she looked at Merlin. "But I just remembered. Morgan said once that your power would be weakened the farther she lured you from your homeland. Is that happening?"

He smiled and enfolded her in a hug. "No. And I have you to thank for that."

"How?"

"You have been drawing me into the new magic, the power that takes its strength from life—and love. Then the staff you made for me wove both magics together—formed from ancient oak, shaped into images of friends, and carved with love. It's helping me make the transition between magics. I realized that in the temple. The power of hate and death there was suffocatingly thick, but I still felt tied to the web of warm magic that links the whole world."

Blanche groaned and rolled over. "Wizards! Talk, talk, talk about magic. Dragons just *do* it. Go to sleep!"

The next day, they headed north to where their memories of geography told them would be Mongolia. After a long stretch of desert, low mountains ahead of them at least promised some visual relief. As they approached them, though, the dragon slowed, her wing beats hesitant and shuddering.

"What's the matter?" Merlin asked.

"There's something . . . something up ahead. I don't know if I like it or hate it . . . but . . . There! Wrapped around that peak!"

Along with the others, Merlin stared at the peak. It seemed wreathed in cloud. He did feel a presence, not evil exactly, but . . . Then he saw it. The dark cloud slowly unwrapped itself from the mountaintop. Menacingly it slid through the air toward them, taking shape as it came.

Long and black, flecked with gold. A dragon.

"Ooh, friend for Blanche!" Troll crowed.

Beneath them Blanche's growl shook her whole body. Merlin said quietly to Troll, "Dragons don't go in for friendship much. They're generally loners and . . . very territorial!" That last was shouted as the black dragon suddenly picked up speed, shooting toward them with mouth open and golden fangs glistening. Blanche swerved aside just as Merlin hastily wrapped a protective spell around the riders to hold them on her back.

"Blanche, should I use—" Merlin yelled, but she cut him off.

"No, boy, stay out of things! This is dragon business."

The black dragon was nearly on them now, his great leather wings slicing the air. He was much larger and slimmer than Blanche. Gold rimmed his black scales and drooped from his muzzle like whiskers. The roar as he rushed down on them was like an approaching hurricane.

Abruptly Blanche rolled upside down and shot a jet of flame at the dragon's belly as he swooped over. His roar turned to a shriek, and he jackknifed around. His golden eyes glared and he opened his mouth. Despite Blanche, Merlin raised a protective shield. A blast of flame from a dragon that size could incinerate them all.

The shield did them no good. What the dragon spewed out was not fire but wind. An icy blast caught them square on, tumbled Blanche over like a leaf, and blew her a mile away. When she recovered herself, she snarled and shot back toward her adversary like a spear. Flame leaped from her mouth.

The black dragon dodged one volley, then countered her next with a blast of arctic air. It froze the flames and sent them falling like shards of bright glass toward the distant ground. Furious, Blanch twisted and swerved, shooting volley after volley of fire. Most were blown aside, but one grazed the black dragon's left hind leg. He roared, battering them with another hurricane blast. Blanche righted herself and charged in again, bellowing fire.

The battle seemed endless. Blanche's riders gave up trying to follow it and just held on, praying Merlin's protective and securing magic would hold. Among the roars, shrieks, and rumbles, they heard snatches of words.

"My territory! Foreign interloper! Invading scum!"

"Greedy, arrogant bully! Inhospitable wretch!"

Merlin tried to make himself heard. "Blanche, go! Get us out of here!"

"Is that an order, boy?" she snapped between blasts of flame.

"Yes! Leave, now!"

"Only for you, then, sniveling cowards that you are." With a parting volley of flame aimed at the huge black dragon, she wheeled away and flew rapidly past the mountain. The four riders turned and looked fearfully over their shoulders. The black dragon had returned to his mountain peak. Rearing up with wings outstretched, he shot off a parting blast, hurrying them on even faster.

When the wind finally died and their pace returned to leisurely flapping, everyone seemed to breathe again.

"That . . . ," Welly said, "that was . . . amazing."

"Yes," Blanche answered dreamily, "isn't he magnificent?"

"But he tried to kill you!" Heather exclaimed.

"Of course," Blanche said matter-of-factly. "He's a dragon—that's what we do."

"But . . ."

In front of Heather, Merlin shook his head. "Don't argue about dragons with dragons. They have their own logic."

Blanche didn't respond, angrily or otherwise. She just flew on, humming happily. Occasionally she sighed and looked back over her shoulder.

As that day lengthened, the desert below began to be furred with gray-green grass. Here and there, round white tents could be seen. What interested Blanche more were the occasional herds of animals. The sun was near setting as they passed over another scattering of black dots.

"Dinnertime!" Blanche announced as she dropped into a steep dive. "Worked up quite an appetite back there."

Heather closed her eyes in terror but suddenly popped them open as she heard a voice in her mind. *Hey, make your flying steed leave my goats alone!*

What? Where are you?

Here, herding my goats. I'll shoot you out of the sky with my arrows! Don't want to. But I'm a good shot.

Looking down, Heather saw a lone horseback rider galloping after the fleeing goat herd. She yelled at Blanche, "Stop! Not those goats."

The dragon kept diving, spreading her talons.

"Earl, make her stop!" Heather screamed. "I'm talking to the herdsman."

"You heard her, Blanche. Hold off! We'll get you some other food."

With an angry snort, the dragon spread her wings and veered off. An arrow arched through the air where she would have been. A second arrow she caught in one claw and crushed to splinters.

"Thank you, Blanche," Merlin said evenly. "Now please land. We need to talk with this boy."

When the dragon landed and her riders clambered off, Blanche turned her back on them and kept an angry, hungry eye on the fleeing goat herd. The young herder urged his horse toward them. The animal was smaller and shaggier than their British horses and seemed very leery of getting any closer to the dragon. Finally the boy dismounted, hobbled the horse, and walked the rest of the way.

"We've talked before, haven't we?" he said to Heather.

"And you talked mostly about horses."

He grinned. "That's what I always talk about." The boy pointed at Blanche. "Where you come from, do you ride those things instead of horses?"

"No, she's special. And we apologize for her. She's been doing a lot of work and is really hungry."

Overhearing, Blanche snorted angrily. "Don't you *ever* apologize for a dragon being a dragon! We do what we do and don't sneak around lying or trying to control others like some humans I've known."

"A dragon?" the boy said. He looked impressed but not particularly terrified. "I heard there was a dragon in some mountains south of here. But I thought it was black."

"He is, a beautiful black," Blanche sighed.

Merlin stepped forward. "I'm sorry we scared your goats, but would it be possible for us perhaps to buy one of them from you? We need to travel quickly, and our mount does need some food."

"No need to buy when you are our guests. Night is coming. You must spend it with my family. Our yurt is just over there." He pointed toward a white mushroom-like tent on the other side of the sparsely grassed valley.

The boy smiled again, showing brilliant white teeth in a weathered brown face. "Grandfather will want to meet all of you. He's the shaman here and is always telling us about fabulous beasts and spirits and about far places. I didn't really believe in those places until I started hearing the voices."

As they walked back toward his horse, Heather eagerly asked, "Do you hear lots of voices? From all over?"

"I do now. Some talk about things I don't know anything about. That's how I guess they are far away."

"Things like jaguars?"

The boy laughed. "You've talked with him too! What is a jaguar?"

"A big spotted cat," Heather explained. "We don't have them where I live either."

The boy stopped and looked back at Blanche, who was still sulking where she'd landed. "Come with us, honorable flying steed," he called. "There will be goat meat at the yurt. Grandfather said this morning that he sensed guests coming. So we have prepared, though we weren't looking high enough."

The boy unhobbled his horse and with a slap sent the nervous animal galloping home. Then the four humans and one troll, with the dragon trailing behind, walked over the dry crackling grass toward the white tent. As they approached, an elderly man, a middle-aged woman, and a girl about Heather's age stepped out. So did a black dog, who barked, looked at the dragon, then with a whimper slunk back into the yurt.

The old man stepped forward, his long wispy mustache fluttering slightly in the chill breeze. He recited ritual greetings, then said, "I foresaw guests, but not such a variety." He looked at Heather and Welly. "Some from far places. And some from far times," he added, shifting his gaze to Merlin and his startlingly pale skin. "Some even from other worlds, it seems," he said, bowing slightly to

Troll. "And a dragon—though not from these parts, I think. Badrack, better fetch our winged guest the extra goat. Good thing we had warning."

As the boy ran off behind the yurt, the old man addressed the rest. "Welcome and come in. Accept our poor offerings."

One by one, they stepped through the low wooden doorway and took up offered places on the tattered and worn rugs that covered the floor. In the center, an ancient iron stove sent more smoke into the tent than found its way out the central smoke hole. The crisscross lattice frame of the round tent showed in the lower walls. The domed cloth ceiling was held up by wooden beams, their once-bright paint now faded. Bedrolls and cupboards lined the base of the walls.

Heather found herself sitting next to the younger girl, whose glossy black braids were twice as thick as Heather's dirty-blond ones. Heather looked at them admiringly, then realized the girl was looking the same way at the embroidered red dress she'd been wearing since fleeing Kali's temple.

Heather smiled. "If you like the dress, I'll trade it for warm leather trousers and a top like yours. Do you have any old ones you don't wear anymore?"

"You'd give up such a fine thing?"

"Gladly."

In an instant, the girl was pawing through a cupboard. Soon the two moved into a shadowed corner, and in a flurry of giggles, the exchange was completed. Dressed in embroidered finery, the girl was soon laughing and spinning around in the crowded tent while Heather was sitting comfortably in fur-lined leather clothes that smelled heavily of goat.

"Watch out you don't get too close to Blanche wearing that," Merlin whispered. "One sniff and she'll think you're another meal."

She cuffed him playfully. "You just try riding astride a dragon wearing a long flimsy dress. Besides, I don't want anything that Morgan gave me. Mostly she gave me lies."

"She's the Mistress of Lies."

The Mongol woman was busy passing out bowls of runny white stuff and hard white stuff. When Heather received her share, she tried not to wrinkle her nose. Both smelled and tasted of goat. The next course was greasy chunks of meat that definitely were goat. As they were eating and trying to nod their appreciation, Badrack came back into the yurt.

"Your dragon finished that whole goat in four bites. But she is polite. She thanked me, then said she needed to sleep."

"She can be very civil when the mood strikes her," Merlin said. "But don't fear for your herd. We must be leaving first thing in the morning."

The old man chuckled. "That is long hours yet. I beg you spend a short piece of it telling us of your travels. I sense there is much worth knowing. As I sense that you, despite your seeming youth, are very old in power."

Merlin smiled at the man, who he felt was clearly a person of power himself. So, briefly he told their tale—about Arthur and Morgan, about waking the dragon, and about pursuing Heather through Baba's underground city and Kali's evil-drenched temple. Finally came their confronting the black dragon and deflecting the attack on Badrack's herd.

During the tale, the old man sat with closed eyes, gently rocking back and forth. At the end, he nodded and looked at Merlin. "Your power and your peril are even greater than I sensed. You must indeed flee this land quickly, for pursuit already sniffs out your trail." When Welly flinched and clutched at his sword, the man laughed. "Not that quickly. There is time for rest. But here we live in sight of the Beautiful Mountain, and the Mountain gives me vision to see what may be coming our way."

Turning to his grandson, he patted him on the back. "Just as the Mountain has given Badrack hearing to reach even farther than I can see. He will make a fine shaman someday."

The boy blushed and hung his head. "But I'd like to have real adventures like these folks have had—before I become a wise old shaman."

Welly shifted slightly so as not to disturb Troll, who'd fallen asleep across his lap. "But you can do both. Look at Earl here. He gets into more trouble than anyone I know— and I suppose that's another word for *adventure.* But he's also as wise and old as they come."

Merlin laughed. "*Trouble* is when it's happening. It's only called 'adventure' after you're home safe and looking back."

Troll opened one eye, then rolled over and curled up closer to the stove. "Then want this be *adventure* soon. Sleep now."

Blankets and shaggy smelly skins were unrolled, and soon hosts and guests were stretched out around the edges of the tent. Sleepily Heather watched the mother poke more fuel into the stove and realized that what they were burning was dried dung. Well, she figured, she probably couldn't get any worse-smelling, and at least she was dry, warm, and safe—for the moment.

She rolled over and tried to hold that warmth and comfort in her mind, but other images kept creeping in. She didn't need the old shaman's warning to sense they were being pursued. The horror of Kali's temple seemed to have burned a hole into her soul. Through it, she felt a cold dark evil blowing ever closer. Shivering, she clutched at her bracelet for comfort, then curled into a tight ball, finally relaxing into troubled sleep.

14

MOUNTAIN

They woke to Badrack flinging open the door from outside and shouting, "The dragon's gone! I went out to see if she could do with a lighter breakfast, but she was already flying off. She yelled back a message 'for the doddering old wizard,' she said. That's you?" Badrack glanced questioningly at Merlin, who was trying to look more awake and alert than he felt.

"What was the message?"

"She said, 'Biology trumps duty. So long.' That was it exactly."

Everyone in the yurt was now awake and looking at him as Merlin groaned.

"What does it mean?" Heather asked, afraid she already knew.

"It means that our Blanche has chosen to put aside honor and go off to seek a mate."

"That black dragon?" Welly questioned. "But he tried to *kill* us—and her."

Merlin shook his head. "That's the way it is with dragons. Mostly they're solitary and avoid their own kind. But they do find mates. And the more a dragon fights another, the more attracted they are to each other."

"That's crazy!" Welly said.

"Trolls same. But me no find lady troll even to fight."

Merlin stood up, clumsily folding his blanket. "Some people are like that too. Look how Arthur and Margaret started out, snarling at each other like dogs. But this does leave us in a bad way." He turned to the old shaman. "Are you certain that pursuit you feel is still tracking us?"

"Yes, and getting closer. The only thing you can do now is appeal to the Mountain."

"How do you mean?" Merlin asked.

"I know nothing of the place you are from, but here in Mongolia, it is the *land* that has the power. It is felt in everything—the rocks, the grass, the rare venerated trees. The Devastation did not change that. Our people were always few and close to the land. Mostly, though, power is in the mountains. Our mountain here, our Beautiful One, has very great power. If you go to it, make the proper offerings, and ask its help, it may grant that help."

After a moment, Merlin nodded. This wasn't quite the magic he knew. It had a foreign accent. But it was familiar too. Magic of place was very old and very powerful. "Where is this mountain? Tell me its name so I can call upon it properly."

All the locals looked alarmed. "No, no!" the shaman said. "Here you must never speak the name of a spirit as powerful as a mountain—not within its sight. That will anger it, and the greater the spirit, the greater the anger. To be safe, we call it only Beautiful One."

"But we know its real name, don't we, Grandfather?" Badrack said.

"As shaman, I do. And as my successor, so do you, though I will flail you if you speak it aloud—if the Mountain doesn't do so first."

By now, the travelers were all up and slipping on the jackets they'd removed in the warmth of the yurt. "We cannot thank you enough for your hospitality," Merlin said. "I wish there was some way to repay it. But the best we can do now is to remove ourselves as fast and far as possible. If Morgan or her minions are indeed on our trail, they will not go easy on any who aided us."

"Do not fear," the shaman said, hobbling to the door. "I can shield us from such things. But you need to travel far and fast for your own sakes. Badrack, go fetch the camels. Our guests can ride them to the base of the Mountain, then set them loose. They'll return on their own."

As the boy ran out, the grandfather guided Merlin outside and pointed to a broad mountain across the grasslands to their west. Its bare white rock was blushing pink in the clouded dawn. "When you reach the base of the Mountain, climb to the top. There are paths of sorts. It is a powerful mountain, but also a faithful guardian and so not too high for people to climb. Once at the top, you will see a great pile of stones. There you must place offerings, each one of you, and walk around the pile from left to right—*not* the other way—three times while asking the Mountain's help. Then climb down the other side. If help is to be offered, it will come."

They all stood outside now, shivering in the dawn chill. From behind the yurt came a gargling roar. Badrack appeared leading two of the most amazing animals Heather had ever seen. At first she thought they looked like tall lumpy haystacks with legs. Then she saw that they were simply covered with shaggy tan hair. There were great wobbly lumps on their backs, and their arched necks ended in long sneering faces.

"Camels," the shaman said proudly. "We are fortunate

to have a pair. The tame ones died after the Devastation, but the wild ones survived, and we have tried to tame them again. Of all the herdsmen on the steppe, only shamans' families have them now because they are too willful without a little power of control. You can do that, wizard?"

"Heather is best at that," Merlin replied. "Animal magic is her specialty."

"Ah, it is the same with my Badrack—that and his crazy voices. Go, then. Each of you powerful ones ride in front with one of your companions behind. That should keep the beasts in line."

The camel that Heather and Welly were given snorted, spat, and backed away. But Heather reached into its grumpy mind. *Gentle now. Go with us on a ride over the grasses, feeling wind in your lovely hair. We are poor stupid things who don't know the beauties of this place. Take us to the Beautiful Mountain. Show us what a magnificent place you are lords of. We hardly weigh anything—not to a strong creature like you.*

The creature didn't deign to answer but snorted and folded itself down so they could clamber onto its back, Heather between the neck and the first shaggy hump and Welly jammed between the two humps. Then the camel suddenly rocked back and forth and stood up, nearly catapulting its riders off.

Welly yelped, and Heather felt the camel's smug mental laugh. *Oh, clever trick,* she thought back, trying to keep annoyance out of her mind. She looked over and saw that Merlin and Troll were also mounted, though their camel seemed to be giving them even more grief.

At the door of the yurt, the family watched with smiles. For the first time, the dog had crawled from its hiding place and joined them. Scurrying forward, the mother and daughter handed each traveler a leather bag of lumpy things. From the smell, Heather feared it was more of the hard goat cheese. Then the woman reverently handed Heather another bundle, a red-clay jar sealed with leather.

"It is our best goat yogurt. Sprinkle it on the stones while you circle them as your offering." Heather thanked her, glad that she wasn't required to eat it herself.

The grandfather raised a hand. "Ride and climb swiftly. If you respect the Mountain's power, it will respect yours. Go!"

Both camels erupted into a rolling swaying gait that had Heather wishing she hadn't eaten all that goat stuff the night before. It still sloshed uncomfortably in her stomach. Then she was diverted by a voice in her head. Badrack's.

May your troubles turn to adventures soon. Let's talk when we can.

Smiling, Heather thought back, *Yes, let's. And may you find some adventure that's not too troublesome.*

I'll do my best. Soon too, maybe.

For all their awkward appearance and painful gait, the camels covered ground swiftly. The brittle grass crunched beneath their broad hooves, and gradually the white mountain loomed closer. Above it, the sky stretched, a rare pale blue. Heather was always a little awed when the high dust thinned enough to show that color. She thought again what the world must have been like when a clear blue sky was normal. But if what the old shaman had said was true, this part of the world hadn't changed that much. These grasslands had never hosted cities, and the sparse wandering herdsmen had attracted no bombs. She could understand how these people would live close to the spirits of their land.

Slowly the white mountain began to fill all their view.

But at the first hint of rising ground, the camels came to a stubborn halt.

Told to go to base of mountain, Heather's said into her mind. *That's here. Get off.*

Doesn't a little politeness go with your taming? Heather asked as she gestured for everyone to dismount.

What taming? We're just hanging out with those people because the food's better. With that, the two shaggy camels turned and loped back toward the yurt, which was now a distant white speck.

"They could have taken us a little ways up," Welly grumbled.

Heather shook her head. "I don't think my mind could have taken the complaining. Let's just walk."

They soon found the base of a worn trail that etched its way up the mountainside. As they climbed, the way got steeper and sometimes disappeared among tumbled pale rocks. But then they'd see its sketchy line continuing farther on and, after much awkward scrambling, rejoin it. Troll seemed to have no trouble scampering over the rocks, and Merlin with his long legs had fairly easy going. Heather struggled to keep up with him.

Welly, despite his constant warrior workouts at home, still found this sort of exertion hard on his plump frame. Straggling along behind everyone, he had slapped his hand onto a rock to hoist himself up when he heard an ominous rustle. Alarmed, he squinted through sweat-smeared glasses.

"Snake!" he cried, and pulled back his hand, nearly losing his balance.

Heather looked back and saw the gray chevron-marked snake coiled and glaring at Welly. He scrambled back farther. "Are they poisonous around here?"

It didn't take much mental probing for Heather to find the answer. "Yes, and proud of it. I'll try to get any nearby snakes to move out of our way."

She didn't know how many might be around, so she just broadcast, *Snakes, out of our way! Now!*

The effect was startling. In an explosion of rustling and slithers, snakes and lizards seemed to scuttle over every rock on the hillside.

"Oh," she said aloud. "Overdid it a little, I think." *Sorry. Just leave the four of us alone, okay?*

The flitting stopped, and Welly proceeded nervously up the mountainside after the others.

Several hours later, they staggered up to the summit. Wind chilled their sweat-soaked bodies, and by then everyone's legs were quivering. Sinking down onto flat boulders, they stared at the tall conical pile of rocks at the mountain's tallest point. Among the fist-sized rocks were scraps of cloth, glinting pieces of ancient glass, and skulls of goats and horses.

Finally Merlin stood up. "All right, everyone needs to make an offering, something of value presumably, and walk three times around the mound clockwise praying for help. There's no point in not believing. So much has happened lately and so many beliefs have been intersecting, I'm willing to believe anything if it works."

He walked over to the mound and, after a moment's thought, removed a ring from his hand. Queen Margaret had given it to him last Yule. It was an old silver ring she'd found at an antiques shop and chosen because it was engraved with a capital *M*. With a sigh, he placed it in a high rocky niche and began circling the mound.

Welly reluctantly unwound the blue and white scarf

he always wore around his neck. The cook's assistant back in Keswick had knit it for him before they left on their long quest to unite Britain. He'd often thought fondly of her when he put on the scarf but was sure that by now she'd taken a fancy to someone else and was probably happily married. He sighed and, reaching up, wrapped the now-grubby scarf around a projecting stone and started around the mound. He'd miss not so much the scarf as the dream it represented. But this was proving to be a very big world. There had to be a girl out there for him somewhere.

Troll sat at the edge of the mound fingering his prized plastic necklace but unable to take it off. When he'd finished his own triple circuit, Merlin knelt down beside him. "The more something is valued, the more worthy the sacrifice. Surely the Mountain will see how much you are giving up."

"Troll see too. Best thing ever had."

"When you get back to Britain, you'll be a hero. Arthur and Margaret will give you something even more splendid. But first we have to get back there. And maybe parting with your necklace will make the difference. It's the heroic thing to do."

Troll's sigh reached to his toes. "Being hero hard thing." Slowly he stood up, pulled the necklace over his head, flung it to the very top of the mound, and began trudging around.

All this time, Heather had been sitting on the same rock she'd first collapsed onto, the pot of goat yogurt waiting beside her. Her eyes rested on the distant horizon, where an ominous black cloud was rippling over the grasslands. Her mind was filled with Badrack's voice. They were talking now, but it was the first call that had frozen her to the spot.

I tried to trick her but don't know if it worked. She knows where you are and is coming fast! Flee!

What happened? What did you do? Heather had asked.

As soon as you left, I rode south. I guess Grandfather was right—I could feel evil flowing from there. I rode as fast as I could, and then I saw it. Like a sooty cloud in the sky. I kept riding till it was over me. And then I looked up. And waved.

Waved? At Morgan? Heather had questioned.

I wanted her to think I was just a dumb friendly native, curious about odd stuff in the sky. Really, I was never so scared in my life. It was like looking up into a great flock of vultures. Only they were uglier. Claws and fangs and ghastly demon faces. Their flapping wings sounded like dried bones clacking. In the middle of it all, a woman rode on a red beast even stranger than your dragon. She was beautiful.

Morgan, Heather thought with a shiver.

At first she ignored me, then she wheeled back and landed beside me. My horse nearly threw me in panic, then he just stood quivering with fear. Black hair, green eyes, very beautiful. But I could feel the poison under it.

"Oh, y-you are more wonderful even than the others," I stammered with this foolish grin on my face. "Are you a friend of theirs?"

Her voice was like bells. "I and the others have known each other for a long time. I am trying to join up with them again. Do you know where they've gone?"

"Yes, they went to the sacred mountain, but I don't know where after that. The mountain spirit will know. It is a very powerful spirit. If you call on it, it will surely answer you since you are clearly a magnificent spirit yourself."

"And how do I call on it?"

"You must go very close to it and yell out its secret name three times."

That seemed to annoy her. "And how do I learn this secret name?"

"My grandfather is a local wise man—he knows spirit names. Once I heard him whisper the Mountain's."

"Tell me!"

"I dare only whisper it," I said, stepping close to her. She bent down from that terrible beast. That close, she smelled of cold and death. I turned my back on the Mountain and spoke its name very softly.

She laughed like a raven and spurred her beast into the air. "Now, with its true name, I will force this spirit to tell me what I need." She surged up to join that flapping black flock, and like a storm cloud, they rolled off your way.

If she uses that name . . . ? Heather questioned.

The Mountain's anger may be great. But if she doesn't, she will find you easily. Either way, you are in danger where you are. Flee!

Heather jumped to her feet and ran to join the others. "Hurry, Morgan is coming! Badrack told me, and you can see her just there." She pointed to the growing smudge of black in the southern sky.

"Quickly, down the other side of the mountain!" Merlin yelled.

Heather was about to follow, then remembered the pot of yogurt she was supposed to sacrifice. Hurrying back for it, she ripped off the leather lid. She ran three times around the pile of stones, sprinkling white liquid as she went, praying for deliverance with every breath. Placing the empty pot at the base of the pile, she ran after the others—but not before turning and looking again at the nearing cloud.

Cold and fear seemed to blow from it like an approaching storm.

15

BRIDGE

The late-afternoon sky had turned to faded gray, and the mountain's rocks and shadows blurred into a confusing jumble. It seemed that they stumbled and slid down the slope more than they ran.

"I never thought I'd miss that cranky dragon," Welly panted, running beside Heather. "But fleeing on foot from Morgan and her nasty flock is not going to be easy."

"Well, at least it'll be night soon," Heather offered. "But there sure aren't many places to hide out here."

As at last they neared the bottom, Merlin raised a hand to halt them. Below were clustered gray shapes. They might have been boulders or tuffets of grass, but they moved.

Heather peered into the thickening dusk. The shapes were animals, large and shaggy, with great back-sweeping horns. She'd seen pictures of something like them once. Deer? No, not plain deer. Reindeer.

The four walked down slowly now. The animals milled about but didn't flee. Then Heather saw that a man was riding one. As they reached more-level ground, the bearded man directed his reindeer toward Merlin.

"You need swift mounts," he said simply. "Take some of my herd, some to ride and some as cover."

"How . . . ?" Merlin began, then dropped the question. Their offerings had been accepted.

Four reindeer were selected and the travelers were helped to mount. The herdsman cut off another half dozen from his herd and with a shout sent them all galloping northeast.

Surrounded by a moving sea of reindeer, Heather lay low on the shaggy back of hers and tightly gripped its antlers. Her mount gave an annoyed shake of its head, and Heather held the antlers more loosely. She didn't know where to steer it anyway. Obviously it was following some directions—but not hers.

Behind them, the sky darkened, but with more than evening. Heather shuddered at the thought of what must be in that black cloud she'd seen approaching. She craned to look behind them. Blackness hung over the mountain—and not simply the blackness of storm.

With a suddenness that shook the earth and sky, lightning cracked over the mountain. A tremendous wind swirled over its peak. It was as if titanic anger was suddenly unleashed. With a jolt, Heather realized what it was. Morgan, unaware of the taboo, must have spoken the secret name!

Their little party rushed on while behind them rain, wind, and thunder battered the far side of the mountain. Again and again lightning silhouetted the peak, dark and beautiful in its anger. Even at this distance, the earth shook with the volleys of thunder. Not even a supernatural army, Heather realized, could withstand the Mountain's supernatural fury.

Their small herd ran on and on until dawn showed they had come to a land of sparse dark trees. For a few hours, the herd rested under their cover, scratching aside dusted snow with their hooves to graze on the crackly grass. Gratefully the riders slipped off their mounts. Slumping at the base of rough tree trunks, they shared provisions. Even the hard smelly goat cheese didn't seem so repellent.

Heather felt she had just drifted off to sleep when an animal voice, a reindeer voice, scratched at her. *Time to go on.*

Where?

Where we're told. To the Bridge. Will take you there but not over.

Heather repeated this to the others as they stiffly mounted up.

Troll was excited. "Bridge! Trolls love bridges. Maybe meet lady troll there. Oh. Or bigger nasty troll. Great Wizard protect us, okay?"

"I'll try," Merlin laughed. "Though I'm having trouble keeping up with the surprises this world's still throwing at us."

They rode through that day, into the night, and through many more days and nights. The reindeer seemed tireless, but the exhausted travelers managed to sleep in fitful snatches with hands tightly wound into their mounts' shaggy pelts. The ground was all white now with snow. Against it, the dark twisted trees they rode past looked like ancient guardians.

Sleepily, one morning, Heather had realized the sky was beginning to pale when a terrified cry jolted her fully awake. Huge winged shapes swooped down on them, grabbed a fleeing reindeer each, then soared away, scattering blood as they went. The rest of the reindeer panicked, breaking in all directions. Merlin struggled to control his mount and to light the air with his upheld staff. Heather tried to concentrate on calming reindeer minds, but her own mind was far from calm.

Merlin was pointing his staff at one of the great flying shapes when a voice cut down toward them. "Hold it, boy! We've just grabbed a quick bite. So leave off the fireworks. We're the good guys, here to rescue you—again."

"Blanche?" all four of them cried from the backs of their flinching reindeer.

"Me and my sweetie. You may call him Hei Se if you want. That means 'black' in his language. He's decided to play along with our heroic honor game for a while. There's not much doing for a dragon in a land where most folk that believed in him are long dead."

The sky was lightening now. Against its sooty pink, the great black dragon hovered like a storm cloud. While Heather mentally worked at herding the reindeer together again, the two circling dragons finished their snacks, then settled onto a snowy slope, rolling around to clean themselves. The snow was left streaked with blood.

The reindeer now huddled close together, and abruptly Heather's mount announced to her, *You're near enough to the Bridge. Get off. We're going back.*

Heather wanted to protest that the dragons wouldn't hurt them now, but she couldn't. Who knew when their ravenous appetites would kick in again?

Right. You've been great. I'm awfully sorry about the other two. We'll be all right from here.

Quickly Heather told her companions to climb off

before their restive mounts threw them off. Then the diminished herd wheeled about and charged back the way they had come, keeping closely to the cover of trees.

The four travelers were left alone looking at the two dragons. Having finished preening, both dragons were looking at them. Twice the size of Blanche but with a more slender build, the black dragon's snout was longer and ended in drooping golden whiskers. His horns pointed backward like gold-tipped daggers instead of curving inward like Blanche's. But they were both undeniably dragons, and Welly felt totally intimidated. He knew he wasn't alone when Troll clambered up his legs and tried to crawl under his loose jacket.

Merlin was the first to recover. He stepped forward and bowed. "Welcome back, Blanche. And we are most honored to make your acquaintance, mighty Hei Se. If indeed you wish to accompany us, we would be doubly honored."

The black dragon's voice was sharp and grating. "It has been so long since I interacted with mortals, I might find this amusing. My dear Blanche tells me you are aiming to return to your home on the other side of the world. I could never bring myself to leave my own home for long even after the fools who lived there managed to destroy it. But the thought of a brief vacation is most intriguing—particularly accompanied by such a charming lady."

Heather could have sworn she saw their dragon's white scales briefly blush pink.

"Then we should be under way," Merlin said, "now that you have dined. I am sure you are aware that we are pursued. A benevolent mountain spirit attacked our pursuers but may have only temporarily delayed them. We were being sent to some sort of bridge. Is that how you recommend going?"

The black dragon laughed, producing not smoke but a swirling gust of wind. "The Bridge, yes. The Land Bridge. It was there eons ago when I was a mere dragonling, and some of my humans crossed it. But then it vanished under the waves and only lately has risen again. It would not be a swift matter to walk it because mostly it is covered in ice and snow. But it would be a good route to fly over. Crossing hundreds of miles of open ocean is not to my taste. Snatching up a quick seal or a dolphin is no easy matter, and there would be no perch to rest weary wings."

Again Merlin bowed. "We will follow your advice, mighty Hei Se, and if you would permit two of us to ride on your back, it will ease the burden on Blanche."

The white dragon snorted. "Don't presume, boy. I'm strong enough to carry twice your number." Then, turning to the other dragon, she added, "But I am happy to share the adventure with dearest Hei Se, if that suits you, my dear."

Merlin suggested that there be a magic worker on each dragon, and Heather quickly chose Blanche. Welly immediately joined her. Troll practically fainted from fear, and Merlin had to carry him up onto Hei Se's back and wedge him into a fold in the scales in front of him.

Soon they were again in the air, soaring toward the newly risen sun. Before long, they saw the gray expanse of ocean approaching to their right. But to their left the land continued in a narrow arch, its surface white with snow that here and there opened into grassy tundra. Small herds of reindeer and other shaggy animals grazed there.

For days, they skimmed over the land bridge, resting briefly when they saw patches of open tundra. Sometimes the dragons would find a herd to snack on, and other times they would sail out over the open sea and return with something slick and blubbery. There were times too when after leaving their riders on land, they simply played in the sky, diving and circling, shooting fire and storms at each other like children playing ball.

As rations picked up at various stops ran low, Merlin reluctantly asked the dragons' aid in supplying food. The result one night was a dead two-headed rabbit dropped beside their fire. Heather was sorry to see it lying there but couldn't resist the enticing smell of roasting rabbit once Merlin and Welly had managed to skin and cook it.

When the last scrap of meat was finished and the greasy fingers were licked, Welly asked Merlin about the black dragon. "From what he said about the land bridge, he sounds really ancient. Can dragons live that long?"

Merlin nodded, collecting the rabbit bones and giving them to Troll to crack for marrow. "Dragons are creatures of Faerie, so they're as close to immortal as anything can be. They can be killed, of course. For a time, in Britain, heroes went around doing that. That's one reason many dragons returned to their Otherworlds even before the Devastation. This Chinese dragon must have a tremendous attachment to his land for him to have stayed with no one left to tell stories about him."

Troll threw aside the last of his cracked bones. "That sad. Humans can be big bother. But tell good stories. Make even small trolls feel big."

Heather laughed. "You mean creatures from the Otherworlds like humans because we tell stories about them, making them out as heroes—or villains?"

"Or gods," Merlin added. "Kali is a goddess, and her power is of a whole different type. Worship is vital to them, and no doubt she was once worshiped as a bringer of both life and death. But the world is badly out of balance now, and she retains power through fear and human sacrifices."

Suddenly Heather went pale. "Was that what Morgan was trying to do, become immortal by drinking my blood?"

Merlin scowled. "Morgan is part human, part Eldritch. Same as I am. But mixed-bloods are mortal. We can use magic to prolong our lives, and Morgan has chosen to do so with the darkest magic."

Gently grabbing Heather's hand, Merlin said, "I foolishly told her about you, about the strength of the new magic. That's why she wanted your blood particularly. And now that she has met you, she might suspect even more about your powers. That army that was beaten back by the Mountain—it was full of demons, demons Kali probably called up for her. I think they're following us now not just for vengeance or even to keep us from revealing their plans to Arthur. They must realize how much power you have and how much threat you pose to them."

"Threat? All I can do is a little animal magic and talk in my mind to a few people."

"But you do it in a different way. Magic based on life, on human relationships, and on communication—that is a threat to them. Their magic depends on fear and hate. That's how they want to unite the world. But if, as the world gradually recovers, people learn to communicate instead of hate and their growing magic feeds on life instead of death—then this new world could develop differently."

"Ah, what a wise sage you are, boy." The black dragon had silently crept up and been listening. He laughed when they all jumped and looked around. "That is another reason, besides the undeniable charms of my beloved, that made me throw my lot in with you. I can feel the hate of those pursuing you. It rises from the same sources that drove humans to destroy their world. Anything I can do to thwart those forces would give me infinite pleasure."

Merlin bowed. "Thank you. We are honored by your support."

"Are they still pursuing us?" Welly asked nervously.

"Of course they are, boy," Blanche snorted. "So if you've all finished philosophizing, mount up. Dear Hei Se says we haven't much farther to go."

"And what will we find when we get there?" Heather asked, trying to keep her voice steady. The great black dragon still made her jumpy.

"Who knows?" He laughed gustily. "It's my first trip beyond China. But if there are human survivors anywhere, there will still be openings to their Otherworlds. This is a voyage of discovery."

As they mounted up, Merlin was still worrying about exactly what they'd discover. If North America had been as badly devastated as he feared, it would be a long bleak trip eastward back to Britain. And then there'd be another ocean to cross. Could they even make it? Yet Heather said she'd heard several voices from the Americas. Maybe they'd find enough life to sustain themselves.

Maybe—if they could escape the evil that was pursuing them. As they rose again into the air, he looked fearfully over his shoulder. The sky behind them was an innocent pale blue. Yet he could feel the black threat beyond it. Shuddering, he looked forward again. In the distance, he thought he saw the faint outline of land stretching from the end of the land bridge toward the south. He couldn't sense what lay there. Newness, certainly. And perhaps hope.

16

FOREST

Another few hours brought them to the coast. After landing on a snow-flecked beach, they pooled what faint sense they had of a desired direction and decided to fly south along the coast until they found either a cluster of humanity or an Otherworld entrance. But flying on until sunset, they found nothing. To their left, the continent stretched under a bleak glacial shroud. Ahead of them, the white fringe of surf beat on rocky barren beaches. Above, the sun was just a pale wraith in the shrouded sky.

They stopped at one beach for the night, huddling among rocks to escape the battering winds from cold ocean and colder land. Food for the dragons was scarce until, in frustration, Blanche blasted a shallow bay with flame and a few fish and odd creatures floated to the surface.

The following days and nights were much the same except that their vague sense of a goal grew stronger and urged them on in the same direction. Then, as they rose into another dawn, a faint column of smoke on the horizon drew their attention. With more confidence, they headed down the coast toward it.

In patches now the snow cover vanished to be replaced by bare rock, waving dune grass, or short wind-twisted trees. Riding behind Heather, Welly squinted through his glasses at the rising thread of smoke. "It seems to be coming out of the top of that mountain. Do you think it's a volcano?"

"Could be. It does sort of look like volcano pictures in books. And I sense there's more life over there. Makes sense, I guess. The area around volcanoes ought to be warmer."

She looked across at Merlin, whose black dragon was flying alongside theirs. The wind and steady flapping of dragon wings made conversation difficult. But he grinned and nodded, pointing toward the smoking mountain.

"Do you hear any voices from up ahead?" Welly asked Heather.

She shook her head. "I heard a squawk in the night almost like a baby crying. But I think it was probably some noisy seabird."

They continued flying south. Beneath them, snow had vanished from the shore. Jutting from the sand were fingers of dark rock smoothed by eons beneath the sea before the waters had drawn back, leaving them bare and exposed.

The smoking mountain loomed closer now. It was set back from the coast at the head of a long valley bounded by steep ridges. Shrouded sunlight glinted off coils of a river that wound down the valley toward the sea. Partly hiding the river and climbing up the valley sides was a carpet of dark green. Trees. Heather and Welly gasped at the same time. More trees than they had ever seen in one place. Heather kept staring, sure she hadn't seen anything as beautiful since leaving Avalon.

The river fanned out into several braids as it cut through sand dunes and spread in muddy fingers into the gray-green ocean. Both dragons circled tightly together over the delta. Wisps of fog were slowly rolling in from the sea but hadn't softened the dark tree-filled chasm.

"Doesn't feel totally right," Hei Se called.

"No, it doesn't," Blanche answered. "Feels hostile."

"Foreign."

"Very."

"Okay, I agree," Merlin interjected. "It feels hostile, very foreign, and layered with fear. But it also feels like a human and Otherworld link. For all we know, it could be the only place on this continent where we can get any help. We need provisions and directions at least. What do you sense, Heather?"

Heather started to answer, then abruptly clamped two hands to her head. "Only thing I sense is an unhappy squawking baby. Not much help there."

Merlin shrugged. "All right. Let's land at the mouth of the river valley—well back from the waves but before the trees get too dense. Then we can explore."

Welly was glad when the dragons broke their close spiraling formation. It was making him airsick. But the thought of landing in hostile foreign territory was not comforting.

The two dragons banked and glided in over the foaming breakers and the braided river mouth. The watercourse came together just before it emerged from the trees, and there the dragons settled onto the grass-held dunes. Stiffly the travelers climbed off their dragons, then stood in silence staring up the river valley.

Welly was the first to speak. "Those are *some* trees. I've never . . . I mean, they're *enormous!*"

Slowly the four walked forward. The stunted trees Heather and Welly had seen seldom were taller than twice their own height. Merlin had known tall pre-Devastation trees, but nothing like these.

Troll summed it up for them. "Trees *big*! Even in Faerie, never see trees like these."

As they walked under the giants, they were engulfed in silence and thin veils of fog. Drooping ferns carpeted the forest floor. The trees' red-brown bark was shaggy and deeply furrowed. On the largest trees, the trunks rose straight and unbroken to great heights before branches emerged, weighed with feathery dark green needles. The treetops were nearly lost to sight as they swayed in and out of swirling fog.

The silence was profound. Even the tumbling river seemed hushed. Suddenly Merlin stiffened. Clutching his Eldritch sword, he whispered, "We aren't alone."

A voice rang out from the forest gloom. "The storied invaders! Attack!"

Figures charged from the shadows of tree trunks and ferns. Most were as dark red as the trees, with long black hair and eyes that held no welcome. They were armed. Spears and swords glinted in the fog-dimmed light. With a raucous cry from high up among the trees, a creature leaped down to join the attackers. Ten feet tall, its human-seeming arms and legs were covered in shiny black feathers. Its eyes gleamed like coals, and its beak of a mouth snapped open.

"Destroy them!"

The four travelers hastily stood back to back, pulling out their own swords. Slowly the forest folk moved in. Then horrendous roaring from the beach turned all attention there as two dragons charged to the attack.

In a mad chaotic flurry, the tall feathered figure and two others like him in gray fur and brown leaped toward the dragons, chanting and drawing power from the air. Ropes of light coiled, solidified, and flung themselves at the dragons. In moments, the beasts were totally ensnared and thrown helplessly on their sides. Then, with a collective howl, the forest people threw themselves at the four travelers.

Welly found himself facing a girl his own age. She grinned like a wild beast and lunged forward with her stone-tipped spear. Welly beat it aside with his sword, then tried to jab at her, but she sidestepped and lunged at him again. The metal sword cracked her spear shaft in two, but she grabbed the bladed half and slashed at him, cutting a long rent in his jacket. Spinning around, he jabbed at her with his now-longer blade. She twisted aside, quickly backing out of range. Welly leaped forward and took another massive swipe at her.

Suddenly he felt his feet sliding from under him. A mossy bank gave way. He tumbled down as the girl standing above him laughed. Flailing at the crumbling earth, Welly caught a root and slashed upward with his sword, cutting the turf from under her feet. The root snapped, and the two tumbled downward through moss, dirt, and ferns.

The others were equally engaged. Troll gibbered and danced among the attackers, just avoiding their blades and poking at some with his own. When too many enemy crowded around, he let out a piercing troll shriek that clearly frightened them more than his weapon. Heather furiously beat two attackers back with her Eldritch blade. Desperately she wished she could focus enough to work some useful magic. She didn't know if she really wanted to hurt these people, but she certainly didn't want to let them hurt *her.*

Merlin had used his sword to fend off several attackers, but now the beings in feathers and fur surrounded him, and he wielded his staff in a flurry of purple energy. But they had power of their own. He could feel its strength and its strangeness. He wasn't sure how long he could hold the three of them off.

The sounds of battle were suddenly sliced through by an ear-piercing squawk. Then a woman's voice rang out. "Stop! My grandchild speaks!"

Abruptly the attackers lowered their weapons and stepped back. The defenders blinked in bewilderment, then joined the others looking to where an old woman stood on a mossy knoll. Her braided gray hair was crowned by a basketwork hat, and she held up a baby in both hands. The child looked at them with wide dark eyes, then burbled into laughing words. "Friends! Friends come!"

Heather clutched at her head as she felt a high voice burst inside. *Good friend. Want help?*

Yes, she thought back. *Thank you.*

The old woman lowered the child, cradling it protectively in her arms. "Kiwilah has spoken for the first time. She was born with the Power. Listen to her!"

The tall being with the black feathers stepped forward. "But, Muweena, the stories have long spoken of danger coming to us on hostile wings over the water. You yourself and we Spirit Folk have felt it nearing. Surely these are the enemies foretold."

Squawking piercingly, baby Kiwilah wiggled in her grandmother's arms until the woman put her down. Then, giggling, the baby crawled down the mossy slope, got unsteadily to her feet, and toddled toward Heather. "Friend!" she burbled, and threw chubby arms around Heather's legs.

Shaking her head, the old woman clambered down the bank as well. "Yes, Raven, the enemy are coming. But these are not the ones." She stopped in front of Merlin and looked him in the eye. "Who are you, then, you with enough power to fend off three of our Spirit Folk?"

Merlin bowed to the three and then to her. "Their power is indeed very great. We are four travelers and our dragon companions seeking only to find our way home. But I fear that there are indeed evil forces pursuing us. Perhaps it is they whom you expect."

The woman nodded. "Perhaps. The stories say, 'Beware the day when evil beings on fearsome wings come from over the sea. They seek vengeance and power and would destroy much.' Is that the sort of thing that pursues you now?"

"It is," Merlin said. "And vengeance, power, and silence is what they are seeking from us. I am sorry if we have brought this evil on you as well."

"Are they close at your heels?"

Merlin looked west, to where dense fog now hid the sea. "I do not think they are close. But they are coming."

"Then there is time to talk and learn things of each other. But you said there are four of you. Have we slain the fourth?"

"No," a girl's voice called from a thicket of ferns. "I tried, but as everyone seems to have made a truce, he is safe now."

Welly and the warrior girl, both covered in moss and dirt, stepped out of the ferns. "Hey," he objected. "I broke her spear. *She's* the one who is lucky for the truce."

Several people laughed, their weapons now lowered. One woman called, "This one with the eye shields must be a fearsome warrior indeed to have held off Takata. She's a wildcat."

As others laughed, Merlin asked Muweena, "Could you release our dragons now? I am amazed that any rope could hold them."

The feathered man snapped his beak and strode toward the angrily twitching bound dragons. "Foreign fool, these aren't ordinary ropes. Only Otherworld power could hold Otherworld beasts."

"Watch who you call a beast, birdbrain," Blanche hissed through bound jaws.

The three Spirit Folk—Raven, Bear, and Wolf—stood around the dragons, chanting and weaving their hands into a snare of patterns. Like smoke, the ropes dissolved. In one fluid move, Hei Se reared up and drew in a gigantic breath.

Merlin raised his staff. "Stop! We've made a truce. Their attack was a misunderstanding."

Hei Se snorted, sending a gust of wind that swirled sand and dust into the air. Beside him, Blanche crouched, flames from her nostrils curling a few ferns into ash.

"*I* have signed no truce," the black dragon growled. "This blow to dragon honor is crushing. Payment must be made."

"Payment in the form of a large meaty meal might be acceptable, though," Blanche added.

"Yes, yes, that could be arranged," Muweena said, hobbling up to the group. She was again holding Kiwilah, who looked at the two dragons with wide eyes.

"Doggies!" the baby cried happily.

Hei Se snarled. "Doggies, is it? Well, babies *do* make good appetizers."

Roughly Blanche shoved him aside and with a toothy smile gazed down at the baby. "Hush, oaf," she told Hei Se. "Even baby humans are cute. Aren't you, cutey-poo?" The dragon blew tiny sparks out of her mouth, and Kiwilah laughed and clapped.

"Well, if my granddaughter approves of you, you must be all right," Muweena said. "Now let us go to the lodge. There is much to talk about and, I think, some feasting to do."

Welly looked around uneasily at the warriors, who moments earlier had been ready to kill them. But he did like the idea of feasting. Then he noticed Takata was limping and decided he'd better offer her his arm. After all, he had been the one who had knocked her into that hole. At first she refused, but when she took a step and nearly fell, she shrugged and took his arm.

Troll strutted happily after them, pleased with the way the forest warriors looked at him almost with awe.

The path they all followed between the enormous trees was narrow, and the dragons grumbled. But in pushing their way through, they discovered how fine the tall rough trunks were for scratching their backs and itchy sides, and after several pleasant stops, they had to hurry to catch up.

The trail led up the valley, with the river gurgling steadily on their right. Night was coming on, and the fog-enshrouded forest grew dark and damp. Ahead, through the massive pillars of tree trunks, they occasionally caught a red glow. The volcano that during the day showed itself with a column of smoke at dusk glowed like an ember.

Walking beside Muweena, Merlin asked about it.

"Fire Mountain," the old woman replied. "She is what

gives us life. Long ago, when fire rained on the world, de-stroying most life, the Earth was angered that humans should be so careless of creation. She shook violently in her anger, and her skin ripped open, pouring out her flam-ing blood. But then she grew sorry that her anger had caused more suffering, so this valley was created, where the warmth of her blood bubbling near the surface could keep back the cold and sustain life."

The old woman laughed. "That's the story, anyway, and in its way, it tells the truth. So much in this land was destroyed by fire or cold or disease. Here bombs triggered earthquakes and they loosed volcanoes, and though that brought more destruction, it also saved a small scrap of life. This is now one of the few places left where the Otherworld is willing to touch ours."

Merlin nodded. "And the Raven, Wolf, and Bear spirits come from there. Is it their story, about evil coming from over the sea?"

The baby in her arms tugged at Muweena's braids as she answered. "It is an old story, told here and in the Otherworld for many years. But I can feel its truth, just as I feel old, old powers surging back into this world. I have some writings here from the times before. But I am also this tribe's Medicine Woman and can feel the even earlier truths."

Now baby Kiwilah was flailing her arms, making it clear she wanted to be carried by Heather, not her grand-mother. Merlin smiled as the transfer was made, and the baby immediately began playing with Heather's braids. "Your grandbaby has inherited the Power, then?"

Muweena laughed. "She could mind-speak from the moment of birth, and what a lot she has had to say! I will be glad now that she is speaking aloud so my head will hurt less. Your companion, Heather, has the same Power?"

"Yes, as have several others we have met. All young ones, though not as young as your Kiwilah."

"And despite your looks," the woman chuckled, eyeing Merlin, "I can tell you are a great deal older. Yes, the world is changing, and a new generation may help with that. Kiwilah will no doubt succeed me as Medicine Woman. My other granddaughter speaks easily with spirits, but it is her other skill she prefers—the warrior's skill. In the end, I pray it is the power to speak and not to kill that will rule the day."

"Which is your other granddaughter?"

"That wildcat Takata, whom your own young warrior has fallen in with."

Merlin smiled. "Welly would be pleased to know that he is seen as a warrior. It wasn't always so."

"One often does not see oneself as others do. Ah, here is the lodge. I fear your large winged friends need to stay outside, but we'll bring them food."

Huge trees circled a clearing where the shapes of several long plank houses were visible in the dusk. In front of the largest house stood several tall poles carved into the stylized shapes of animals standing on top of one another. Several women came out of the main house carrying torches, and by their light, the entire party, minus the dragons, was led inside. A fire burned in a long stone hearth in the center of the lodge, its smoke lazily coiling its way toward a hole in the plank roof.

Heather smelled wood smoke and marveled that any place still could have enough wood to build houses with it and even to burn. But then, this valley felt special, not just from the volcanic warmth but from the faint current of Otherworld power she sensed tingling in the air.

Down, please, Kiwilah's voice sounded in her head.

Gladly. Just don't squawk in my head anymore. Words only.

She put the baby down to toddle unsteadily on her chubby legs toward several women with other babies sitting by the fire. When Merlin took her hand, Heather smiled up at him. She had never thought of herself as very maternal, but little Kiwilah was fun, as long as there was no magnified mental squalling.

The party of four travelers took up seats by the fire pit, and several of the warriors who had fought with them did as well. Welly managed to find a seat beside Takata. Heather smiled at this but pretended she hadn't noticed.

More people kept coming into the lodge and finding places to sit by the fire or along the walls. The three Spirit Folk stood in the shadows at the end of the long room where the roof was highest. Finally Muweena stood up. All talking stopped as she raised a hand. "We welcome travelers from distant lands. They are not the enemy foretold, but they may herald that enemy. So now we must talk and learn—and of course feast, as is proper to welcome guests."

Happy chatter broke out again, and soon women and children brought in wooden platters heaped with slabs of smoked reddish fish. There were also berries, small hard fruit, and fried balls of nutty dough.

As the eating went on, Merlin told the Medicine Woman about their travels and the view of the world he'd formed along the way. In the end, she nodded and said, "I understand what you mean about seeing unjoined pieces of a big picture. And I think what you guessed is right. That woman who first stole your friend now realizes more is at stake. She and her allies will do much to shatter any picture you and the others like your Heather and my Kiwilah might help create."

For a time, she sat in silence, staring into the swirling smoke. Then she smiled and looked back at Merlin. "So our job, young old man, is to stop them."

When everyone had eaten their fill, an elderly man brought out a long wooden flute and began to play. The notes were clear and high and soared through the smoky room as if they sought to burst out and rise to the towering trees. Several drums joined in, and Heather couldn't help feeling how different these were from the drums of Kali's temple. There the rhythm had been of fear and throbbing hate. Here it seemed to be the steady heartbeat of the ancient forest.

After a time, Merlin asked if he might try the flute, and soon his magicked music filled the hall with the lilting rhythms and flickering images of ancient Britain. Younger people got up and danced, and despite her injured leg, Takata let Welly pull her into the light steps of a jig. Even the tall Spirit Folk swayed to the power-filled foreign music.

As the music died, people gradually went out to their own houses. The guests were given animal skins to wrap up in and shown sleeping places along the wall. But before they were settled to sleep, Raven walked stiffly up to Merlin and bent close to his ear.

"We sense the truth of your story, but it only heightens our fear of what is coming. Will you know when the enemy is near?"

"I believe so, but they will try to cloak themselves, some no doubt using powers with which I am unfamiliar."

The raven head nodded. "Then we will set watchers. Shark will patrol the sea, and Gull will send his flocks into the air above. I have called for more help from our Otherworld. But the forces you hint at are fearsome."

Merlin frowned, looking at his sleeping friends and hosts. "They are. They take pleasure in destruction."

The Raven croaked, "Then we must seek to create—which is always harder. Rest now. There may be little enough time for that."

17

BATTLE

It was a strange, oddly beautiful time of waiting. The air felt heavy with power, as if a storm was coming. But for the next few days, the western horizon remained clear. The fog thinned to show a faintly blue sky. Watery sun sent golden shafts of light through the trees, splattering the ferns underneath with moving patches of softly glowing green.

The three Spirit Folk took most of the men and women to a nearby clearing and trained them further in warrior skills. Welly eagerly joined them, somehow always managing to do his training near Takata. Troll, to his surprise, acquired several younger warriors to be his special training partners. They were impressed to meet someone from another Otherworld and gave him a name that translated as Small but Feisty Spirit Warrior. This pleased Troll enormously, and he kept chanting it over to himself.

Heather occasionally joined the training, hoping and failing to work off her rising restlessness. More often, she stayed near Muweena and Merlin, though she tried not to get swept into their deep discussions of magic. Instead she tried to focus on the beautiful trees, the fun of playing with baby Kiwilah, and the quiet pleasure of simply being near Earl again.

She also worked on her mind-talking, trying to deliberately contact some of her voices rather than letting them just randomly fall into her mind. It worked better with some than with others. Badrack reported that the evil storm had been dispersed by the Mountain but that his grandfather feared it was reassembling and becoming even stronger. It was harder to reach Padma, but at least Heather picked up the feeling that Padma's people had not been blamed for Heather's escape. The strength of young Ivan's sending faded in and out, but he did say that Baba was talking more and more about their moving eventually to the surface. The jaguar boy had had mixed feelings about having just been presented with a new baby sister, and the African priestess in training was excited about a proposed trip to trade with a distant village.

Merlin was pleased to learn about Heather's progress and what it promised for the future. But their immediate future filled him with doubt and uncertainty. Despite enjoying his discussions of magic with the Medicine Woman, he kept fighting a nagging certainty that their little party should move on.

"And where to?" Muweena asked after he'd suggested that again. "There is practically nowhere to go on this continent unless you like blasted ruins, plains of melted glass, or icy winds that howl with ghosts. Better that you stay here awhile."

"But we are bringing danger upon you. We appreciate your warriors' training and the willingness of your Spirit Folk to call on Otherworld aid. But this little haven of life is beautiful. It seems to stand for everything that those who are after us hate. I fear what that hate could do to you."

Slowly she shook her head. "Do not be troubled. We are not without our strengths—our warriors, the Spirit Folk, who refuse to abandon their ancient people, and even the land itself. The magic of place is very strong. It is something you should study more. There is much power in this valley. It may help us if called upon."

After a time, Muweena retired to an underground sweathouse to purify herself with steam and commune with the spirits. Merlin declined her invitation to do the same. When the Medicine Woman had left, he asked Heather to come sit with him on a large boulder overlooking the tumbling river.

"Muweena is fortunate," he said once they had settled onto the mossy rock. "She has a calm certainty about her. Perhaps it comes from generations of linkage to this land and its spirits. Or perhaps she's just not the sort of person to be troubled by doubts."

Heather looked at Merlin and the dark brooding that often shadowed him. She wrapped an arm around his waist. "And you are, I know. But that's just the way you are. You look at all the possibilities—which means you can never be *certain* of anything. But you still figure out the right thing to do in the end."

"Do I? I don't seem to have done a lot right lately. I put you in danger in the first place by bragging about you to Morgan, and then I became distracted and let you be kidnapped from under my nose. I failed to take you from Morgan when she was without the strength of allies, and I would have failed to save you from being sacrificed if you hadn't used your own magic in time. And now I've only just realized the extent of the danger Morgan and her alliances pose to the world. Part of me wants to flee homeward as quickly as possible, but another part wants to take a stand here even though by doing so we endanger one of the few bright places left in the world."

Heather snuggled closer and kissed him on his haggard cheek. "Earl, you keep telling me that magic is something I have to open myself to. If I think about it too hard and try to force it, nothing will happen. Life is like that too, isn't it? You can try to plan and make good decisions, but in the end, you have to let it take you where it will."

He looked at her and smiled his thin lopsided grin. "Here I am, a couple thousand years old, and you have to keep teaching me the basics." He kissed her back. "Today life and magic *are* the same. So, what do you say we work together and try to whip up some magic defenses for this little island of life?"

Through that afternoon, into purple evening, the two sat on the rock weaving a web of light and power. Its strands enmeshed the towering trees and the winged and crawling lives around them. They stretched out over the dunes to the crashing waves and the life that surged beyond them and soared over them. The tendrils of power drew strength from every life and hope they touched within the web.

Until full darkness fell, the web was spun, the warriors trained, and the Medicine Woman spoke with the spirits. Then came a night of readiness and waiting.

With the dawn came the dark.

It began as a cloud along the western horizon. A cloud of darkness that the rising sun could not dispel. From the waters, whales and seals cried of its coming. From the sky, birds flocked in warning and terror. Among the trees, the village houses emptied. Everyone headed in near silence to the beach to watch the dread approach.

Merlin surveyed their small army as it assembled on the sand dunes that stretched between the forest and the crashing sea. Two dragons, four travelers, a few hundred native warriors, and now a dozen spirit animals, some representing beasts he had never seen except in books. He looked beyond them to the vastness of the enemy. Hopelessness threatened to choke him.

Relentlessly the darkness rolled toward them, veins of lightning flickering in its depths, a myriad horrid shapes half visible in its roiling mass. In its center, a winged beast and its rider glowed a putrid green.

"Morgan," Merlin whispered as he stood beside Heather on a sandy knoll. "Kali seems to have recruited for her a whole new army—demons and spirits of the tormented dead. But I don't see the Goddess herself here."

Heather stared into the darkness but didn't see the many-armed deity either. "Perhaps she doesn't like to leave her temple. Morgan did say she's very changeable, like the moon. Maybe she's not in the killing mood herself just now." Heather tried to sound light and confident, but her voice shook slightly.

"Her good friend Morgan can make up for that," Merlin said drily. Then, feeling Heather shiver, he squeezed her hand. "But we'll hold them off. We have to."

Their web of power was scarcely visible in the morning light. Only a faint spangling caught the eye, like a billowing curtain of dust motes. But when the front of the dark cloud reached it, electric charges cracked and sizzled across the sky. Glowing darkness spread toward the barrier like a stain. It battered the shield until the sky throbbed with power. Waves of purple energy and green thrummed against each other until the air threatened to shatter with the sound.

Beyond their protective shield, the ocean churned in violent upheaval. But around the defenders, the air was still, and at their feet, placid waves lapped the sand.

As they struggled to maintain their defense, Heather felt it thinning in places. Fear began to bubble through her, but she fought it down, trying to replace it with numb determination, if not with hope.

Merlin's upraised staff shook with strain. Sweat trickled into his eyes as he stared into the tumultuous cloud. Darting in and out among the writhing demons, Morgan launched bolt after bolt of power, an evil green glow billowing about her like a cape. Under yet another blast of power, the shield seemed to buckle. But then it snapped back into throbbing shape. They could see, though not hear, Morgan's snarl. Slowly the sorceress unclasped something from her belt. A long curved sword, its edge dripping with blood.

"Kali's sword!" Heather gasped.

Brandishing the sword above her head, Morgan drew strands of glowing power into its blade. With a shriek, she slashed the sword downward. Blood-red light smashed into the sparkling shield. For a moment, the web held, then it shattered. Thousands of glittering fragments fell to the sand. For long seconds, silence hung over the world. Then came the storm.

Darkness surged forward. Wind battered the beach. Demons and ghouls tumbled free of the cloud, trailing black fear with them. The defending army cried its defiance. Chaos erupted in the sudden twilight. Bodies surged, spears and swords clashed, arrows flew, claws and fangs struck. The churning air filled with screams and with sprays of blood.

A squadron of horned and scaly demons headed straight for the knoll where Merlin and Heather stood back to back. They both drew out their Eldritch swords, and Merlin ignited them with power. The glowing blades hacked and scattered the attacking demons, but others kept coming.

Nearby, Troll and his band of followers defended another dune. An ancient troll war cry rang over the battlefield and was taken up by human throats around him. To Welly, fighting at Takata's side, it sounded as bloodcurdling as the cries of the demons. But then his attention shifted as their small band of warriors was attacked from another side by pallid hollow-eyed creatures. Ghouls, he realized, the unquiet dead. How could you fight such things?

One answer came immediately as a blast of flame shriveled the creatures to ash. Blanche and Hei Se had positioned themselves on tumbled rocks that jutted into the sea. While Blanche sprayed fire, the black dragon battered the enemy with storm wind that blew clumps of them from the beach into the churning waves. Here and there about the embattled beach, Spirit Folk, yelling their own unearthly cries, hacked and clawed and wielded spears of magic.

For a moment, the attack on their knoll had lessened. Merlin looked into the storm-black sky. Morgan still hovered amid the cloud, content for the moment to watch her minions work.

And Merlin could not deny that though his forces

were holding their own, Morgan's way outnumbered them. In time, sword arms would fail, spears and arrows would be spent, and the dragons and spirits would tire. Morgan's forces, on the beach and still waiting in the clouds, seemed endless.

Despair clawed at Merlin's mind. This was *not* the place to make a final battle. The stakes were too high and their forces too unmatched. He should never have let this happen! Not here, not now. In his carelessness, had he failed the world? Had he failed Arthur—again?

Suddenly Muweena was at their side, shouting over the storm. "Come! You four and your dragons have done well. But you must flee now. Hurry!"

"Flee?" Merlin yelled back. "It's too late for that. We can't leave the others. We can't retreat!"

"It's not retreat. It is the only *way*. Come!"

When Merlin still hesitated, the old woman grabbed his arm. "Trust me. You may know this enemy, but I know this land."

Scowling into the turmoil around them, he finally nodded. Resigned, Merlin clutched Heather's hand.

Forcing herself into desperate focus, Heather mentally called the two dragons. *Come! Follow us now. No questions. There's no time. Come!*

Muweena and Merlin called to several fighting nearby. Confused and angry, Welly, Takata, and Troll withdrew from the battle. Hacking and blasting their way through the enemy, they finally gathered where sand met the trees. Muweena shouted over the deafening battle, "Quickly, everyone onto the dragons. Takata, you join them on one; I will ride the other. Then we fly east, low over the trees."

"Why not through the forest?" Heather questioned. "Above the trees, we will be seen."

"That is my hope," she yelled back. "Now hurry!"

They scrambled onto scaly backs. A few mighty wing strokes brought them level with the giant treetops. "East!" Muweena shrieked. Her voice was barely a whisper against the tumult of battle below, but her arm pointed to where the pale sun disk had risen beyond the smoke-wreathed mountain.

They flew low and fast, skimming over feathery tree-tops. The uppermost branches lashed in the wind of battle behind them. As they passed, Heather peered down into the darkness below, wondering if even this storm could reach into the calm depths of the forest. Then a change came in the noise of battle. Tightening her grip on the white dragon scales, she twisted to look back.

The darkness had risen from the beach like a cloud of flies startled from a corpse. The cloud pulsed, tightened, and slowly began moving their way. She called a warning. Seated behind her, Welly and Takata turned and stared. On the black dragon flying at their side, the others turned as well. Merlin looked worried, Troll terrified, but Muweena only grinned.

They flew on over the forest until the great trees thinned. Below them, now the ground looked black and crusty. Steam rose in ragged puffs from clefts in the rock, and here and there, mud bubbled and popped in gray pools. The bare slope of the volcano was drawing nearer.

Studying it now, Heather could see that there were in fact several peaks. Smoke rose from all of them, but the uppermost glowed a sullen red. The air smelled sulfurous and thick. Turning again, Heather saw that the dark cloud was still pursuing them. Even in the muted daylight, its edges flickered with lightning.

At a shouted order from Muweena, the black dragon

dropped lower. Blanche followed through air flecked with gray ash. They dropped lower and lower until they circled for a landing on a flat plateau between two of the volcanoes' lesser peaks. Above the noise of the pursuing storm, the Medicine Woman yelled for them to dismount. Soon the five humans and one troll were huddled between the encircling wall of two dragons. They all looked skyward, feeling horribly exposed.

The black cloud rolled nearer, and again shapes could be half seen in its roiling mass. Welly looked at it and tried to swallow his fear. He turned to Takata, who stood beside him, spear ready. Gruffly he said, "I guess it's better that we die here and draw them away from your people."

She shook her head. "Our warriors will be sorry to miss this battle." Then she grinned. "But *I* am here, their wildcat warrior. You've nothing to fear."

Welly laughed grimly and unsheathed his sword. "Right. A ferocious warrior, and modest too. How can we lose?"

The cloud descending above them rolled with thunder. Over it, a single sharp voice cut like a bolt of lightning. "Merlin! Die now, finally die! You and your plans are at last ended. My world begins today!"

Defiantly Merlin raised his staff toward the green figure glowing amid the cloud. But Muweena grabbed his arm. "Wait!"

Angrily he looked at her. "Wait for what? This ends now."

Before she could answer, the earth they stood on gave a tremendous shake. All were knocked from their feet. The dragons bellowed, but the noise was drowned by the great rumbling rising from the mountain. The ground kept convulsing. Jagged cracks snaked over the rock. The frightened group clung to the heaving ground, but their attention was drawn upward.

The tallest peak was no longer simply smoking. Its summit had split open. A fierce red glow lit the underside of the descending cloud. Then, with a violent shudder, the mountain belched fire. Flames and molten rock spewed upward.

The darkness flinched back, but too late. Flames scorched the edges, then spread with hungry fury into the mass. Below, the dragons cowered and the others threw arms over their heads. But the bellows of the Earth and the screams of its victims could not be shut out.

The horror in earth and sky felt like it would never end.

18

JOURNEY

Slowly silence descended—as did a cloud of gray and drifting ash. The earth ceased to shudder. Coughing and gasping, the survivors sat up. A clean breeze from the sea steadily blew the ash eastward, and slowly their vision cleared. The top of the mountain, wider now, still glowed red. A throbbing river of lava flowed down the far side, but already it seemed to slow and cool. The sky was clear.

"Are they gone?" Heather whispered. "Really gone?"

"Gone?" Merlin said, then coughed, trying to clear his throat of ash and the dregs of dying fear. "Perhaps not totally. Evil is not easily extinguished, and Morgan has survived much. But her army and its strength—at the moment, both seem quite gone." Then he turned to Muweena, who was still crouched at his side. "And we have you to thank."

A grin etched even more wrinkles across the old woman's face, but she shook her head. "We have the Earth to thank, and all of our power to call on it. The Earth can only put up with so much suffering before it strikes back, you know."

"Well, I do now," Merlin laughed as he stood up, "and am grateful."

She nodded and stood as well. Removing her basketry cap, she shook off the ash before settling it back onto her head. "I must return to the village now. There are other healers among us, but I fear there will be enough wounds to heal for us all. And there will be dead to bury."

"We can help with the healing," Heather said.

"No. Your way lies elsewhere now. And this is the time for you to go."

Merlin looked to the east. Under the silvered sun, the volcanic plain merged into snow-covered wilderness. "Flying eastward to the ocean and over that to Britain. A long journey. We would happily postpone it if we could be of help to you here."

"No, no!" the old woman insisted. "There is another way, but you must take it *now*. The Fire Mountain is more than just our protector. It is our opening to the Otherworld. Right now the opening has widened. It may admit friends, even those with different Otherworlds."

Merlin looked at the mountain, still oozing lava down one side. The heat could be felt even where they stood. "It would be a privilege to visit your Otherworld. But our home lies on the other side of this globe. It is there we must return."

The Medicine Woman chuckled. "For all your great age and wisdom, it seems there are things you do not know, young man. The Otherworlds are connected. The pathways are seldom used and dangerous without a guide. But it is possible to travel from one to another."

"Troll know that!" Troll piped up. "Mama always say never go near paths. Too dangerous. Get lost."

"And she was right," Muweena said. "But you have all helped us here and helped the world, I think. If asked properly, spirit guides could show you the way."

"And how do we ask properly?" Heather said.

"You take someone with you who knows the entrance-way and how to speak to spirits. Takata, for example."

Startled, Welly looked at the warrior girl standing beside him. She smiled, then lowered her eyes in mock shyness. "I would be honored, Grandmother. It sounds as if, in the land these people come from, they can use warriors even more than we do here."

"And we would be honored to have you with us, Takata," Merlin said. "But is the way wide enough for dragons?"

A voice rumbled from above. Hei Se arched his head down toward them. "Otherworld spaces accommodate Otherworld creatures. Size is of no concern. Blanche can travel with you. But I fear I must return to my own land."

"Sweetie, must you?" Blanche wailed.

"It is my land. In time, life will return to it, and I must prepare."

"Won't you even come for a visit?" Blanche asked coyly. "When the little ones are hatched, perhaps?"

Heather gasped. "Blanche, you're expecting?"

The dragon huffed a sooty cloud. "How do you think dragons come about? Not everything in this world is done with magic, you know."

Merlin smiled and nodded to the dragons. "Depends on how you define *magic*. Congratulations, you two. Perhaps when her brood hatches, Blanche can take them on a world tour to visit their papa. Somehow this world doesn't seem as dauntingly large as it once did."

"And perhaps, in time, the thin net you and others are weaving can bind it closer yet," Muweena said. "But come, you beautiful black creature. If you will carry me back to my village, we will send you off with a feast to carry you across your ocean. The way time passes for you, it will be a mere nothing before you see your beloved again."

With a deep humming song, the black dragon reached his neck across the clustered people and wrapped it around Blanche's long white one. For a moment, the two hummed together a tune so deep and old it seemed to sink into the rock. Then he pulled away, and the Medicine Woman scrambled onto his back. With a few mighty wing beats, the black dragon soared into the sky.

"Keep in touch," Muweena called to those on the ground. "Little Kiwilah will be listening for you."

They watched as the black shape grew smaller until it was a tiny speck over the valley and the forest of dark green it guarded. Blanche's keening song followed it, then lapsed into empty silence.

Takata's voice was husky when she spoke. "I'll miss her and my people. So, your world had better be good, or I won't stay and lend you my warrior skills."

"Or your modesty," Welly added.

She cuffed him, then turned to the others and cried, "All right, follow me. That opening won't just hang there while we get sentimental."

She led them to the edge of the plateau. A few rocks and masses of pebbles loosened by the earthquake still slid down the slope, but, deftly sliding with them, Takata headed down at a breakneck pace. Blanche, after a last longing look to the west, glided down and met them at the bottom.

A jagged crevasse, hidden by the overhanging cliff, lay before them. Glowing heat and the smell of sulfur gushed from it. When the others hesitated, Takata taunted, "You can face hordes of evil but are afraid of Mother Earth's indigestion? Come on!"

They followed her lead into the opening and scrabbled down a pile of jagged boulders, warm to the touch. Tunnels branched off in several directions, but heat and a fiery glow spilled from all of them. Striding ahead, Takata ignored the tunnels and climbed up a pile of tumbled rock into a dark cool cleft. The opening widened, the air blurred, and what had looked like stalactites on the rock walls now seemed to be long tangled roots.

"Climb," Takata ordered. Surprisingly, foot- and hand-holds were easily found and the party climbed. In the rear, Blanche wedged her way up but found that each time the passage seemed tight, it eased away from her, just allowing her to pass with wings tightly folded.

Roots gave way to shelves of fungus sprouting like steps up the inside of a great hollowed tree. They seemed to climb forever, but when their legs were quivering almost too badly to work, they reached a great knothole in the side of the tree. Light poured through. One by one, they crawled out. They were still in a cave, but through an opening, they could see a colorful world beyond. The light was clear, clearer than any light in their own dust-clouded world.

Takata looked out the opening and sighed. But she did not lead them through. Instead she turned to a furred figure that had been sitting on a boulder, unnoticed by the rest. She spoke to it in a language none of the others knew— spoke and sang and spoke again. Then she turned to them.

"I've never gone beyond this point, but Mole Spirit will guide us through the passages. Try not to touch the walls—there are hazards there. And *do not* step into any of the Otherworlds you see, tempting as they may seem. The passageways, he says, are more or less neutral, but the Otherworlds themselves do not tolerate intrusions."

From then on, their lives seemed nothing but a series of tunnels in stone or snow or leafy mold. Shapes that might be snakes or worms or writhing roots poked from the passage walls, jabbing at them unexpectedly. Patches of glowing moss gave off a sickly bluish light. At times, the enclosing walls vanished and their path turned into a bridge—a thin ribbon of a bridge spanning dark deep chasms. Then tunnels began again. Time lost all meaning. Even the air around them quivered with unreality.

As they trudged ahead, numerous passages branched off, but their guide ignored them. Through occasional gaps in the walls, they glimpsed other places. Worlds of light and color and strange yet half-familiar creatures. They all felt the pull of these places, but also their strong lack of welcome.

At one gash in the rocky wall, Troll stopped his numbing trudge and peered in. He could see a mossy grotto where a spring bubbled up and poured a crystal clear stream over rocks that glistened in the sun. A meadow stretched from streamside to a wall of trees, and beyond it, tiers of mountains rose into the purple distance.

He took a few hesitant steps, feeling damp moss squelch between his toes. The tumbling water sang a luring tune. The air smelled sharply of pine, wood smoke, and roasting meat.

Another step, and another. A scaly white tail suddenly

wrapped around him and yanked Troll back into the gloomy passage. "Dolt! Don't you ever listen to warnings? I ought to leave you to be zapped by whatever guards that place, except that I pledged to get you *all* back safely."

"But it troll-friendly place. Maybe have lady troll . . ."

"Oh, right. Or maybe a giant guardian lady ogre would bop you with her club. Otherworlds, particularly *other* Otherworlds, are dangerous places. March!"

They all continued marching. Then, after days or months or years, the Mole Spirit stopped scuttling ahead of them. He gestured in two directions. To their left was an opening screened with a cascade of spring-green willow branches. Through it, they glimpsed lush grass, a sun-sparkling stream, and creatures from their most ancient myths.

Together Heather and Welly gasped.

"Avalon," Heather whispered. "We've been there."

Beside her, Merlin sighed. "Yes, but it is not our time to go there again." He gestured toward the right side of their passage. Two roughly worked stones guarded a dark entrance. The light that filtered through it was coldly gray.

The Mole Spirit nodded, then stepped forward and bowed to them all, launching into a squeaking song. Takata translated. "He prays that all of our worlds may grow together again, and he wishes us well in ours—now and for all time."

With that, their spirit guide scuttled back the way they had come, leaving the others to look at the two entrances. Pushing her way through, Blanche stuck her head into the Avalon portal.

"My Otherworld," she sighed. "Nearly all dragons are there now. I wouldn't be alone there."

Merlin put a hand on her scaly flank. "You are free to choose, dear Blanche. Your debt has been more than paid. But in our world, you would never be alone. You would have friends there, and you would be part of our story."

The white dragon took one last long look at the glistening world beyond the willows. Then, shrugging her winged shoulders, she turned to the darker entrance.

"That's the trouble with dragons. Curiosity. We hate not knowing how a story will end."

The light they emerged into was cold and dim. A low afternoon sun shone as a clouded disk. The pale grass was coarse, and patches of snow huddled in shadows. Those shadows were cast by huge blocks of stone jutting from the earth in a broken circle. Spanning some of them were other stone blocks, making the semblance of giant empty doorways.

"Stonehenge," Merlin whispered. "This was ancient even when I was here before. I should have guessed that one of the other doors to Faerie would still be here."

Rising on her haunches, Blanche craned her neck, gazing beyond the stone circle. "Company's coming."

They all turned to look. In the distance, they saw a company of horsemen headed their way. Three banners fluttered among them. One Merlin recognized as the blue eagle banner of Salisbury. The others brought a cry of joy from his lips. The gold Dragon banner of Arthur Pendragon and the red Lion of Margaret, Queen of Scots.

The party was now galloping toward them, but in their lead loped a grotesque two-headed dog. Making a direct charge for Heather, it soon barreled her over, licking the girl frantically with both tongues. She struggled to pull a bag free from her belt and enticed Rus off by offering two handfuls of hard goat cheese. Both heads gobbled these up and snuffled for more.

The mounted party was not far behind. As soon as his white stallion skidded to a stop, Arthur was out of the saddle and hugging Merlin.

"Salisbury's Druids insisted we come here today. They couldn't say why. You obscure magic workers are infuriatingly alike. Oh, how I've missed you, old man!"

By now, the red-haired queen had joined them. "It's been months! I'd almost given up hope. But they're all back—and Heather too!" Bounding from her horse, she hugged the girl. "I was so worried for you!" She looked at Takata and added, "And you have brought somebody new, I see."

Welly stepped forward. "This is Takata, Your Majesty. A fearsome warrior from the Americas."

The girl nodded. "I am that. One of our best. I am at your service, if we suit each other."

Margaret laughed. "Well, modesty never suited me much. We are happy to have you with us."

From horseback, the Duke of Salisbury looked down at them all and smiled. "My Druids didn't think to advise that I bring extra horses. So, everyone, let's double up and get back to town. I think a feast is in order."

"A large feast, I trust," Blanche huffed. "After all, I am eating for *four* now."

When Arthur cast her a questioning look, Merlin said, "Dragons usually lay three eggs to a clutch. We do have a good deal to tell you about."

When they returned to their horses, Arthur asked, "Can you start telling me any of it now?"

"What? And spoil the prolonged storytelling?" Then the wizard laughed, and added, "But I can tell you that there is a big world out there, and it's full of more dangers and more possibilities than we could ever imagine. But you first. How goes the uniting of Britain?"

The King smiled. "Well. Only a few holdouts remain— your friend Nigel of Glamorganshire, for one. But I think eventually our unity and strength will persuade them, perhaps without war."

"Good. War is something we've had enough of. But don't rest on your accomplishments just now, Your Majesty."

"What? You're still prodding me to do things, aren't you, old man? Got something more in mind than finally bringing unity and peace to this land?"

Laughing, Merlin helped Heather onto the red horse, behind Margaret. He and Heather smiled at each other for a long moment, then Merlin turned back to his king.

"The world we've seen is big, badly wounded, and much in need of that same unity and peace. But the foundations are there to build upon. It will take more than our lifetimes—even our second ones—to make it happen. But we can get started."

"Start now?" Troll questioned. "Eat first, maybe?"

King Arthur smiled. "True. Even with magic, we can't save the world on empty stomachs. But, Merlin, old friend, are you really sure about this?"

"Our world's been given a second chance, Arthur. That might be more than we deserve. But we have to try."

The King shook his head, then sighed. "You're always saying things like that, Merlin, grand impossible-sounding things. But usually you're right. So . . . why not try it one more time?"

"After dinner," Troll pleaded.

"Right!" King Arthur laughed. "We'll save the world after dinner."

PAMELA F. SERVICE grew up in Berkeley, California, and spent three years in England studying archaeology. She, her husband, Bob, and their daughter, Alex, lived for years in Bloomington, Indiana, where Pam worked as a museum curator, served on the city council, and wrote. Now back in California, she has published over twenty children's books, works as a museum director in Eureka, acts in community theater, and is still writing.

THE LAND I LOST

THE LAND I LOST

ADVENTURES OF A BOY IN VIETNAM

by Huynh Quang Nhuong
with pictures by Vo-Dinh Mai

1 8  1 7

——— HARPER & ROW, PUBLISHERS ———
Cambridge, Philadelphia, San Francisco, London, Mexico City, São Paulo, Sydney
——— NEW YORK ———

The Land I Lost

Library of Congress Cataloging in Publication Data
Huynh, Quang Nhuong.
   The land I lost.

   Summary: A collection of personal reminiscences of
the author's youth in a hamlet on the central highlands
of Vietnam.
   1. Central Highlands (Vietnam)—Social life and
customs—Juvenile literature.   2. Huynh, Quang Nhuong—
Juvenile literature.   3. Central Highlands (Vietnam)—
Biography—Juvenile literature.   [1. Huynh, Quang Nhuong.
2. Central Highlands (Vietnam)—Biography]   I. Vo-Dinh
Mai, ill.   II. Title.
DS559.92.C46H88 1982   959.7 [92]   80-8437
ISBN 0-06-024592-1   AACR2
ISBN 0-06-024593-X (lib. bdg.)

For my mother

CONTENTS

THE LAND I LOST

I was born on the central highlands of Vietnam in a small hamlet on a riverbank that had a deep jungle on one side and a chain of high mountains on the other. Across the river, rice fields stretched to the slopes of another chain of mountains.

There were fifty houses in our hamlet, scattered along the river or propped against the mountainsides. The houses were made of bamboo and covered with coconut leaves, and each was surrounded by a deep trench to protect it from wild animals or thieves. The only way to enter a house was to walk across a "monkey bridge"—a single bamboo stick that spanned the trench. At night we pulled the bridges into our houses and were safe.

There were no shops or marketplaces in our hamlet. If we needed supplies—medicine, cloth, soaps, or candles—we had to cross over the mountains and travel to a town nearby. We used the river mainly for traveling to distant hamlets, but it also provided us with plenty of fish.

During the six-month rainy season, nearly all of us helped plant and cultivate fields of rice, sweet pota-

toes, Indian mustard, eggplant, tomatoes, hot peppers, and corn. But during the dry season, we became hunters and turned to the jungle.

Wild animals played a very large part in our lives. There were four animals we feared the most: the tiger, the lone wild hog, the crocodile, and the horse snake. Tigers were always trying to steal cattle. Sometimes, however, when a tiger became old and slow it became a maneater. But a lone wild hog was even more dangerous than a tiger. It attacked every creature in sight, even when it had no need for food. Or it did crazy things, such as charging into the hamlet in broad daylight, ready to kill or to be killed.

The river had different dangers: crocodiles. But of all the animals, the most hated and feared was the huge horse snake. It was sneaky and attacked people and cattle just for the joy of killing. It would either crush its victim to death or poison it with a bite.

Like all farmers' children in the hamlet, I started working at the age of six. My seven sisters helped by working in the kitchen, weeding the garden, gathering eggs, or taking water to the cattle. I looked after the family herd of water buffaloes. Someone always had to be with the herd because no matter how carefully a water buffalo was trained, it always was ready to nibble young rice plants when no one was looking. Sometimes, too, I fished for the family while I guarded the herd, for there were plenty of fish in the flooded rice fields during the rainy season.

I was twelve years old when I made my first trip to the jungle with my father. I learned how to track game, how to recognize useful roots, how to distinguish edible mushrooms from poisonous ones. I learned that if birds, raccoons, squirrels, or monkeys had eaten the fruits of certain trees, then those fruits were not poison-

ous. Often they were not delicious, but they could calm a man's hunger and thirst.

My father, like most of the villagers, was a farmer and a hunter, depending upon the season. But he also had a college education, so in the evenings he helped to teach other children in our hamlet, for it was too small to afford a professional schoolteacher.

My mother managed the house, but during the harvest season she could be found in the fields, helping my father get the crops home; and as the wife of a hunter, she knew how to dress and nurse a wound and took good care of her husband and his hunting dogs.

I went to the lowlands to study for a while because I wanted to follow my father as a teacher when I grew up. I always planned to return to my hamlet to live the rest of my life there. But war disrupted my dreams. The land I love was lost to me forever.

These stories are my memories. . . .

—H.Q.N.

TANK, THE WATER BUFFALO

My family had land on which we grew rice. During July to January, the rainy season, the rice field was flooded, and only water buffaloes could be used to till the soil.

We owned three water buffaloes, one male and two females. One day our male died of old age. My father decided to look for the ideal water buffalo to replace him: a bull that was both a hard worker and a good fighter. Fighting ability was important because tigers raided the herd near the edge of the jungle. Buffaloes born and raised among mountain tribes had the reputation of being excellent fighters, but they were often too fierce, violent, and impatient to handle. On the other hand, buffaloes born and raised in the lowlands were patient and obedient, but they did not make good fighters, for they lived in an area where fierce predators

1

did not exist. Neither type of buffalo would meet my father's needs.

However, it was possible to have the ideal buffalo if a young bull had a fierce father from the mountains and a patient mother from the lowlands. This unusual mixture occurred if a fierce mountain bull wandered down to the lowlands and met a female which would bear its offspring. The owner of the female might not know that he had a mixed-blood calf until the calf grew older and the thickness of its coat indicated the mountain origin of its father. So sometimes a farmer who had more buffaloes than he needed would unwittingly sell a valuable mixed-blood calf.

My father, by a combination of luck and patience, discovered a mixed-blood buffalo at the ranch of a buffalo merchant in a town far below the river and bought it at a good price.

I was six years old when my father brought the new calf home. He let me give the young buffalo food and water, and sometimes he allowed me to pat its shoulders. But he told me never to approach it when I was alone, for calves were unpredictable. Although they usually obeyed everybody taller than they were, they did not obey small children and sometimes might hurt them.

I listened to my father, but I trusted our calf. I knew he and I would become great friends.

Our calf grew into a handsome and powerful buffalo. He not only became the head of our small herd, but also became the head of all the herds in our hamlet after many ferocious and successful fights with the other males. We named him "Tank," because when he hit another male during a fight, he struck as heavily as a tank.

One day a young bull from a nearby hamlet trespassed on Tank's territory and challenged his authority. Tank roared a few times to warn the intruder, but the other buffalo was determined to fight. When we heard Tank's roars we knew that there was trouble in the field. Everyone in the hamlet rushed to a hill to watch the fight. We could not prevent it, so we stayed on high ground to protect ourselves; for a defeated buffalo would often run to humans to be rescued and, in its panic, trample them.

Tank left his herd and faced the arrogant intruder. The other buffaloes stopped eating and waited. Suddenly the two bulls charged and ran into each other head on. I heard a mighty thud. Both buffaloes fell back. My heart was pounding. It was the first time any of us had ever seen Tank fall back. Tank was the pride of the hamlet, and we would be very ashamed if he lost the fight; or worse, if Tank were killed, some of our female buffaloes might follow the victorious bull home to the other

hamlet, and it would be very hard to bring them back.

The two buffaloes recovered from the powerful collision and ran at each other again. This time they locked horns and tried to twist and break each other's necks. Next, each pushed the other and tried to overturn him. At first the intruder sustained Tank's push very well. But then, little by little, he began to lose ground. Tank pushed him farther and farther backward. Unfortunately for the other buffalo, who had fought quite well so far, there was a deep trench behind him. When his two hind legs fell into the trench, the animal was helpless. Tank's sharpened horns hit first his neck, then his shoulders; but unlike other buffaloes, this one did not call for help.

My father felt sorry for the bull, and he asked my cousin, whom Tank loved the best, to try to stop Tank from killing him. My cousin rushed to Tank's side and called his name. Tank, furious because he was hurt himself, nevertheless listened to my cousin and let him lead him away. The defeated intruder was rescued from the trench and set free, and we never saw or heard from him again.

Tank became so famous that people from far away brought females to breed with him. Buffalo thieves also considered him a prize. One day it rained very hard and Tank did not come home. The next morning we went to look

for him. We asked a friend who had a hound dog to help us. My father, my cousin and I, and a few well-armed friends followed the hound and found Tank near a river crossing about fifteen kilometers from home, tied to the root of a tree.

When we untied Tank, he was very happy and licked everybody who had come to rescue him. But we were puzzled. There was blood scattered all around, but Tank himself was unharmed. And why, if thieves had taken Tank so far away from our home, had they finally left him there?

Weeks later these questions were answered. At a local wedding we heard a drunken man tell the story of how he had been hurt by Tank during his attempt to steal him. First, he and two accomplices had spent many days observing the clothes and mannerisms of my cousin, who took care of Tank and his herd. Then, helped by the pouring rain, which prevented Tank from seeing him clearly, and wearing the same clothes and whistling the same song my cousin did, he approached Tank in the field. When he was close enough he seized the rope that passed through the buffalo's nose. Tank was helpless. If he resisted, the rope would hurt his sensitive nose badly. With the help of his two accomplices, the thief led Tank away. When they reached the river crossing, he loosened the rope so Tank could drink some

water. But instead of drinking, Tank hit him with his horns, gashing the man's leg from his knee to the upper thigh. Since the man could not walk, the other thieves had to carry him and leave Tank behind. They knew that we would soon be on their trail with a hound dog. But before they left, they managed to tie Tank's rope to the root of a tree so the angered buffalo couldn't attack them again.

When the thief finished his story, one of the wedding guests asked him why he had not killed Tank, since Tank had hurt him so badly. The thief answered that to kill a buffalo, under any circumstances, would bring bad luck. Besides, he admired Tank too much to kill him. He said that if they had succeeded in stealing Tank, they would have been able to sell him for ten times the price of any ordinary buffalo. Then he added that sometimes he still came to our hamlet just to have a look at the magnificent bull. No other bull was intelligent enough to fool him, a man of many years' experience as a buffalo thief. When asked if he would attempt to steal Tank again, he said no, because this time he would be risking his life for sure. He was right. My father had removed the rope passing through Tank's nose, just in case anyone tried to steal Tank again.

To our surprise, we learned we did not need the rope to command Tank. He continued to till the soil and guard the herd. We com-

manded Tank orally now. He quickly learned
the meaning of "Left," "Right," and "Stop,"
and did exactly what my cousin wanted while
working in the field. When my cousin put
crops on his back and said, "Go," he would
walk straight home by himself. And at home
after we had unloaded the crops and said,
"Go," he would return to the field.

Other buffaloes might be able to do the
same job, but not as well as Tank. Most of
them could not resist the green grass that bor-
dered the path leading home. When they lingered to eat, they would be late for their tasks.
Or sometimes on their way to the field they
would see a female buffalo and would stay
around and forget everything. But Tank was
so exact about his work that one day an angry
housewife said she wished that her husband
would be as dependable as Tank.

My cousin also trained Tank to fight jungle cats. He made a stuffed tiger with straw
and old linen, and simulated a tiger attack from
different angles. He taught Tank to roll over,
for without this trick a buffalo was helpless
if a tiger or a panther jumped on its back. But
a well-trained buffalo could make a tiger jump
away by rolling over, or crush it under its
weight. And every morning, my cousin attached a razor-sharp knife to each of Tank's
horns before he let him go to the pasture on
the edge of the jungle.

One afternoon all the buffaloes began roaring. Everyone rushed toward the pasture. Hunters blew their hunting horns, and hunting dogs raced out of houses to follow their masters. When we reached the pasture we saw all the adult buffaloes forming a circle to protect their young, and Tank apart from them, fighting with a huge tiger. As we approached, the tiger quit the fight and limped back into the jungle. We examined Tank and found blood on his horns. There was blood scattered all around the ground too, but it was the tiger that had been badly hurt, not Tank. Tank had only a few scratches on his neck.

After this tangle with the tiger, Tank never had to till the soil again. Other inhabitants of the hamlet told my father that if his two other buffaloes were not enough to till the land he owned, they would send theirs to help. Tank's only responsibility now was to guard the hamlet's herd during the dry season.

MY COUSIN

My cousin stayed with my family from the time that he was a little child because my aunt died during his birth, and my uncle was killed while hunting a wild hog. My parents loved him dearly and tried to give him as much education as they could. They sent him to a good school in the lowlands, but he did not like going to school so far away from the jungle where he was born. My parents finally realized how miserable he was. So my cousin returned home and lived with us.

Even though he was ten years older, my cousin and I were perfect companions, and the best times of my childhood were the times I spent with him. We roamed the jungle behind our hamlet in search of birds' nests, wild hens' eggs, mushrooms, edible fruits; or crossed the river on the backs of water buffaloes to pick green mangoes; or caught fish in the rice fields during the rainy season.

One of my cousin's favorite pastimes was hunting. If the hunt was not to be too danger- ous or tiring he would ask my father to allow me to join him. At the end of the rainy season we went hunting wild chickens with a few other boys from the hamlet. Each of us carried a long stick to beat every bush in sight until a frightened chicken was flushed out, and then we chased it, yelling as loud as we could. At this time of the year wild chickens lose their feathers and cannot fly. We just ran after them until they were tired, and we caught them.

When we had enough chickens for the day, we chose a place where we could cook them. We covered their bodies with clay until they looked like soccer balls, and left their legs, necks, and heads free. The bewildered chickens looked comical and pitiful at the same time. We threw them all into the fire until the clay that covered their bodies became white. Then we broke open the white ball of clay and ate the chicken inside. They were delicious!

* * *

One day my cousin climbed a tall banyan tree and brought down a nest of three baby birds. They were all covered with lice. First he got rid of the lice, and then he dug three large holes in the ground and into each hole he put a cage containing a baby bird. He cov- ered the holes with boards, so that each bird would hear only the sounds that he wanted

it to imitate. Every day, after feeding them, he let each one hear the same song, again and again. The first bird heard "The Blue Danube Waltz"; the second, "The Bridge over the River Kwai"; and the third, "Malegueña."

After three months, each bird knew its song. My cousin took the cages out of the holes and hung them in three corners of our house. All day long we heard them singing. Sometimes my mother had a headache and would have to ask my cousin to hang the cages in the garden. When guests came to our house they always asked us about the birds. Once in a while we brought the three cages into the sitting room and urged them to sing at the same time. The birds became the celebrities of our hamlet.

One day Tchen, the boy living in the next house, sneaked into our garden and stole the bird that sang "The Blue Danube." He opened the cage door and plucked a few feathers off the bird and scattered them around, to make us think that the bird had been eaten by a cat.

But my cousin noticed that there was no blood around the cage, and instantly suspected Tchen. So when it got dark my cousin posted himself near the window of Tchen's room. He saw Tchen holding the bird in both hands and urging it to sing, but the bird remained silent. My cousin came home looking very pale, and spent the remainder of the night pacing in his room.

Early the next morning, my cousin hid behind a tree on the road that Tchen had to use
to go to school. When Tchen walked by, my
cousin grabbed him and told him that he'd better return the bird immediately. If he didn't,
my cousin would kill him.

Tchen was very frightened, but he still
tried to deny he had the bird. My cousin told
Tchen what he had seen the night before in
his room, and he added that Tchen better not
kill the bird to destroy the proof. He meant
what he said: the bird back, or death.

Tchen returned the bird. Later on I asked
my cousin whether or not he had really meant
to kill Tchen. My cousin said: "Yes, I did mean
that."

* * *

One day my cousin told me that a man
from a tribe nearby had taught him the technique of catching a live python and taming
it. Pythons, like wild elephants, can be tamed
and become faithful friends to people. My
cousin said that when a python attacked you,
you should raise both hands high to keep them
free while the python coiled around you. Then,
with one hand you should grab its tail, and
with the other hand you should hold its head
away from you, to avoid getting bitten. As the
python started squeezing, you should lightly
bite its tail. For some reason that would keep
the python at bay. Afterward you could call

for help if the python was too big, or better yet, walk home with the python wrapped around you. But, my cousin added, you should never make the mistake of biting the python's tail too hard. If you did that, the python would get very angry and squeeze you to death.

A few months later we heard one of our roosters cry very loudly. We rushed out of our house and saw a python squeezing the rooster. My cousin used the technique he had learned and caught the python easily.

We kept the python in a cage, and every day my cousin approached it in a very gentle way. About a week later he succeeded in feeding it a live rat. After that, the python and my cousin quickly became very good friends.

When my cousin was not busy, he applied shoe polish to the python's skin to make it shiny. Sometimes, to entertain a guest at our house, he would make the python into a coil and use it as a pillow. In fact, pythons make very good pillows. Their skins are soft, and their cool blood makes it seem as if your head is resting on an air-conditioned pillow.

I too was very much impressed by my cousin's python and wished I had a smaller one that I could bring with me to the lowlands, where I went to school. It would certainly impress my friends at the boarding house, especially the young daughter of my landlady!

The next time I was home from school,

my mother asked my cousin and me to go to the edge of the jungle to gather some firewood. At the jungle's edge we saw birds hopping on the ground and singing in the bushes, a sign that there were no dangerous beasts around. So we went a little farther into the jungle and looked for a type of mushroom my parents were very found of. But secretly, I hoped we might find a small python.

We did not find any mushrooms or pythons, and since we had gathered enough firewood, we started the journey home. A little later we stopped and rested on a fallen tree trunk half buried in dead leaves. My cousin whistled a song and I beat the time to it on the dead tree with my sharp woodcutting knife. Suddenly the tree moved. We looked at each other. Each of us thought that the other had moved the tree. Then we realized that it was not a tree we were sitting on but a very angry python!

We threw everything into the air and ran as fast as we could. When we were far enough away, we looked back and saw the python raising its head about two meters above the ground and opening its huge mouth in our direction. This python certainly wasn't the one I wanted for a pet! And after that whenever we went into the jungle my cousin and I looked very carefully at any tree we wanted to sit on.

THE LONE WILD HOG

The wild hogs living in the jungle near our hamlet were a constant problem because they sometimes attacked people or cattle without provocation. As the guardian of all the buffaloes in our hamlet, Tank once had to fight a huge wild hog when the herd was grazing at the edge of the jungle. He defeated the hog, but the victory was not an easy one.

A fully grown male hog can weigh almost three hundred kilos, and its skin is covered by a thick coating of the sap from a tree we called the "oil tree." A combination of instinct and parasitic itches causes a hog to rub itself up against the oil tree, which oozes sap when its bark is broken. The sap, when condensed and dried, becomes an extremely tough covering that acts like armor, making the wild hogs immune to wounds from short knives or bullets from small guns. The older the hog, the thicker

its armor. The only part of the wild hog's body that is not covered by this special sap is its throat and most of its neck, for dry sap would hinder its movement when it wanted to bend its head to drink or to eat roots. That is why the wild hog always rubs away any sap that drops on its neck or its throat.

The head of the wild hog is its most powerful weapon. When a wild hog charges, it may knock down its opponent, but that usually does little damage. It is the follow-up slap of its head that is lethal. The tusks of the wild hog grow in such a way that the sideways slap of its head can rip away the abdomen of a pursuing hunting dog. And even though the tips of an old hog's tusks will tend to curve in toward its head, when an old wild hog is cornered, it will break off the curved parts of its tusks by smashing them against a tree so that the jagged tips will point outward.

Wild hogs live in groups and each group has a leader, or dominant male. Usually, wild hogs try to avoid people, fighting back only when cornered. But every once in a while there will be a lone male that either is not strong enough to challenge the dominant male of the herd and prefers to live alone, or has been a dominant male of a large group itself, but because of old age has been beaten by an upcoming young male and has had to leave its harem. And it is this lone wild hog that is the most

ferocious animal of the jungle. Even a tiger avoids a lone wild hog unless it is very hungry, for it will attack every animal, or person, in sight.

One day a young farmer from our hamlet was working in a cornfield near the edge of the jungle. He had his little daughter and his watchdog with him. His daughter was playing with the dog when suddenly the dog stopped playing and became very nervous. The farmer looked around. He saw a huge wild hog charging down the hill.

There was no place in the field big enough for both the farmer and his daughter to hide, so the farmer picked her up and put her in a small clump of elephant grass. He quickly ran away from the place where he had hidden her, hoping the wild hog would follow him and leave his daughter alone.

As he ran, the farmer yelled as loud as he could for help, while his brave watchdog tried to defend him from the wild hog. The dog was strong, but it was no match for the angry hog. In a few seconds it lay dead on the ground, its chest and its abdomen torn open.

The farmer continued to run toward a tree, but the tree was too far away and the wild hog overtook him. It knocked him to the ground and broke his shoulders and neck with powerful slaps of its head. Four other farmers

working in a field nearby rushed over to help their friend, but it was already too late.

The wild hog left the dead farmer and charged the newcomers. They jumped into a deep ditch and tried to hide. By chance, one of them carried with him the horn he used to gather his herd of buffaloes. He blew three blasts on his horn and alerted our hamlet to the danger.

Immediately the whole hamlet was on its feet. Sounds of hunting horns summoning hunting dogs were heard from one end of the hamlet to the other. Meanwhile the man in the ditch kept blowing his horn to let us know exactly where they were.

When the wild hog could not figure out a way to come down into the ditch to attack the men, it stomped around the edge, snorting at them menacingly. As the barks and howls of the hunting dogs became louder and louder, the wild hog gave up and ran back to the jungle. But the dogs saw the wild hog, and the lead dog immediately ran after it.

The village rescue party, including my father and my cousin—whose own father had been killed by a wild hog—pulled the four men out of the ditch. Everyone became very angry when they saw the mangled body of the dead farmer in the field. They found his frightened little daughter hiding in the elephant grass, but they decided not to let the girl see the body

of her father. Instead they told her that her father would be okay after a few days of treatment in the hospital, and then someone took the little girl to a neighbor's house.

Judging from the barking of the leader of the hunting dogs, the hog was now far away. It would take a long time for the villagers to catch up with it and then a very long and hard fight to kill it. Nevertheless, even though it was late in the afternoon, they immediately organized the hunt.

First they called in most of their hunting dogs, except for the lead dog and two bloodhounds. The men did not want to tire all the dogs at the same time and thereby maybe lose track of the hog. There was some of the dead farmer's blood on the tusks of the hog, so even if the lead dog were killed, the two bloodhounds would be able to follow the hog's trail.

Next they sent four men to carry the body of their friend home. Then all the rest, armed with knives, quickly moved toward the noise made by the barking lead dog.

The knives they carried were special. Each knife had a long, sturdy handle that ended in a wooden crescent that fit over the hip, and a blade with two sharp edges and a pointed tip, designed to penetrate the hog's throat as far as possible. When a wild hog attacks a hunter he can hold his knife, crescent handle against his hip, and try to stand up to the

charge. Or he can sidestep the charge and let the animal come close enough to him to try and slap him with its head. A skillful hunter will let the animal pierce its own throat by slapping it against a well-placed knife.

It was midnight when the men caught up with the hog. They could hear that the dogs had it cornered. It could not run any farther because a steep cliff blocked its way.

The men cut down trees and blocked the only path leading to the hog. Then they let loose ten fresh dogs and called off the lead dog and the two bloodhounds. The fresh dogs harassed the hog for the rest of the night and kept it at bay, tiring it out for the attack at dawn. The men knew they would lose a few dogs, but they had no other choice. If they did not let the dogs attack the hog, it might sneak out of their trap, or even if it did not, fighting a fresh wild hog in the morning would be just as dangerous as fighting a tired hog in the dark.

The night seemed endless. The pandemonium of barking dogs and snorting wild hog kept everyone awake. Once in a while the painful howling of a wounded dog made them sit up with a start and wonder which dog had just been hurt, how many were already dead. The men loved their dogs very much, but they would not hesitate to send in more if the first ten had all been killed. All the rest of the

dogs seemed to share the anxiety and the determination of their masters. They lay side by
side now without any quarrels; sometimes
one licked the nose of another to show that
it was friendly. Normally they never got along
with each other.

By dawn four dogs were dead, and a fifth
was dying. It had a ghastly wound in its stomach, but still it refused to let go of the tail of
the angered hog. The other five dogs relentlessly continued to attack.

The hog had a stone wall behind it. Its
mouth foamed and its tusks were broken in
half. It had prepared itself to fight to the death.

The men let loose all their dogs and then
formed two half circles blocking the hog's escape. They let the dogs harass the hog for a
while longer and lost a few more dogs; one
dog had its two hind legs torn away, but it
still tried to crawl forward to bite the hog.

Then, without warning, the hog stopped
fighting the dogs and charged the first line of
men. The man closest to the hog was lifted
off the ground, thrown on his back, and
knocked unconscious. The men on either side
of him quickly positioned their knives. The
hog ignored the unconscious man and slapped
its head at one of the other men instead, cutting
itself near its ear on his knife. It was a very
deep wound, but not a fatal one. The hurt animal ran back to the stone wall, where it was

immediately surrounded again by the dogs.

The second line of men quickly replaced the first line, and the unconscious man was carried to safety. He had a broken leg and a bruised hip, but his condition was not critical. Meanwhile the hog, looking very tired now, knelt down and no longer seemed to be bothered by the dogs.

The men called off all the dogs and prepared for the final assault. Two of them slowly approached the hog from either side of its head. The hog got up on its feet again, and moved backward. Then suddenly it charged the man on the right. He jumped aside, but instead of turning, the hog continued its charge and crashed into the first line of men. The two men behind the hog threw away their knives and grabbed its tail and tried to slow it down. The hog quickly turned, but in doing so it slapped into the knife of a man from the first line. It tried to shake off the knife, but the more it tried, the deeper the knife cut into its throat. Finally it succumbed to the fatal wound.

The hunters ignored the dead hog. Instead, some tried to comfort their wounded dogs, while others stared at their dead ones. One of my father's three dogs had had its chest torn open, and died shortly after the fight. His two other dogs stayed next to it and growled at everyone who came close to their dead friend

except my father and my cousin.

The men broke into two groups. Some gave first aid to the wounded dogs, while the others cut bamboo trees and vines and built makeshift stretchers to carry the wounded men, the hog, and the wounded and the dead dogs home. The village chief called a young man to his side and told him to signal on his buffalo horn that the hunting party was safe. The young man blew one long blast followed by one short one and then repeated the signal several times, hoping a favorable wind would carry the happy message home to the hamlet.

When everything was ready, the village chief gave the signal to start the journey home. The blasts on the horn were repeated until the party came in sight of our hamlet. The hunters heard children shouting their names and welcoming them home, and the women ran forward to help the men carry their wounded or dead dogs.

We all gathered at the village chief's home, where the wounded men and dogs were given further treatment and where a big feast of hog meat was prepared. Everyone, including the dogs, had some meat. But the heart of the hog was saved. We placed it on the altar of the young farmer killed in the field. Then we hung the hog's broken tusks in front of his tomb as a reminder to all of us of the constant danger we faced from a lone wild hog.

MISTER SHORT

The river in front of our hamlet was full of crocodiles. These crocodiles were so intelligent that they avoided suspicious live bait or dead poisoned animals, so the villagers abandoned the idea of getting rid of them and we simply learned how to live with them.

Along our stretch of the river lived a crocodile, an old-timer, which the villagers named "Mister Short." Mr. Short—before he became short—used his long tail to knock people out of their boats and then proceeded to eat them.

Our villagers, when going to the town below, always used small boats, and with a small boat one must travel near the riverbank, standing precariously balanced on the moving boat and pushing the boat with a long bamboo stick. It was very easy to be knocked off the boat by one well-placed smack of a crocodile's tail.

Mr. Short had a very simple but ingenious

technique for accomplishing this. When a boat passed by his territory, the cunning crocodile stuck his head firmly into the mud of the riverbank and knocked the man off his boat with one powerful lash of his tail. Mr. Short was very successful and had managed to eat quite a few people.

Villagers going downriver through the territory of Mr. Short could avoid the riverbank by poling out to the middle of the river and then letting the current carry the boat. But when they traveled upriver, against the current, they could not avoid poling along the riverbank. It was very difficult to crouch down to avoid the strike of the crocodile and still push the boat against the current with a stick.

One day a young man of our hamlet, Hung, my cousin's friend, was fed up with being terrorized when passing through Mr. Short's territory and decided to do something about it. First he went to the local blacksmith and asked him to forge a very long and sharp knife. During the next few days, with the help of my cousin, Hung spent hours practicing with his new knife. He lay on his back holding his long knife in both hands, and asked my cousin to swing at a gourd hanging over his head with a long branch of a banana tree. When Hung was skilled enough to cut the banana leaf every time it passed overhead, he next made a dummy of a standing man with a pole in his

hands. At sundown Hung and my cousin put the dummy on his boat and traveled to the area where Mr. Short plied his trade.

It was twilight when they got there. Hung lay on his back, facing the standing dummy, and my cousin, holding another knife, hid at the other end of the little boat. They let the boat slide downriver, very close to the riverbank where Mr. Short usually waited in ambush.

In the twilight Mr. Short did not see clearly and mistook the dummy for a real person. The crocodile struck at the dummy with a powerful sideways blow of his tail, and at that very moment Hung swung at the tail with his long knife. He succeeded in cutting off a big portion, which fell into the boat, where it wriggled comically.

After that Mr. Short stopped attacking people, but he lived on for many years, feeding on animals that came to drink at the river. Once in a while people saw him crawling awkwardly into the river, a crocodile with a little tail growing out of the stump of a big tail.

RIVER CREATURES

When my father did not need Tank to till the rice fields during the rainy season, I liked to ride on his back and look for an otters' party. There were many otters living on the river-banks in front of our hamlet because fish were plentiful in the deep river. Normally the otters lived in twos. But once in a while they all gathered together, caught a great number of fish, and threw them up on the riverbank. Then they all sat down around the fish and ate them. We called this unusual gathering an otters' party.

One day my cousin and I thought up a plan to capture the otters' fish. It would be hard to do because if the otters saw people approaching to try and take their fish, they jumped back into the river and took all the fish with them. But otters did not worry about other animals, so I decided that because Tank's

back was wide and high above the ground I could lie flat on his back and approach an otters' party without attracting their attention. To make detection of me even more difficult, I would wear clothes that blended in as much as possible with the color of Tank's back. I would also carry a sturdy stick to scare the otters away in case they turned on me. I had to take this last precaution because I knew that otters, when gathered in a large group, had attacked people who passed by them in small boats.

A few days later I spotted an otters' party on the riverbank. I found a good stick and climbed onto Tank's back. After I showed Tank the direction I wanted him to go, I lay facedown and let him carry me to the party. When Tank was about three meters from the group, I slid down to the ground and chased all the otters into the river. That day I caught them thoroughly by surprise, and I got twenty-four fish, all different kinds, and most of them still intact and fresh.

After that I repeated my raids as often as I could and usually with great success. But one day, after I had surprised the otters and put all the fish on Tank's back, I noticed that one female did not leave. She just swam up and down the river and seemed very anxious to return to where I was. Sensing something unusual, I carefully looked around and discovered

three otter cubs in a very deep, narrow hole under a thick thistle bush. I was very excited. Otter cubs were priceless, for one could train an otter cub to catch as many fish as one wanted.

When I had squeezed myself into the hole and had almost reached the cubs, the mother otter came up behind me and bit my toes, very hard! It was so painful that I had to crawl out of the hole as quickly as possible and shake her off. The mother otter jumped back into the river, but when I crawled into the hole again I received the same painful bite on my toes. Suddenly, I came up with an idea. I took some mud from the riverbank and wrote on Tank's back, *Otter cubs—come quickly.* Then I gave Tank a little tap on the back and said, "Go." Tank trotted straight home.

When Tank arrived home my parents saw the fish he carried, but no me. They panicked. Then they discovered the message on Tank's back, and they were very happy. My cousin and Tank soon returned to where I was. My cousin prevented the mother otter from biting me while I took the three cubs out of the hole, one by one.

We sold two of the cubs at the marketplace to two rich merchants, and kept the third one to train to catch fish for us.

The cub we kept quickly learned its job, but we always kept it in an iron cage for fear

that it would run away from us. Unfortunately, when I caught the cub its eyes had already opened. If it had just been born and its eyes had not yet opened, we would have been the first beings it saw, and it would have considered us as its parents and remained with us for the rest of its life.

Afterward, whenever we wanted fish we just brought our otter to the riverbank, tied it to a long rope to prevent it from escaping, and let it dive into the river. When it caught a fish, it surfaced and gave the fish to us.

Since it was always easy for us to get fish, we gave them to friends whenever they wanted any. Sometimes, when we had free days, we let our otter fish all day long. It caught a great number of fish, which we then dried and sent to our relatives who weren't as lucky as we to have a trained otter for a fisherman.

* * *

In the river in front of our hamlet there lived a type of catfish that weighed more than one hundred kilos when fully grown. Gourmets sought them, but they were difficult to catch because they often broke the fishline or tore up the fishnet. We called them white catfish in order to distinguish them from black catfish, which were darker and smaller.

To catch white catfish we used a squirrel or a big frog as bait. We couldn't use fishing

poles made of light bamboo trees because they would break. And big, heavy poles were too tiring to hold. Thus a fisherman who wanted to catch a white catfish just held the fishline firmly in his hands. When the catfish bit, the fisherman held the line for a while. If the line did not break and the catfish tired, he slowly pulled it to the riverbank and used a big net to pull it onto dry ground.

One day I left Tank and the other buffaloes grazing near the river while I talked with a friend of my family's. He was old and could not do hard work in the field, so he fished for white catfish to help out his family. I had just finished saying that if a fish took the bait, I would help him, when I saw his face turn pink and his hands shake very hard. Immediately I jumped next to him, grabbed the line, and started pulling.

The fish fought back like a devil, and one of its powerful jerks almost dragged both of us into the river. I yelled to Tank to come and help us.

Tank came quickly. We tied the fishline to his horns and signaled him to walk backward. Tank lowered his head and pulled with all his strength. Luckily, the line held, and Tank dragged the fish closer and closer to shore. Suddenly we saw a huge white catfish jump into the air and then fall back into the

water with a tremendous splash. Tank kept pulling and the old man kept yelling, "That's right, son. That's right, son." Moments later we saw the head of the fish come out of the water, then the body, and finally the tail.

When the entire fish was on the riverbank, we stopped Tank and untied the line from his horns. Our old friend was so happy that he jumped up and down like a child. He said that without me and Tank he knew that the catfish would have gotten away from him. Then we brought Tank closer to the fish so that he could see it clearly. Tank looked at the fish and pricked up his ears in a funny way.

My old friend called it a day, because he had made a big catch and he wanted to go home immediately to show his family. But the fish was too heavy for him to carry. Although it was still early, I decided to bring the herd home so that Tank could help our friend carry the fish.

I told our friend that we should load the fish on Tank's back. He was very happy with the idea, but said that first he had to cut off the fish's pectoral fins. He explained to me that each pectoral fin has a spine with venom in it that made a cut from the fin very painful. He took a knife out of his pocket, cut off the two pectoral fins, and thereby prevented Tank from being hurt.

When we arrived at my house, where I left the herd, the old friend wanted to give my parents part of the fish. But my parents refused his offer, telling him that our otter caught all the fish we needed. They said he should keep the whole fish and sell it at the marketplace, where he would get a good price for such a delicacy.

Tank and I accompanied our friend to his house. When we arrived, his family was very happy to see the big fish. The old man kept repeating how wildly the fish had fought and how helpful Tank and I had been.

Soon all his children got busy. Several carried the fish inside, one prepared tea for him, and another hung his fishing line on the wall. When the boys and girls were tired of looking at the fish, they surrounded Tank and asked me endless questions about him: Why was Tank's stomach so big? Was he pregnant? Why were the hairs at the end of his tail longer than those on his head? And so on.

My friend's wife wanted me to stay for dinner, but I refused because my parents had told me to be back as soon as possible. My mother wanted to use Tank to draw some water from the well. But as I said good-bye, my friend's wife made sure I didn't refuse a piece of cake to eat on the way home, and a lump of brown sugar for Tank. Tank was very fond of

brown sugar—more than he was of fishing, I think!

* * *

From the time Tank helped our old friend to get the white catfish, I had considered the idea of catching golden eels with Tank's help. There were two kinds of golden eels living in our area—one kind had bulging eyes, the other had beady eyes. Both were very much sought after because their meat was excellent. These eels, when matured, reached two meters in length and weighed about five kilos.

The eels lived in muddy ditches that brought water to the fruit gardens, the banana groves, and the coconut groves when the level of the water in the river in front of our hamlet was high. They hid in deep holes that they dug in the hard clay soil beneath the mud of the ditch, usually near a tree planted on the border of the ditch. The roots of the tree were a natural barrier against intruders, and when an eel coiled its body around the root of a tree, it was almost impossible to pull it out. Each eel's nest had several openings to allow it to escape in case of danger, and inside a nest there were many zigzag corners, which allowed an eel to hook its body around a corner and resist someone's trying to pull it out by its head or tail.

Eels lay constantly in ambush near the main entrance of their nest, waiting for prey

to pass by—fish, shrimp, crabs, even baby
ducks if a mother duck was foolish enough
to lead her young brood over an eel's nest. Then
the eel would shoot out of its nest like an arrow, snap up a baby duck, pull it down into
its nest, and swallow it moments later. Sometimes an eel even tried to attack an adult duck
if food was scarce. It would bite the duck's
foot and try to pull the frightened fowl down
into the nest, where it would drown. The duck
might survive if someone heard it quack and
rushed to rescue it, but it would often lose
one foot because the teeth of a golden eel are
very sharp.

One could lure an eel with almost any kind
of bait, but we used earthworms because they
were easy to find. We would dangle the worm
at the nest's entrance, and sooner or later the
eel would come out and bite the bait. We allowed the eel to swallow the bait far down
into its stomach, instead of pulling the line
right away, for if we pulled the line too soon
we would only succeed in tearing off the eel's
jaw during the struggle to pull it out of its
nest. But with a hook in its stomach, it could
not get away—no matter how hard it tried.
Sooner or later, unless the fishing line broke,
we would drag the eel out of its nest, dead
or alive.

In our hamlet, whenever an eel was
hooked, the children of the neighborhood had

a good time. They ran out of their houses when they heard the yell for help. Two or three boys would help pull out the eel, and everyone else yelled or laughed. Sometimes adults came to help too, if they were not busy. It took at least one hour to pull the eel out of its nest, and by this time, it was usually dead.

But a live eel got a better price than a dead one in the market, and since Tank had easily succeeded in pulling the white catfish out of the river for our old friend, I came up with the idea of letting him drag eels out of their nests for me. If he could pull an eel out quickly, I had a better chance to get the eel alive instead of dead.

First I had to find an eel's nest, but this was not difficult. One can know roughly the location of a nest by listening carefully to the sound an eel makes when it snaps at a victim. The sound made by its closing jaws is similar to that of a loud click and can be heard clearly from thirty or forty meters away, especially at night.

After finding the general area of a nest, I pinpointed the exact location by examining the mud. The mud around the main entrance of the nest is always more disturbed than the rest. Then I tied the end of a fishing line to Tank's horns and made the bait jump up and down on the mud covering the hole. The eel stuck its head out of the mud first, saw the bait

clearly, snapped it up, and returned to its nest below. I loosened the line to let the eel swallow the bait into its stomach, then I signaled Tank to pull. Despite his tremendous strength, Tank needed quite a bit of effort to pull the eel out of its nest. But it was the most exciting sight to see the wagging head of the eel stick out of the mud first, and then its big, trembling golden body come slowly out of the hole. When the eel was on dry ground, it yanked, turned, and squirmed like an earthworm attacked by a swarm of fire ants.

Using this method, I caught several big eels; none of them could resist Tank more than fifty counts. When Tank started pulling, I counted, One, two, three . . . Some strong eels reached forty-five, but the weaker ones were already on dry ground, wriggling, when I had not yet reached twenty. Often, when an eel had taken the bait, I yelled to my friends to come to see Tank's work. When everybody arrived, I signaled Tank to pull. Some of my friends counted with me while the others yelled, clapped their hands, or cheered loudly for Tank.

It was difficult to tell whether Tank enjoyed fishing for eels as much as we did, but he always accomplished his task extremely well.

THE HORSE SNAKE

Despite all his courage there was one creature in the jungle that Tank always tried to avoid— the snake. And there was one kind of snake that was more dangerous than other snakes— the horse snake. In some areas people called it the bamboo snake because it was as long as a full-grown bamboo tree. In other regions, the people called it the thunder or lightning snake, because it attacked so fast and with such power that its victim had neither time to escape nor strength to fight it. In our area, we called it the horse snake because it could move as fast as a thoroughbred.

One night a frightened friend of our family's banged on our door and asked us to let him in. When crossing the rice field in front of our house on his way home from a wedding, he had heard the unmistakable hiss of a horse snake. We became very worried; not only for

us and our friend, but also for the cattle and other animals we raised.

It was too far into the night to rouse all our neighbors and go to search for the snake. But my father told my cousin to blow three times on his buffalo horn, the signal that a dangerous wild beast was loose in the hamlet. A few seconds later we heard three long quivering sounds of a horn at the far end of the hamlet answering our warning. We presumed that the whole hamlet was now on guard.

I stayed up that night, listening to all the sounds outside, while my father and my cousin sharpened their hunting knives. Shortly after midnight we were startled by the frightened neighing of a horse in the rice field. Then the night was still, except for a few sad calls of nocturnal birds and the occasional roaring of tigers in the jungle.

The next day early in the morning all the able-bodied men of the hamlet gathered in front of our house and divided into groups of four to go and look for the snake. My father and my cousin grabbed their lunch and joined a searching party.

They found the old horse that had neighed the night before in the rice field. The snake had squeezed it to death. Its chest was smashed, and all its ribs broken. But the snake had disappeared.

Everybody agreed that it was the work of

one of the giant horse snakes which had terrorized our area as far back as anyone could remember. The horse snake usually eats small
game, such as turkeys, monkeys, chickens, and
ducks, but for unknown reasons sometimes it
will attack people and cattle. A fully grown
horse snake can reach the size of a king python.
But, unlike pythons, horse snakes have an extremely poisonous bite. Because of their bone-
breaking squeeze and fatal bite they are one
of the most dangerous creatures of the uplands.

The men searched all day, but at nightfall
they gave up and went home. My father and
my cousin looked very tired when they returned. My grandmother told them to go right
to bed after their dinner and that she would
wake them up if she or my mother heard any
unusual sounds.

The men went to bed and the women prepared to stay up all night. My mother sewed
torn clothing and my grandmother read a novel
she had just borrowed from a friend. And for
the second night in a row, they allowed my
little sister and me to stay awake and listen
with them for as long as we could. But hours
later, seeing the worry on our faces, my grandmother put aside her novel and told us a story:

Once upon a time a happy family lived in a small village on the
shore of the South China Sea. They

respected the laws of the land and
loved their neighbors very much. The
father and his oldest son were wood-
cutters. The father was quite old, but
he still could carry home a heavy load
of wood.

One day on his way home from
the jungle he was happier than usual.
He and his son had discovered a wild
chicken nest containing twelve eggs.
Now he would have something
special to give to his grandchildren
when they pulled his shirtsleeves and
danced around him to greet him
when he came home.

The father looked at the broad
shoulders of his son and his steady
gait under a very heavy load of wood.
He smiled. His son was a good son,
and he had no doubt that when he
became even older still his son would
take good care of him and his wife.

As he was thinking this he saw
his son suddenly throw the load of
wood at a charging horse snake that
had come out of nowhere. The heavy
load of wood crashed into the snake's
head and stunned it. That gave them
enough time to draw their sharp
woodcutting knives. But instead of
attacking the horse snake from the
front, the elder shouted to his son
to run behind the big bush of ele-

phant grass nearby while he, who was a little too old to run fast, jumped into the front end of the bush. Each time the snake passed by him the old man managed to hit it with his knife. He struck the snake many times. Finally it became weak and slowed down; so he came out of his hiding place and attacked the snake's tail, while his son attacked the snake's head. The snake fought back furiously, but finally it succumbed to the well-coordinated attack of father and son.

When the snake was dead, they grabbed its tail and proudly dragged it to the edge of their village. Everyone rushed out to see their prize. They all argued over who would have the honor of carrying the snake to their house for them.

The old woodcutter and his son had to tell the story of how they had killed the snake at least ten times, but the people never tired of hearing it, again and again. They all agreed that the old woodcutter and his son were not only brave but clever as well. Then and there the villagers decided that when their chief, also a brave and clever man, died, the old woodcutter was the only one who deserved the honor of replacing him.

When my grandmother finished the story, my little sister, and I became a bit more cheerful. People could defeat this dangerous snake after all. The silent darkness outside became less threatening. Nevertheless, we were still too scared to sleep in our room, so my mother made a makeshift bed in the sitting room, close to her and our grandmother.

When we woke up the next morning, life in the hamlet had almost returned to normal. The snake had not struck again that night, and the farmers, in groups of three or four, slowly filtered back to their fields. Then, late in the afternoon, hysterical cries for help were heard in the direction of the western part of the hamlet. My cousin and my father grabbed their knives and rushed off to help.

It was Minh, a farmer, who was crying for help. Minh, like most farmers in the area, stored the fish he had caught in the rice field at the end of the rainy season in a small pond. That day Minh's wife had wanted a good fish for dinner. When Minh approached his fish pond he heard what sounded like someone trying to steal his fish by using a bucket to empty water from the pond. Minh was very angry and rushed over to catch the thief, but when he reached the pond, what he saw so petrified him that he fell over backward, speechless. When he regained control he crawled away as fast as he could and yelled loudly for help.

The thief he saw was not a person but a huge horse snake, perhaps the same one that had squeezed the old horse to death two nights before. The snake had hooked its head to the branch of one tree and its tail to another and was splashing the water out of the pond by swinging its body back and forth, like a hammock. Thus, when the shallow pond became dry, it planned to swallow all the fish.

All the villagers rushed to the scene to help Minh, and our village chief quickly organized an attack. He ordered all the men to surround the pond. Then two strong young men approached the snake, one at its tail and the other at its head. As they crept closer and closer, the snake assumed a striking position, its head about one meter above the pond, and its tail swaying from side to side. It was ready to strike in either direction. As the two young men moved in closer, the snake watched them. Each man tried to draw the attention of the snake, while a third man crept stealthily to its side. Suddenly he struck the snake with his long knife. The surprised snake shot out of the pond like an arrow and knocked the young man unconscious as it rushed by. It broke through the circle of men and went into an open rice field. But it received two more wounds on its way out.

The village chief ordered all the women and children to form a long line between the

open rice field and the jungle and to yell as loudly as they could, hoping to scare the snake so that it would not flee into the jungle. It would be far easier for the men to fight the wounded snake in an open field than to follow it there.

But now there was a new difficulty. The snake started heading toward the river. Normally a horse snake could beat any man in a race, but since this one was badly wounded, our chief was able to cut off its escape by sending half his men running to the river. Blocked off from the river and jungle, the snake decided to stay and fight.

The hunting party surrounded the snake again, and this time four of the best men attacked the snake from four different directions. The snake fought bravely, but it perished. During the struggle one of the men received a dislocated shoulder, two had bruised ribs, and three were momentarily blinded by dirt thrown by the snake. Luckily all of them succeeded in avoiding the fatal bite of the snake.

We rejoiced that the danger was over. But we knew it would only be a matter of time until we would once again have to face our most dangerous natural enemy—the horse snake.

OPERA, KARATE, AND BANDITS

When she was eighty years old my grandmother was still quite strong. She could use
her own teeth to eat corn on the cob or to
chew on sugar plants to extract juice from
them. Every two days she walked for more than
an hour to reach the marketplace, carrying a
heavy load of food with her, and then spent
another hour walking back home. And even
though she was quite old, traces of her beauty
still lingered on: Her hands, her feet, her face
revealed that she had been an attractive young
woman. Nor did time do much damage to the
youthful spirit of my grandmother.

One of her great passions was theater, and
this passion never diminished with age. No
matter how busy she was, she never missed a
show when there was a group of actors in town.
If no actors visited our hamlet for several
months, she would organize her own show

in which she was the manager, the producer, and the young leading lady, all at the same time.

My grandmother's own plays were always melodramas inspired by books she had read and by what she had seen on the stage. She always chose her favorite grandson to play the role of the hero, who would, without fail, marry the heroine at the end and live happily ever after. And when my sisters would tell her that she was getting too old to play the role of the young heroine anymore, my grandmother merely replied: "Anybody can play this role if she's young at heart."

When I was a little boy my grandmother often took me to see the opera. She knew Chinese mythology by heart, and the opera was often a dramatization of this mythology. On one special occasion, during the Lunar New Year celebrations—my favorite holiday, because children could do anything they wanted and by tradition no one could scold them—I accompanied my grandmother to the opera.

When we reached the theater I wanted to go in immediately. But my grandmother wanted to linger at the entrance and talk to her friends. She chatted for more than an hour. Finally we entered the theater, and at that moment the "Faithful One" was onstage, singing sadly. The "Faithful One" is a common character in Chinese opera. He could be a good minis-

ter, or a valiant general, or someone who loved and served his king faithfully. But in the end he is unjustly persecuted by the king, whose opinion of him has been changed by the lies of the "Flatterer," another standard character.

When my grandmother saw the "Faithful One" onstage she looked upset and gave a great sigh. I was too interested in what was happening to ask her the reason, and we spent the next five hours watching the rest of the opera. Sometimes I cried because my grandmother cried at the pitiful situation of the "Faithful One." Sometimes I became as angry as my grandmother did at the wickedness of the "Flatterer."

When we went home that night my grandmother was quite sad. She told my mother that she would have bad luck in the following year because when we entered the theater, the "Faithful One" was onstage. I was puzzled. I told my grandmother that she was confused. It would be a good year for us because we saw the good guy first. But my mother said, "No, son. The 'Faithful One' always is in trouble and it takes him many years to vindicate himself. Our next year is going to be like one of his bad years."

So, according to my mother's and grandmother's logic, we would have been much bet-

ter off in the new year if we had been lucky enough to see the villain first!

* * *

My grandmother had married a man whom she loved with all her heart, but who was totally different from her. My grandfather was very shy, never laughed loudly, and always spoke very softly. And physically he was not as strong as my grandmother. But he excused his lack of physical strength by saying that he was a "scholar."

About three months after their marriage, my grandparents were in a restaurant and a rascal began to insult my grandfather because he looked weak and had a pretty wife. At first he just made insulting remarks, such as, "Hey! Wet chicken! This is no place for a weakling!"

My grandfather wanted to leave the restaurant even though he and my grandmother had not yet finished their meal. But my grandmother pulled his shirt sleeve and signaled him to remain seated. She continued to eat and looked as if nothing had happened.

Tired of yelling insults without any result, the rascal got up from his table, moved over to my grandparents' table, and grabbed my grandfather's chopsticks. My grandmother immediately wrested the chopsticks from him and struck the rascal on his cheekbone with her elbow. The blow was so quick and powerful

that he lost his balance and fell on the floor. Instead of finishing him off, as any street fighter would do, my grandmother let the rascal recover from the blow. But as soon as he got up again, he kicked over the table between him and my grandmother, making food and drink fly all over the place. Before he could do anything else, my grandmother kicked him on the chin. The kick was so swift that my grandfather didn't even see it. He only heard a heavy thud, and then saw the rascal tumble backward and collapse on the ground.

All the onlookers were surprised and delighted, especially the owner of the restaurant. Apparently the rascal, one of the best karate fighters of our area, came to his restaurant every day and left without paying for his food or drink, but the owner was too afraid to confront him.

While the rascal's friends tried to revive him, everyone else surrounded my grandmother and asked her who had taught her karate. She said, "Who else? My husband!"

After the fight at the restaurant people assumed that my grandfather knew karate very well but refused to use it for fear of killing someone. In reality, my grandmother had received special training in karate from my great-great uncle from the time she was eight years old.

Anyway, after that incident, my grandfa-

ther never had to worry again. Anytime he had some business downtown, people treated him very well. And whenever anyone happened to bump into him on the street, they bowed to my grandfather in a very respectful way.

* * *

When my father was about ten years old a group of bandits attacked our house. There had been a very poor harvest that year, and bandits had already attacked several homes in other hamlets. My grandmother had a premonition this would also happen to them, so she devised a plan. In case of danger, she would carry the children to safety, and my grandfather would carry the bow and arrows, a bottle of poison, and the box containing the family jewels.

It was night when the bandits came. My grandfather became scared to death and forgot his part of the plan, but my grandmother remained very calm. She led her husband and children to safety through a secret back door that opened into a double hedge of cactus that allowed a person to walk inside, undetected, to the banana grove. When they were safely inside the banana grove, my grandfather realized that he had forgotten the bow and arrows and the bottle of poison. So my grandmother stole back into the house and retrieved the weapons.

The bandits were still trying to smash

through our very solid front door when she sneaked out of the house for the second time. She dipped one arrow in poison and crawled around to the front of the house near the bandits. But, upon second thought, she put the poisoned arrow aside and took another arrow and carefully aimed at the leg of the bandit leader. When the arrow hit his thigh the bandit let out a loud cry and fell backward.

The night was so dark that none of the bandits knew where the arrow had come from. And moments later, friends started arriving and began to attack them from the road in front of our house. The bandits panicked and left in a hurry. But my grandmother spent the rest of the night with her family in the banana grove, just in case the bandits came back.

*　*　*

When my grandmother became older she felt sick once in a while. Before the arrival of the doctor, she would order everybody in the house to look sad. And during the consultation with the doctor she acted as if she were much sicker than she really was. My grandmother felt that she had to make herself look really sick so that the doctor would give her good medicine. She told the doctor that she had a pain in the head, in the shoulders, in the chest, in the back, in the limbs—pain everywhere. Finally the doctor would become confused and wouldn't know what could be wrong with her.

Whenever the doctor left, my mother would sneak out of the house, meet him at the other side of the garden, and tell him exactly where my grandmother hurt.

Two or three days later my grandmother usually felt much better. But before the doctor arrived for another visit she ordered us to look sad again—not as sad as the first time, but quite sad. She would tell the doctor that her situation had improved a little bit but that she still felt quite sick. My grandmother thought that if she told the doctor she had been feeling much better he would stop giving her good medicine. When the doctor left my mother sneaked out of the house again and informed him of the real condition of my grandmother.

I don't think my grandmother ever guessed it was my mother's reports to the doctor, and not her acting, that helped her get well.

*   *   *

One morning my grandmother wanted me to go outside with her. We climbed a little hill that looked over the whole area, and when we got to the top she looked at the rice field below, the mountain on the horizon, and especially at the river. As a young girl she had often brought her herd of water buffaloes to the river to drink while she swam with the other children of the village. Then we visited the graveyard where her husband and some of her children were buried. She touched her hus-

band's tombstone and said, "Dear, I will join you soon." And then we walked back to the garden and she gazed at the fruit trees her husband had planted, a new one for each time she had given birth to a child. Finally, before we left the garden my sister joined us, and the two of them fed a few ducks swimming in the pond.

That evening my grandmother did not eat much of her dinner. After dinner she combed her hair and put on her best dress. We thought that she was going to go out again, but instead she went to her bedroom and told us that she didn't want to be disturbed.

The family dog seemed to sense something was amiss, for he kept looking anxiously at everybody and whined from time to time. At midnight my mother went to my grandmother's room and found that she had died, with her eyes shut, as if she were sleeping normally.

It took me a long time to get used to the reality that my grandmother had passed away. Wherever I was, in the house, in the garden, out on the fields, her face always appeared so clearly to me. And even now, many years later, I still have the feeling that my last conversation with her has happened only a few days before.

SO CLOSE

My grandmother was very fond of cookies made of banana, egg, and coconut, so my mother and I always stopped at Mrs. Hong's house to buy these cookies for her on our way back from the marketplace. My mother also liked to see Mrs. Hong because they had been very good friends since grade-school days. While my mother talked with her friend, I talked with Mrs. Hong's daughter, Lan. Most of the time Lan asked me about my older sister, who was married to a teacher and lived in a nearby town. Lan, too, was going to get married—to a young man living next door, Trung.

Trung and Lan had been inseparable playmates until the day tradition did not allow them to be alone together anymore. Besides, I think they felt a little shy with each other after realizing that they were man and woman.

Lan was a lively, pretty girl who attracted the attention of all the young men of our hamlet. Trung was a skillful fisherman who successfully plied his trade on the river in front of their houses. Whenever Lan's mother found a big fish on the kitchen windowsill she would smile to herself. Finally she decided that Trung was a fine young man and would make a good husband for her daughter.

Trung's mother did not like the idea of her son giving good fish away, but she liked the cookies Lan brought her from time to time. Besides, the girl was very helpful; whenever she was not busy at her house Lan would come over in the evening and help Trung's mother repair her son's fishing net.

Trung was happiest when Lan was helping his mother. They did not talk to each other, but they could look at each other when his mother was busy with her work. Each time Lan went home Trung looked at the chair Lan had just left and secretly wished that nobody would move it.

One day when Trung's mother heard her son call Lan's name in his sleep, she decided it was time to speak to the girl's mother about marriage. Lan's mother agreed they should be married and even waived the custom whereby the bridegroom had to give the bride's family a fat hog, six chickens, six ducks, three bottles of wine, and thirty kilos of fine rice, for the

two families had known each other for a long time and were good neighbors.

The two widowed mothers quickly set the dates for the engagement announcement and for the wedding ceremony. Since their decision was immediately made known to relatives and friends, Trung and Lan could now see each other often.

One day as Trung helped Lan to plant a mango tree behind her house, he asked her: "Have you ever looked at those dainty town boys who pass by your house all the time?" Instead of answering Trung, Lan poked a hard finger at his ribs and laughed. Then she said: "You are not bad looking at all; so don't bother about them. Besides, my mother said that in darkness everything, everybody looks the same!" To a shy young man like Trung the remark was quite bold, but he was very pleased and happy.

At last it was the day of their wedding. Friends and relatives arrived early in the morning to help them celebrate. They brought gifts of ducks, chickens, baskets filled with fruits, rice wine, and colorful fabrics. Even though the two houses were next to each other, the two mothers observed all the proper wedding day traditions.

First Trung and his friends and relatives came to Lan's house. Lan and he prayed at her ancestors' altars and asked for their blessing.

Then they joined everyone for a luncheon.

After lunch there was a farewell ceremony for the bride. Lan stepped out of her house and joined the greeting party that was to accompany her to Trung's home. Tradition called for her to cry and to express her sorrow at leaving her parents behind and forever becoming the daughter of her husband's family. In some villages the bride was even supposed to cling so tightly to her mother that it would take several friends to pull her away from her home. But instead of crying, Lan smiled. She asked herself, why should she cry? The two houses were separated by only a garden; she could run home and see her mother anytime she wanted to. So Lan willingly followed Trung and prayed at his ancestors' altars before joining everyone in the big welcome dinner at Trung's house that ended the day's celebrations.

Later in the evening of the wedding night Lan went to the river to take a bath. Because crocodiles infested the river, people of our hamlet who lived along the riverbank chopped down trees and put them in the river to form barriers and protect places where they washed their clothes, did their dishes, or took a bath. This evening, a wily crocodile had avoided the barrier by crawling up the riverbank and sneaked up behind Lan. The crocodile grabbed her and went back to the river by the same route that it had come.

Trung became worried when Lan did not return. He went to the place where she was supposed to bathe, only to find that her clothes were there but she had disappeared. Panic-stricken, he yelled for his relatives. They all rushed to the riverbank with lighted torches. In the flickering light they found traces of water and crocodile claw prints on the wet soil. Now they knew that a crocodile had grabbed the young bride and dragged her into the river.

Since no one could do anything for the girl, all of Trung's relatives returned to the house, urging the bridegroom to do the same. But the young man refused to leave the place; he just stood there, crying and staring at the clothes of his bride.

Suddenly the wind brought him the sound of Lan calling his name. He was very frightened, for according to an old belief a crocodile's victim must lure a new victim to his master; if not, the first victim's soul must stay with the beast forever.

Trung rushed back to the house and woke all his relatives. Nobody doubted he thought he had heard her call, but they all believed that he was the victim of a hallucination. Everyone pleaded with him and tried to convince him that nobody could survive when snapped up by a crocodile and dragged into the river to be drowned and eaten by the animal.

The young man brushed aside all their ar-

guments and rushed back to the river. Once again, he heard the voice of his bride in the wind, calling his name. Again he rushed back and woke his relatives. Again they tried to persuade him that it was a hallucination, although some of the old folks suggested that maybe the ghost of the young girl was having to dance and sing to placate the angry crocodile because she failed to bring it a new victim.

No one could persuade Trung to stay inside. His friends wanted to go back to the river with him, but he said no. He resented them for not believing him that there were desperate cries in the wind.

Trung stood in front of the deep river alone in the darkness. He listened to the sound of the wind and clutched the clothes Lan had left behind. The wind became stronger and stronger and often changed direction as the night progressed, but he did not hear any more calls. Still he had no doubt that the voice he had heard earlier was absolutely real. Then at dawn, when the wind died down, he again heard, very clearly, Lan call him for help.

Her voice came from an island about six hundred meters away. Trung wept and prayed: "You were a good girl when you were still alive, now be a good soul. Please protect me so that I can find a way to kill the beast in order to free you from its spell and avenge your tragic death." Suddenly, while wiping away his tears,

he saw a little tree moving on the island. The
tree was jumping up and down. He squinted
to see better. The tree had two hands that were
waving at him. And it was calling his name.

Trung became hysterical and yelled for
help. He woke all his relatives and they all
rushed to his side again. At first they thought
that Trung had become stark mad. They tried
to lead him back to his house, but he fiercely
resisted their attempt. He talked to them inco-
herently and pointed his finger at the strange
tree on the island. Finally his relatives saw the
waving tree. They quickly put a small boat into
the river and Trung got into the boat along
with two other men. They paddled to the island
and discovered that the moving tree was, in
fact, Lan. She had covered herself with leaves
because she had no clothes on.

At first nobody knew what had really happened because Lan clung to Trung and cried
and cried. Finally, when Lan could talk they
pieced together her story.

Lan had fainted when the crocodile
snapped her up. Had she not fainted, the crocodile surely would have drowned her before carrying her off to the island. Lan did not know
how many times the crocodile had tossed her
in the air and smashed her against the ground,
but at one point, while being tossed in the air
and falling back onto the crocodile's jaw, she
regained consciousness. The crocodile smashed

her against the ground a few more times, but Lan played dead. Luckily the crocodile became thirsty and returned to the river to drink. At that moment Lan got up and ran to a nearby tree and climbed up it. The tree was very small. Lan stayed very still for fear that the snorting, angry crocodile, roaming around trying to catch her again, would find her and shake her out of the tree. Lan stayed in this frozen position for a long time until the crocodile gave up searching for her and went back to the river. Then she started calling Trung to come rescue her.

Lan's body was covered with bruises, for crocodiles soften up big prey before swallowing it. They will smash it against the ground or against a tree, or keep tossing it into the air. But fortunately Lan had no broken bones or serious cuts. It was possible that this crocodile was very old and had lost most of its teeth. Nevertheless, the older the crocodile, the more intelligent it usually was. That was how it knew to avoid the log barrier in the river and to snap up the girl from behind.

Trung carried his exhausted bride into the boat and paddled home. Lan slept for hours and hours. At times she would sit up with a start and cry out for help, but within three days she was almost completely recovered.

Lan's mother and Trung's mother decided to celebrate their children's wedding a second

time, because Lan had come back from the
dead. All their friends came and sang to the
happy couple. At midnight, at the end of
the last serenade, "The Wedding Night," the
bride and bridegroom were supposed to open
the windows of their room to thank the min-
strels. But Lan and Trung kept the window
closed. Perhaps they were too tired or too busy
to open it. The serenade party left good-hu-
moredly, saying one could do well only one
thing at a time!

LITTLE ALTAR ON
THE ROADSIDE

When I went to the rice field with Tank, my mother often wanted me to burn some incense at a little altar along the roadside. Sometimes I lingered there for a while and cut off the vines that crawled over the altar. But I never lingered if it was growing dark, for at night the deserted road leading to the field seemed too sad and lonely because of the presence of the little altar.

In a little house near the southern end of our hamlet lived a widow and her young son. With the help of her relatives and friends she had brought up her son since the death of her husband, who was killed by a lone wild hog. This woman was still very young at the time of her husband's death, but she refused to remarry, despite many proposals from other men, because she dearly loved her husband. The image of his mangled body remained as

vivid in her mind as if the accident had happened yesterday.

When her son was old enough she told
him of her wish to see him married. She told
him that she became lonely when he was working in the field, that her eyes were not good
enough anymore to sew his torn clothes, that
he needed a wife to help him at home, and
that she needed grandchildren to make her life
less lonely. She also told him that since he
was the only male left in his family, if something happened to him there would be nobody
to continue his father's line and no one to take
care of the tombs of his ancestors.

Her son listened to his mother. He agreed
that the greatest disgrace for the dead was for
nobody to take care of their graves, or burn
incense in front of their tombs after having
cleared the weeds away during the Lunar New
Year. So a few weeks later a go-between found
him a bride in a nearby village.

Three days before the wedding the son
went to the jungle to cut down some bamboo
trees to make a new bed for himself and his
bride. He built the bed but he did not use it,
because according to tradition the wedding bed
had to remain as virginal as the bride and the
bridegroom. So for three nights he slept on a
bench on the veranda of his house.

The night before the wedding his mother
could not sleep because of a strange sense of

foreboding. She got up and walked to the side of her sleeping son. In the semidarkness, she could not see his face clearly at first. When she looked closer she saw a large banyan leaf entirely covering his face. She jumped back and leaned on the door and tried to recover from the shock of this dreadful sight. She was upset because people always covered the face of the dead with a banyan leaf. When she felt calm enough she tiptoed to her son's side, gently took the leaf away, and then stayed near him for a while before going back to her room.

But once again the mother could not fall back to sleep. So in a little while she got up and came to see her son. For the second time she saw her son's face covered with a banyan leaf. This time she decided to find out who had done this most unlucky thing.

She removed the leaf and pretended to go back to her room, but when she had passed the half-opened door she turned back and hid behind it. A few minutes later she saw a mouse dragging a large banyan leaf and covering her son's face with it. Struck by terror at this omen, she fell down and lost consciousness.

When she came to, the night was still young, so she decided to spend the rest of it at her son's side. She decided not to tell him what she had seen, because if she did she would spoil his wedding. But after the wedding she would persuade her son to give up his profes-

sion as a woodcutter and convince him to become a carpenter or a blacksmith. Then he would have nothing to do with the hazardous jungle or the unpredictable river.

Early in the morning of the day of the wedding, she went to visit her husband's grave and prayed to him to protect their only son. Next she went to the village chief and told the chief what she had seen the night before. She asked the chief to forbid her son to perform any dangerous duties during the next few months. Then she went home and prepared the food and drink for the wedding.

Everyone in our hamlet came to the wedding and brought gifts, except the minstrel. He did not bring anything because his gift was to entertain the others with his songs. The rest of the day the mother was distracted by the laughter and cheerful conversation of the guests and by the minstrel's songs instructing the bride and the bridegroom in their new responsibilities as husband and wife. She was even happy with the appearance of the bride, whom she saw for the first time that day. The young girl was not pretty, but she looked very healthy. There was no doubt in the mother's mind that she would soon have grandchildren and that they would brighten her house in the days ahead.

However, her son seemed not to be in touch with what was going on. He laughed and

forced himself to smile at his friends' silly remarks about the wedding night, but his smiles
always turned into strange grimaces at the end.

In the evening when the last guest had
gone, the mother went to her room. She was
exhausted. Suddenly at midnight the hysterical
cries of the bride woke her. She ran to their
room and found her son convulsing uncontrol-
lably, saliva coming out of his mouth. Her son
tried to hold on to his mother's hands. In a
barely audible voice he whispered, "Mother,
help me. Mother, help me."

She quickly pushed the bride out of the
room and told her to yell as loudly as she could
to alarm the neighborhood. By the time the
closest neighbor arrived the son had let go of
his mother's hands and his bewildered eyes
had become empty. And while the first arrival
looked on, the mother closed her son's eyes,
touched his face, and then dropped dead at
his side.

The death of the bridegroom apparently
had been caused by poison, since his skin grew
pink and there was no insect bite or injury
of any sort on his body. The bride was charged
with murder, and according to the laws of the
land she would be hanged if she could not
prove her innocence. All during the funeral
the bride clung to the coffin of her husband
and kept begging him to wake up and tell people that she had not killed him.

The coroner felt sorry for the young bride and made a special effort to look into the matter. First he went to the hamlet where her parents lived and made a thorough inquiry about her life before her marriage. He learned that she had had no lover and that her parents had been glad she was getting married because they still had many more daughters who needed husbands. After his inquiry he did not find any reason why the girl should have killed her husband.

Returning home, the coroner made one last effort to save the girl by examining the wedding bed. He spotted a little hole in the bamboo near the head of the bed. He held his breath and examined the hole closely. Suddenly he jumped back. His vision was blurred by some invisible vapor coming out of the little hole.

With the consent of the village chief he broke the bamboo bed, and out jumped a small two-steps snake. It tried to get away, but the villagers chased after it and killed it. The snake must have been in the bamboo tree since hatching. Its mother, in her wandering life, had laid an egg in the hole created by some insect while the tree was still young. The taller the tree grew the narrower the hole became, and when the baby snake hatched it was trapped in the tree forever. It must have stayed alive by depending upon the rain and dew and the stray

ants or insects that accidently fell into the hole. Since it didn't use its venom often it had built up a lot of poison, and the breath of the snake would be strong enough to kill a person who breathed it. So the bridegroom, sleeping with his nose near the hole, had been killed by the snake's breath, and not by his wife.

The bride sold the little house and returned to her parents. At first she came back every once in a while to visit the graves of her husband and his family and to clear the weeds which grew on them. But then she did not come anymore. She remarried and lived with her new husband far away from our hamlet. So the people of our hamlet built a little altar on the side of the road leading to the graves of the son and mother and father, and during the holidays someone always burned incense at their altar, and from time to time travelers stopped by and prayed at the roadside altar, hoping their prayer would make their long journey less hazardous.

But most importantly, the lonely little altar on the roadside reminded us that just down the deserted road there were three tombs to take care of, especially during the Lunar New Year.

THE HERO

Horse snakes, despite their strength and venom, have one soft spot. They are very fond of the burning oil made of the fat of the hogfish. We call it that because this fish, when fully grown, can get as big and fat as a well-fed hog. However, to catch a hogfish you need to do it in a special way.

When a hogfish takes the bait it always fights very hard, and most of the time it succeeds in getting off the hook. But a wise fisherman will very slowly coax a hogfish to the surface and then gently scratch its belly. After having been sufficiently scratched, the fish will let four or five men take it wherever they wish.

The flesh of the hogfish is very good to eat. But its fat is even more precious because the smell of the oil made from this fat will, when burned, intoxicate a horse snake. So at night, whenever we went from one place to

another in our hamlet, we used lamps filled with hogfish oil to ward off any sudden attacks by horse snakes. If we crossed the path of a horse snake, the smoke of the lamps would make it tipsy. The snake might follow the lamp for a while in order to inhale more smoke, but it would totally forget about attacking us.

During the six-month rainy season, most of the river fish swim into the shallow water of the rice field and live there, feeding on all kinds of insects. Then during the dry season they return to the river. In addition most of the tropical fish in the area also have the ability to live out of the water for more than two hours, staying on paths and dikes where they can find more insects at night.

My cousin and I liked to go out into the field and catch fish at night. Whenever we went out we always carried a hogfish oil lamp. Since I could not catch fish as well as my cousin, who was ten years older, I carried the lamp and a bucket to put the fish in, and my cousin carried a long knife to kill any fish that we found near the edge of the water. But he preferred to catch them alive.

One evening when we were in the field, my cousin began teasing me, saying that since I carried the hogfish oil lamp, a horse snake would follow us home. I knew that he was teasing, but I was frightened and looked back every so often to make sure that there was no

horse snake following us. Then suddenly I saw a huge horse snake, coming from nowhere, and following me with its head waving unsteadily. I was so terrified that I couldn't speak; I could barely drag my feet. Luckily my cousin stopped and tried to catch a fish lying in the middle of the path. I bumped into him and almost knocked him over. Surprised at my unusual clumsiness, he looked back and saw the horse snake behind me. He was terrified too, but instinctively he swung his knife and struck the snake in the head. We dropped everything and ran home as fast as we could, more frightened than ever by the great noise the snake made behind us.

When we reached home my father gathered all his friends to search for the snake. He felt that since it had been discovered so nearby they ought to try to destroy it as soon as possible.

When we returned to the place where my cousin and I had encountered the snake, we saw, to our great surprise and relief, that the snake was lying there dead. With extraordinary luck, my cousin had hit the snake right in the middle of its head and split its brain.

The snake was so heavy that it took eight men to carry it home. The next day it was on display in front of our house. Everybody was impressed by its size. To fight against a

snake of this length twenty men usually were needed.

My cousin put some coconut oil on his hair to make it shinier and he stayed around near the snake. The young girls smiled at him a little bit more than usual, and the young men seemed jealous.

My cousin was a hero!

THE MONKEY AND THE
OLD LADY

During the harvest season, Tank and I often hid behind a thick bush and waited for monkeys to come to steal the crops. When they sneaked into the field, I would give the signal to Tank to charge the monkey thieves. Tank would roar really loud while I yelled and shot at them with my slingshot. We tried to scare them away, but they always came back a few days later. Sometimes they knew where we were hiding and made faces at us from a distance or did somersaults on the plants to taunt us.

The river that crosses the rice field in front of our hamlet was a lifeline, not only for the people of our hamlet, but also for all the animals from the nearby jungle and mountains. Man and beast came to the river daily. But unlike the other wild animals, which came to the river only at night in order to avoid hu-

mans, monkeys came to it any time they wanted to, often after having just stolen some food from the field.

These monkeys were so intelligent that the farmers could not get rid of them. They avoided the most ingenious traps, and there were not enough guns to shoot them down from a distance. So we had to learn how to live with them and to make the best use of them we could.

A fully grown male monkey can weigh fifty kilos. With its intelligence and agility it can be a good fighter, but it usually has no heart for fighting. However, although it can be the most cowardly of all the animals in the jungle, it can also be the most malicious! A small boy with a stick can chase a whole herd of wild monkeys, if he acts brave and looks fierce. But if he doesn't look fierce, the monkeys will turn on him and kill him.

Nevertheless, most of the people in our hamlet kept a monkey or two in their houses for certain purposes, such as picking coconuts or hunting squirrels, or just as pets. But they were kept in strong cages or chained to sturdy poles or trees.

One day an old lady who was a friend of our family's showed my mother a baby monkey that had been born in captivity. Because the old lady had no children or other relatives left, she dearly loved her baby monkey. Each day

she carried the monkey around in one hand, like a newborn child, and in the other hand she carried a bottle of milk.

Things went well for six months, and then the monkey began to behave mischievously. My mother suggested the monkey be chained to a tree, because if it tried to run away, the old lady was too slow to catch it. When the old lady hesitated, my mother said: "My good friend, you should not only chain your monkey to a tree but also inspect the chain every day. You came to live in our hamlet only a short while ago and you may not know how mischievous, malicious, and unpredictable these monkeys can be.

"Quite a few years back when I was still a young girl there was a butcher living with his wife and his two-year-old daughter at the edge of our hamlet. The butcher had a monkey chained to a pole above his pigsty. He had the strange idea that its tricks might entertain the hogs below and make them grow faster. Each day he went about his job cutting up meat, under the watchful eyes of the monkey.

"One evening his neighbor next door invited him and his wife to dinner. Because they were afraid their two-year-old daughter might disturb their hosts, they left her sleeping quietly in the cradle. Since the two houses were separated only by a thin bamboo wall, they could get back immediately to their house if

the child woke up and wanted them.

"During the dinner the monkey managed to get loose from its chain. It grabbed the same knife that the butcher used to kill hogs and ran into the house and slaughtered the child, cutting it into pieces exactly as the butcher did the hogs. The child did not cry or make any noise, so perhaps the monkey killed it when it was sound asleep.

"When the couple got home the sight of their dismembered child horrified them. Their cries of distress gathered many friends who began a thorough search of the area for the monkey, but the monkey had already disappeared into the jungle, a few hundred meters away.

"The butcher was never the same again. For many years afterward he constantly looked for his monkey, but he never found it. Sometimes people saw him, haggard, roaming the jungle."

Reluctantly, the old lady listened to my mother's story, but she seemed to love and trust the little monkey as much as the day it was born. She continued to take good care of it, and she was so proud when it learned how to shake hands with her.

When the monkey was two years old it was much bigger and stronger than most monkeys in the area because the old lady had fed it well. People saw her talking to the monkey for hours as if it understood everything she

said. Sometimes she woke up in the middle of the night and missed her monkey so much that she lit a candle and went out to see if it was all right.

Every three days she went to the market-place to buy food for herself and bananas for her monkey. Since matches were very scarce at the time, whenever she left home for such a journey, she buried the burning embers in the hearth under a thick layer of ashes in order to keep the fire going.

One morning she buried the burning embers, said good-bye to her monkey, and left for the marketplace as usual. But that day the monkey managed to get free from its chain after she had left, and the first thing it did was to dig out the burning embers and put them on the thatched roof of the house. The house burned down completely. Meanwhile, the monkey seemed to know what it had done to the old lady, because it disappeared immediately.

When the old lady returned, both her monkey and her house were gone. She cried so hard, not only from sadness but also from anger. My parents invited her to stay with us until we could raise enough money to build her a new house.

After that day she always carried a stick with her, intending to beat the monkey any time she could lay a hand on the unfaithful

beast. My mother thought that she would be too slow to catch the monkey, but she did not try to discourage her from attempting to punish him.

One day the old lady came home very excited. "I saw him! It was him! With a bunch of other wild ones. He made fun of me by jumping up and down. I wanted to teach him a lesson but he ran away quickly. The next time he will not be so lucky as this time!"

Soon afterward a friend of hers recognized her monkey among the wild ones and killed it with a poisoned arrow. He thought that it would please his old friend very much. But when he showed her dead monkey to her she wasn't happy. Instead she stared at the dead body and cried and cried for hours.

WHAT CAN YOU DO
WITH A MONKEY?

Our family had a small coconut grove near the edge of the jungle and my father trained a monkey to pick coconuts for him. But it took my father quite a while to train our monkey for the job.

One day a peddler from the lowlands stopped by our house to show my father his goods. Since my father was very proud of our monkey, he showed it to the peddler. When the peddler heard that my father had taken several months to train our monkey he told us that he wouldn't need that much time to train not only one, but even a bunch of monkeys to do different useful tasks. My father was very interested in what the peddler said and invited him to stay with us overnight so that he could show us how to train a monkey quickly.

Early the next morning the peddler, my

father and a few of his friends, my cousin, and I went to the riverbank near a big tree that had branches hanging above the water. We hid ourselves carefully and waited for the monkeys to come to the river for their morning drink.

Monkeys never come right down to the river because of the mud. Instead they use a special technique to reach the water. The first monkey hangs on to a branch over the water with one hand while the other hand holds the hand of the second monkey. The second monkey holds the hand of a third monkey and so on until one of the hanging chain of monkeys is close enough to the water to drink. The rest of the monkeys drink by changing positions in the chain.

That morning the level of the water in the river was quite low. Fifteen monkeys were needed to form a complete chain. A friend of my father's shot the topmost monkey, and the rest of the chain fell into the river. Since monkeys cannot swim well we caught all fourteen, tied their hands behind their backs, and marched them home like prisoners of war.

When we reached home the peddler chose one monkey that looked very mean and seemed to be the leader of the group. Then he lined up the others in front of the mean-looking one. Next he tried to teach the mean-looking monkey how to use a spoon to eat rice. He repeated the process about ten times, but the sullen

monkey refused to learn. So the peddler asked for a knife and cut off the head of the stubborn monkey in front of the others.

The other monkeys trembled and remained extremely quiet. Then when the peddler handed each of them a spoon and a bowl of rice they all used the spoons and ate the rice properly.

During the rest of the day the peddler quickly taught them to draw water from the well with a bucket, pick up trash and carry it to the dump, and so on. Sometimes the monkeys were slow to learn something new or became unruly; but when the peddler showed them the knife, they all became orderly and the learning proceeded in a proper way.

The next day a friend of my family's who liked tea very much asked if he could have one of the captured monkeys to use to pick tea leaves in the mountains for him. Because of the cooler temperatures, tea grown on mountaintops is much better than tea grown at the foot of the mountains. My father said yes.

Our friend began training the monkey by feeding it a mixture of water and opium residue every evening. After one week the monkey became addicted. Then he took it into the mountains.

At first our friend had to climb to the top of the mountain each day with the monkey to show it how to tell tea leaves apart from

other leaves by smelling them, and then how to pick the leaves and put them into a light basket attached to its back. In the meantime, the monkey kept drinking the opiated water every night when it got back to its master's home.

After a week the monkey knew its job exactly. Our friend set it free in the morning, and in the evening it brought home a basketful of tea leaves. Some days the monkey did not pick enough tea leaves, and on those days our friend did not allow it to drink the special water. The next day the monkey would do a better job.

Since our friend could not drink all the tea his monkey picked, he sold some of it. He made quite a bit of money by doing so. If someone criticized him he would say: "It is better to be an addicted monkey than a chicken beheaded and eaten!"

My father decided to teach one of the newly captured monkeys how to hunt squirrels. Anyone who owns coconut groves knows that squirrels are the most destructive animals. Of course some young coconuts were always lost to giant bats and rats, but when the coconuts that escaped damage became ripe and were ready for market, the squirrels would come. They would eat through the coconut shells with their sharp teeth, drink the milk, eat the coconut meat, and then relax inside the shells,

which made very comfortable nests.

Squirrel hunting required a very well trained monkey, a dog, and hunters with sling-shots. Hunters shot at squirrels with their sling-shots. They were happy if they could hit one and slow it down, but their main purpose was to tire out the squirrel by constantly harassing it until it would hide on the top of a coconut tree. Then the hunters would send the monkey up the tree to catch the tired squirrel and throw it down to the dog below. The owners of the coconut groves gave the hunters some money for each squirrel and then hung the dead squir-rels on the coconut trees, hoping to scare away other squirrels.

In order to train his new monkey how to hunt squirrels, my father organized a special hunt and brought the new monkey along with him. My father waved a knife in front of it and the new monkey quickly learned to catch squirrels and throw them to the dog. The mon-key seemed a little bit bewildered when it went up the tree to get the first squirrel, but by the time it caught its third squirrel it seemed to enjoy the work. It held the frightened squirrel by the tail, swinging it to and fro and making faces at it before throwing it to the waiting dog. Everybody agreed that the monkey had become a full-fledged hunter in record time.

THE "UNFAITHFUL BIRDS"

Often, when I was in the fields and the sun was high in the sky, I would stay in the shade of a tall banyan tree and listen to the song of a bird we called the "unfaithful bird." And just as often, when I woke up in the middle of the night and listened to the sounds of the jungle, the confused noises of the deep forest would be interrupted by a few clear, lonely notes from the song of an unfaithful bird. Usually, their song was lively and made me forget everything. But sometimes they would sing a melancholy song. Then I longed for something other than the world I lived in. Maybe it was just their night song that stirred this longing in me, for some people say unfaithful birds are not really awake at night; they say they are just singing their dreams. . . .

We called them unfaithful birds because they never stayed with people, no matter how

hard you tried to keep them. But first you had to catch them! They built their nests on trees where wasps and killer bees lived, making the task of reaching their nests nearly impossible. Nevertheless, some villagers managed to catch baby birds, even before they had opened their eyes, hoping that when they did—four days after they were hatched—the birds would consider the humans their parents and stay with them. But that never really worked. As soon as the birds learned to fly they would flee immediately.

When I was seven years old, my cousin gave my younger sister and me a nest of six young unfaithful birds. He avoided the wasps and killer bees by stealing the nest at night. My father built us an attractive cage, and my sister and I spent hours every day catching grasshoppers, crickets, and other insects to feed to the ever-hungry baby birds.

One day I told my cousin that we were very tired of catching insects. I asked him whether he knew a better way to keep the birds. My cousin said yes, there was a way; the birds had to be addicted to opium. He told me that the merchant living on the other side of our garden smoked opium and that I should ask him for the sticky residue inside his opium pipe. If I could get the merchant to give me the residue, my cousin would show me how to use it to make the birds stay with us.

As a matter of fact, the merchant was a friend of mine. From time to time my mother allowed my sister and me to cross the garden and peer through the hedge to watch him smoke opium in his small room. He always smoked at six in the evening, with all the windows open. Sometimes my sister and I arrived a bit early and watched how he prepared for his smoking session. We tried to hide from him, but he usually saw us. Instead of being angry, he simply smiled vaguely.

He owned a black dog and had four white lizards that lived on the ceiling of his room. The dog and lizards looked restless and unhappy until he started smoking. Then the opium smoke hung around the room and the animals became relaxed and happy. The dog slowly wagged his tail and got a dreamy look in his half-shut eyes, which were as dreamy as those of his master. The lizards made chuckling noises and little taps on the ceiling with their little tails.

So the next day when my sister and I saw the merchant sitting in front of his house, we went over to him immediately. I brought along my mandolin even though I hardly knew how to play it. But I played my best to accompany my sister, and she sang as loudly as she could. When we finished the song the merchant smiled at us and said, "Young lady and young gentleman, it was very nice of you to sing a

song for me. Now what can I do for you?" I said, "Sir, we have six unfaithful birds and my sister and I have had a hard time catching insects to feed them. As you know, they will fly away if I set them free and let them feed themselves. But my cousin told us that if you gave us the residue that sticks in your opium pipe, he knows a way for us to keep the birds without feeding them."

The merchant gave us what we wanted, adding that if we needed more we should simply let him know. When we returned home my cousin mixed the residue in a liter of water. Then each day at six P.M. he let the birds drink the water from this bottle. Within six days, the birds would become restless around six o'clock and wait anxiously for their opium drink. But after having drunk the water they looked very happy and preened themselves or sang nicely. My cousin told us that now it was time to set them free.

The next morning we opened the door of the cage; all six birds quickly escaped and flew straight ahead without looking back at us. Even though we knew beforehand this would probably happen, my sister and I were still upset. We remembered all those weeks we had worked very hard to take care of them. But around six o'clock, just as my cousin had predicted, one by one they flew back to the cage and waited restlessly for their special drink. When

we gave it to them they drank it greedily, and then looked very contented with themselves. Some sang, some preened themselves. At one point four or five of them sang at the same time, and produced a very beautiful symphony.

This situation lasted for many months, and the birds became the talk of our small hamlet. Neighbors would drop in around six o'clock and watch the birds return for their drink and then listen to their singing.

But one day a very strong storm hit our hamlet around six o'clock. When it was over our birds did not come back. My sister and I waited for them all evening until finally our parents made us go to bed. The next day we found our birds, one by one, a few steps from each other, lying dead on the ground. They were killed because the storm had hit just when they were flying back to their cage. Maybe they were weak after months of having their special drink, or maybe they needed the special drink so much that they couldn't wait until the storm was over to fly back.

We looked at them for a long time and cried. We buried them in six little tombs, side by side, in a corner of our garden.

THE TWO-STEPS
SNAKE

When there wasn't much work to do in the fields, my cousin and I often went into the woods, looking for birds' eggs. We always brought Tank with us because then I could sit high on Tank's back and inspect the tops of bushes while my cousin could explore the areas underneath on foot. We were almost always successful and brought home all kinds of eggs: wild duck eggs, wild chicken eggs, songbird eggs, and once, an egg we had never seen before.

On that day, my cousin and I found an egg a little too big for any kind of songbird and a little too small for a chicken or duck. We decided to bring it home and ask my parents what it was. After examining it my father guessed that it could be a snake's egg. My mother wanted us to throw it away immediately, but my father said we could keep it in

a little glass case, for he was quite curious about it himself.

A few days later to our great excitement, a two-steps snake broke out of the shell. My mother was scared and insisted that we keep the baby snake in its case somewhere in our garden, for two-steps snakes belonged to the most poisonous species of snakes in our region.

It got its name from the fact that if it bites someone, he will walk only two more steps, then fall dead. A fully grown snake will measure about one meter. In general it is not aggressive. But it's dangerous because it also never runs away from anything, especially when it sheds its skin and hides either underwater in the rice field or under dead leaves in the forest to protect its tender new skin. A person may go out at that time of the year to catch fish in the rice field or to gather firewood in the forest and, by accident, step on a newly molted snake. And in self-defense, it will bite.

The two-steps snake does not live in the same place for very long, unlike most other snakes. Instead it wanders around to look for frogs or mice, and when its hunger is satisfied it finds a new hiding place and stays there for a while. Therefore, during the mating season the female may scatter her eggs over quite a large area. In most cases these eggs are hatched by the heat of the sun. But a bird on a nest may wake up to see a small snake come out

of one of the eggs it considers its own, or a housewife may find a few eggs under her pile of firewood, or a woodcutter may be surprised when a small snake jumps out of a hole in a piece of wood he has just chopped. Of course, many of the scattered eggs will be swallowed by other snakes, or eaten by monkeys, wildcats, birds, or other animals. Only eggs that are well hidden survive.

Our two-steps snake grew quite fast. Every day either my cousin or I went to the far end of our garden, where we had placed the glass case, and fed the snake. Each time we threw in a live fly or small grasshopper, the insect was killed instantly by the breath of the snake, which had poisoned the air in the case.

A few weeks passed and our snake started to become restless. One day when we approached the case to feed the snake, it angrily opened its mouth and we saw its sharp fangs. We were frightened because the glass was fragile, and there would be little chance for us to get away from the quick-moving snake if it broke the case.

When we told my parents what had happened they made us get rid of the snake at once. We covered the case with piles of straw and burned it. When the snake was dead, my father took it out of the case and burned it again, thoroughly. Afterward he threw its ashes into the river. He said that if we threw the

snake away without burning it, one day someone might step on its jaw and be killed. The
poison in the fangs always remained, and many
people had been killed by stepping on dead
two-steps snakes.

Months later we found another two-steps
snake under the bamboo bush in front of our
house. The bamboo bush was intertwined with
other bushes that surrounded the house, so we
could not easily uproot it in order to kill the
snake. Besides, it would have been useless work
if the hole in which the snake lived reached
under other bushes too. We just hoped that
the snake would go away in a week or so, for
according to an old belief, if one set out to
kill a two-steps snake and failed, it would sneak
into the house at night and kill all of the family. We did not believe in this legend, but since
we could not find a sure way to kill the snake,
we did not like to tempt the fates.

However, unlike other two-steps snakes,
this one seemed to choose the shelter beneath
the bamboo bush as its semipermanent nest.
It did go away, once in a while, for a week
or ten days, but it always came back. Little
by little we accepted its presence and gave up
the idea of killing it.

The snake seemed not to be bothered by
us either. Occasionally we saw it sunbathing
or receiving a friend. Its friend was a bit longer,
but we did not know whether it was a male

or a female. Sometimes in the moonlight the two snakes danced together. First, each one made a coil and faced the other. Then they raised their heads at the same time and swayed backward and forward. After a while the heads would move up and down, or sometimes they stayed still with their mouths nearly touching. After each visit our snake would accompany its friend to the gate of our house.

We had a watchdog who was very fascinated by the snake, and vice versa. When the snake disappeared, the dog seemed to miss it. The dog looked into its hole or walked around the bamboo bush, making a whining sound. But when the snake was around, the two always kept a certain distance between themselves; the dog could kill the snake by snapping its neck, and the snake could kill the dog by biting him. When the snake was sunbathing, the dog came as close as he dared and watched the snake with a funny look in his eyes. Sometimes he wagged his tail, pricked up his ears, and barked at the snake in a friendly way. The sunbathing snake kept its eyes half shut in a dreamy way. But in reality it watched every move of the dog warily.

One morning we found the dog dead in the courtyard. At first we thought that the snake had bitten him, but we couldn't find any bite on the dog's body. When we opend the dog's stomach we found a poisoned piece

of meat. We suspected that a thief had poisoned our dog in order to get into our house.

That evening we asked a few friends to stay overnight for a couple evenings to help us watch for the thief. On the next two nights nothing happened. But at two o'clock in the morning on the third night my cousin, who was on watch, heard a loud shriek followed by a heavy thud. He woke up everybody, and we all grabbed weapons, but decided not to go out into the dark. The rest of the night was still except for a few calls of night birds and the occasional roaring of tigers in the jungle.

Early in the morning we found the dead body of a man near the two-steps snake's nest. We carefully examined the body of the stranger and found a snake bite on his ankle. Quickly the news spread that the snake had avenged the death of its friend, the dog, by killing the thief who had poisoned him.

Within a few days the snake had become our "guardian," one who would punish anyone who tried to hurt us. The news spread so fast that soon travelers came from afar to visit the place where the snake lived. Parents would bring their newborn children to see the snake so that the children would grow up free from evil. When farmers came, they would bring a chicken or a duck and set it loose near the snake as a sacrifice to the "guardian."

In a short time there were so many chickens and ducks that we didn't know what to do with them. Ducks filled the ponds, and there were chickens in the rice field, chickens in the garden, chickens in the bamboo bushes. Sometimes a hen disappeared for about three weeks and suddenly reappeared with a very noisy brood of chicks. The chickens and ducks made so much noise in the morning that it was quite impossible to sleep past dawn.

I was going away to school in the lowlands by then, and from time to time I asked a friend: "Would you like to have a chicken?" When he or she said yes, the next Monday I brought a very big chicken from home for my friend. After a while everyone began calling me "Chicken Boy."

The snake worshippers kept coming and the number of chickens and ducks kept increasing. There was no way to convince other people that the snake was not a "guardian genius." Once, during the endless years of fighting in Vietnam, a rocket blew up the bamboo bush. But the snake escaped without any injury and its prestige increased in the eyes of its worshippers.

As time passed the snake trusted us more. From time to time my nephew threw it a live frog or a mouse. Sometimes it came as close as half a meter from my nephew to pick up a crippled frog and to swallow it on the spot.

The last time I heard from my mother, the snake was still alive but quite old. Perhaps because of its old age, its snake friend had stoppcd coming to visit. In its loneliness it seemed to be more attracted to our new watch-dog, which was as friendly to the snake as our first one had been.

SORROW

Winter nights on the central highlands of Vietnam are very cold. Sometimes when the wind was howling outside and we were huddling around the fireplace, I worried about Tank and the rest of the herd. But my father told me that water buffaloes adapt themselves very well to the cold weather, because they are much bigger and stronger than we are. And sure enough in the morning when I touched their shoulders, I found they were quite warm. And when I gave them food and water they drank and ate heartily.

One day when I was in the field with the herd, fierce fighting between the French forces and the Resistance led by Ho Chi Minh erupted in our hamlet. The battle was so close that I tried to run away and find shelter in the river nearby.

I led Tank and the rest of the herd toward

the river, but suddenly I noticed that Tank was lagging behind and limping. I ran back and saw that Tank had been hit by a stray bullet which had passed through his chest. With my urging, Tank made it to the river, but he looked very weak when he lay down. I tapped Tank's neck slightly to let him know that I was still with him, and I also tried to tell him that he would be okay. I saw tears in Tank's eyes, but I did not know whether he suffered from the bullet wound or whether he was sad because he was going to die. When the battle was over, Tank could not get up. He died about an hour later.

We buried Tank in the graveyard where we buried all the dead of our family, and every Lunar New Year my father burned incense in front of all the tombs, including Tank's.

About the Author

HUYNH QUANG NHUONG was born in Mytho, Vietnam. Upon being graduated from Saigon University with a degree in chemistry, he was drafted into the South Vietnamese army. Mr. Huynh was permanently paralyzed by a gunshot wound received on the battlefield, and in 1969 he came to the United States for additional medical treatment.

Since then Mr. Huynh has earned bachelor's and master's degrees in French and comparative literature from Long Island University and the University of Missouri and now makes his home in Columbia, Missouri. THE LAND I LOST is his first book.

About the Artist

VO-DINH MAI was born in Hue, Vietnam. He studied at the Lycée of Hue, and at the Sorbonne, the Académie de la Grande Chaumière, and the Ecole Nationale Supérieure des Beaux-Arts in Paris.

Mr. Vo-Dinh is a professional artist whose works have been exhibited in thirty-six one-man shows both here and abroad and have appeared on UNICEF greeting cards. He has illustrated a score of books, including his own THE TOAD IS THE EMPEROR'S UNCLE and the Christopher Award-winning book written by his wife, Helen Coutant, FIRST SNOW.

He and his wife have two daughters, Phuong-Nam and Linh-Giang, and currently live in Burkittsville, Maryland.

92   Huynh, Quang Nhuong
HUY
        The land I lost